LCCN: 2026904899

ISBNS

E-book: 978-1-970894-65-3

Paperback: 978-1-970894-66-0

Hardcover: 978-1-970894-67-7

This Book is Dedicated To

My parents, who molded me into the person I am. To be honest, loyal, helpful, and a lover of God and Country. To always look for the good in people and to be a leader, not a follower. To my brothers and sister, my wife Diane, my children Leslie, Nikki, and Fred, for their love and support throughout my journey.

Foreword

I go through life every day asking myself, "What will I do today that will make a positive difference in someone's life?"

Every day I ask myself one question,

What will I do today that makes a positive difference in someone's life?

I was raised on faith, discipline, and responsibility. Long before I knew what leadership meant.

I learned early that nothing is handed to you, you earn it every day.

Work taught me pride; sacrifice taught me value.

Leadership isn't about power; it's about character and the courage to change culture.

This is my story, not to impress, but to remind.

Time doesn't wait, but it does teach, if you are willing to listen.

HOUR GLASS

Fernando "Butch" Lecuona III

Why Do People Write Books?

It's a question that delves far beyond the simple act of putting words on paper. The motivations are as diverse as the authors themselves, encompassing personal expression, societal commentary, historical documentation, and financial gain, to name just a few.

Many authors feel an intrinsic need to share their unique perspectives and experiences, crafting narratives that resonate with readers on an emotional and intellectual level. Books can serve as a powerful vehicle for self-discovery, allowing authors to process complex emotions, explore existential questions, and ultimately, find meaning in their lives. For others, the act of writing is a form of catharsis, a way to grapple with personal struggles and emerge with a renewed sense of self-awareness.

Beyond personal expression, books frequently serve as crucial platforms for social and political commentary. Authors often use their writing to challenge prevailing norms, spark conversations about critical issues, and for social justice. This can range from overtly political works to subtly embedded messages woven into fictional narratives.

Moreover, books play a vital role in preserving history and culture. They act as repositories of knowledge, documenting events, preserving languages, and transmitting cultural traditions across generations. Biographies. Historical fiction and academic texts all contribute to this vital preservation process.

Finally, it's important to acknowledge that for some authors, writing is a profession. It's a means of earning a living, and their books are a product of their craft, their skills, and their dedication to their audiences.

In conclusion, the motivations for writing books are richly textured and deeply personal. They encompass self-expression, social commentary, historical preservation, and professional endeavors, weaving together to create the vast and varied literary landscape we enjoy today. [OBJ]

Part One of Hour Glass
Introduction

I am delighted to introduce a comprehensive two-part exploration that transcends conventional discussions on professional development. This unique journey offers an intimate and deeply personal lens through which to examine the profound interplay between an individual's core character and the intricate processes of leadership and organizational transformation.

Drawing upon my own experiences and foundational principles, I delve into how personal integrity, resilience, and vision are not merely desirable traits but essential catalysts for driving sustainable change within any organization. This two-part book isn't just about strategy; it's about understanding the intrinsic human element that underpins effective leadership and shapes the very fabric of institutional evolution. Prepare to gain a fresh, integrated perspective that empowers you to approach challenges with renewed insight and purpose.

The first part is deeply personal, detailing my own path and the experiences that shaped my leadership philosophy. It's a candid account of the challenges I faced and the lessons I learned along the way, offering a glimpse into the human side of leadership.

The second part delves into the significant cultural shift I spearheaded during my time leading the Nebraska Department of Labor. This section provides a detailed, insightful look at the strategies, challenges, and ultimate successes of implementing transformative change within a large-scale public organization. I've included specific examples and lessons learned that are applicable to a wide range of leadership contexts. My hope is that this section will serve as a valuable resource for anyone striving to create a more positive and productive work environment.

Allow me to open a window into the initial chapters of my life, offering an unfiltered and deeply personal account of the memories that marked my formative years. This is a genuine narrative, meticulously woven from the threads of my earliest recollections, exploring the very dawn of my consciousness and the foundational experiences that shaped the person I would eventually become.

I've found myself in a period of profound reflection, and a question has repeatedly surfaced in my mind: 'Why has my life felt so uniquely special?' It's a sentiment that goes beyond mere good fortune; it encompasses a tapestry woven with extraordinary experiences, meaningful connections, unexpected challenges that forged resilience, and moments of sheer, unadulterated joy.

I often ponder the intricate threads – the invaluable lessons learned, the unwavering support from those around me, and the unique path I've been fortunate enough to walk. This deep sense of appreciation fills me with immense gratitude, and I am continuously seeking to understand the beautiful serendipity and purpose behind it all. It truly is a remarkable feeling to recognize the distinctive journey one is on.

Over the course of my extensive journey, I have been incredibly fortunate to traverse a path rich with remarkable experiences and profound encounters. As I reflect upon the many facets of this life, the triumphs, the unforeseen challenges, and the invaluable lessons gleaned, I feel a compelling and sincere desire to document these narratives. It is my deepest hope that by sharing the insights and perspectives accumulated over a lifetime exceptionally full of growth and discovery, I might offer a measure of inspiration or a fresh viewpoint to those who engage with my reflections. 🖼️

Table of Contents

Chapter One

My Formative Years

I've embarked on a project that's been close to my heart for many years – the writing of my memoirs. This isn't just a chronological recounting of events, but a deeply personal exploration of my life's journey, from my earliest childhood memories to the present day.

It's been a profoundly enriching experience to revisit pivotal moments, examine my growth and evolution, and reflect upon the relationships and experiences that have shaped who I am. The narrative encompasses aspects of my life, my family's influence, my career path, significant personal challenges, and triumphs.

This manuscript is a compelling and honest portrayal of my life lived to the fullest, with its share of joys, sorrows, and lessons learned along the way.

Born in Omaha, Nebraska

My life journey began at Offutt Air Force Base in Omaha, Nebraska, on August 13, 1951, where I was born, and it was a fortunate start I often reflect on. My father's service in the U.S. Marines and the years I spent growing up in Omaha instilled in me a deep appreciation for the values and opportunities afforded by life in the United States.

My mother provided a supportive and nurturing environment, fostering a strong sense of community and belonging. The experiences of my childhood and the unwavering support of my family shaped my character and instilled a work ethic that has served me well throughout my life. The opportunities presented to me in America, while certainly not guaranteed, were significantly greater than those available in many other parts of the world. This access to education, personal freedom, and the ability to pursue my dreams fueled my ambitions.

While I recognize that my narrative is one of self-reflection, I firmly believe in the American ideal of achieving success through hard work, dedication, and perseverance. My faith in Jesus Christ provides me with strength and guidance, underpinning my personal values and guiding my decisions. The unique aspects of my upbringing in Nebraska helped shape who I am today, and I remain profoundly grateful for the countless blessings I've experienced. I was born here, and this will be my final resting place.

My Father, Fernando Lecuona Jr.

My father (deceased), a man whose life was a testament to unwavering dedication and service, profoundly shaped my upbringing. His experiences as a Sergeant in the United States Marine Corps, serving with distinction through the end of World War II and the Korean War, instilled in him a deep patriotism and a strong sense of discipline that permeated our family life. These values weren't simply preached; they were living.

His commitment to providing for our family was unwavering. After a period working in construction as an operating engineer, he transitioned to a career as a Douglas County Deputy Sheriff, a role he held for over three decades. His bilingual skills, a fluency in Spanish, proved invaluable, leading to his involvement in the Douglas County Court System alongside his regular duties. He further honed his expertise by attending the FBI Training Academy in Quantico, Virginia, where he became a certified fingerprint classification expert. His contributions to the Sheriff's Department extended to serving as a criminologist, meticulously processing crime scenes.

Beyond his professional achievements, he imparted invaluable life lessons. He taught us the importance of lawfulness, respect for others, and the value of physical fitness. His philosophy on conflict was simple yet profound: never initiate a fight, but never back down from one either. This strength of character stemmed from his own formidable background; he was a Marine boxer and a Golden Gloves Champion. His toughness, however, was tempered by a deep well of respect earned from his peers, friends, and neighbors alike. He was a man who commanded respect while simultaneously inspiring affection. His legacy is one of unwavering dedication, strength, and quiet dignity, a legacy that continues to inspire me to this day.

My Mother Violet Lecuona

I'm writing to share some reflections on my remarkable mother, Violet Lecuona. Her influence on my life, and the lives of my siblings, has been profound and enduring. More than simply a mother, she was the unwavering heart of our family, a constant source of nurturing and unwavering support.

From our earliest days, she instilled in us a deep sense of self-worth and encouraged us to strive for excellence in all that we did. Her love was, and remains, the bedrock of our family.

This wasn't simply a matter of providing for our physical needs – although, despite our family's modest means, she always ensured we were well-fed, clothed, and cared for. It was a love that nurtured our spirits, fostered our creativity, and shaped our character.

Her deep spirituality, expressed through daily prayers for each of us, infused our lives with a sense of peace and purpose. Her unwavering moral compass, shaped by a principled refusal to engage in gossip or negativity, created a safe and supportive environment where we could grow and thrive. Even the seemingly small things – teaching us our letters and numbers, preparing us for kindergarten – speaking volumes about her dedication and foresight.

She instilled in us a profound appreciation for our diverse heritage – a rich tapestry woven from Mexican, Irish, German, and Italian threads. She taught us to be proud of who we are, and to embrace the unique perspectives that our varied backgrounds offered. Her faith was fundamental to our upbringing, shaping our values, and encouraging us to appreciate the blessings in our lives.

Even at 74, I still feel the warmth of her love and the comforting presence of her devotion. We remain her "little kids," forever bound by the unbreakable bonds of family, forged in the delight of her love and unwavering dedication. It is a legacy I cherish deeply, and one I strive to emulate in my own life.

Learning How to Handle Money at a Young Age

My mother's career in banking and credit unions profoundly shaped my financial understanding and habits. More than just learning about debits and credits, or the mechanics of balancing a checkbook – skills I still utilize today – her influence instilled a deep appreciation for responsible money management. She taught me not only the practical aspects of budgeting and saving, emphasizing the importance of a financial reserve for unforeseen circumstances, but also the underlying values of fiscal responsibility and timely bill payments. This early education has been instrumental in shaping my financial life, providing a solid foundation that has served me well throughout my adult years. The lessons she imparted extend far beyond mere transactions; they represent a fundamental philosophy of financial prudence and planning that continues to guide my decisions.

Learning to Save Money from My Mom Using Bank Books

I've been reflecting lately on some of my earliest financial milestones and wanted to share a foundational experience that shaped my perspective. It was a formative time in my life, specifically when I was just sixteen years old, that I opened my very first savings account at Ames Bank. This wasn't merely a transaction; it was a deeply proud moment, signifying a tangible step towards financial independence and personal responsibility.

I still vividly remember receiving my first bank book – a small, unassuming ledger that would become my personal financial diary. Each deposit I made, often from my early jobs, was meticulously recorded, and I found genuine satisfaction in tracking my growing balance. It was through this hands-on experience that I first truly grasped the concept of compound interest.

Seeing how my money could, in essence, work for me, even in small increments, was an eye-opening revelation that transformed an abstract financial principle into a concrete, empowering reality.

Not long after, a new ambition took hold: I desperately wanted to upgrade my band equipment. This desire led me back to Ames Bank, but this time, for a different purpose – a loan.

With the invaluable support of my parents, who co-signed for me, I secured the necessary funds.

The commitment was substantial for a teenager, but the joy of acquiring the equipment was matched by the diligent process of repayment. I dedicated myself to making timely, regular payments, and there was an incredible sense of accomplishment with each installment.

Watching the outstanding balance progressively dwindle, each payment entry stamped into my bank book, was a genuinely thrilling and gratifying experience. It wasn't just about paying off debt; it was about honoring a commitment and seeing tangible progress towards a goal.

This entire journey, from saving to borrowing and repaying, deeply ingrained a fundamental lesson my parents imparted: true appreciation for something that comes from the effort and work you put into acquiring it. It's a principle that has guided many of my decisions, both personal and professional, ever since.

What Did We Learn from Our Parents While Growing Up?

Reflecting on the profound influence our parents have on our lives, I find myself contemplating the multifaceted lessons they impart, often without explicit instruction. These lessons extend far beyond the practical skills they might teach us, reaching into the core of our values, beliefs, and understanding of the world.

From them, we absorb perspectives on relationships – how to navigate conflict, express affection, and maintain healthy boundaries. Their approach to work ethics, financial management, and resilience in the face of adversity shapes our own habits and expectations.

We internalize their communication styles, learning how to express ourselves, and understanding the nuances of conversation. Their coping mechanisms, both healthy and unhealthy, become part of our own emotional toolkits, influencing how we manage stress and challenges.

Furthermore, the unspoken lessons are equally significant. We learn about self-worth through their actions and words, often unconsciously mirroring their self-perception. Their approach to personal growth and continuous learning models our own path to self-improvement. Their demonstration of empathy and compassion, or lack thereof, influences our ability to connect with others. Even their flaws and mistakes provide valuable insights, teaching us the importance of self-awareness, accountability, and continuous growth.

MANNERS

While reflecting on my upbringing the other day, I realized how truly formative those early years were under Mom and Dad's watchful eyes. They instilled in us, with an unwavering firmness, a profound sense of decorum and a deep reverence for our elders that seem increasingly rare in today's world.

I recall the daily lessons in etiquette vividly: the expectation to always open doors for women, to pull out a chair for Mom at the dinner table, and the cardinal rules of dining – no elbows on the table, the proper use of a napkin, and the absolute necessity of eating quietly with our mouths closed.

When we were out in public, especially at restaurants, silence and impeccable behavior were not just encouraged; they were demanded.

It's amusing now, but I still remember those proud moments for Mom and Dad when strangers, on more than one occasion, would approach our table, genuinely impressed by the quiet composure and excellent manners of all of us children. It was a testament to their dedication.

Swearing, of course, was an absolute taboo, and any slip of the tongue would invariably lead to swift and memorable consequences.

There was always the looming threat of having one's mouth washed out with soap, or a quick, firm reminder delivered to our backside to ensure the lesson truly sank in. These weren't acts of cruelty, but rather effective, albeit stern, methods to impress upon us the gravity of our words and actions. We were taught to address any adult with the utmost respect, using "Mister" or "Misses," and our responses to questions were always an automatic "yes, sir" or "yes ma'am," demonstrating a deference that went beyond mere politeness.

Looking back, those stringent lessons weren't just about good manners; they were about cultivating character, respect, and discipline. They shaped us in ways we probably didn't appreciate then, but certainly do now, providing a solid foundation that has served us well throughout our lives. It's a legacy that truly stands apart.

My Grandfather, Fernando Lecuona, Sr.

My grandfather, Fernando Lecuona Sr. (deceased), embodied the American Dream. Born in Mexico in the late 1890s, he immigrated to the United States with a singular vision: to become a citizen. His journey was arduous, beginning with the grueling life of a migrant farmworker traversing the fields of Nebraska. He later transitioned to the demanding work of the meatpacking industry, a testament to his unwavering determination.

He met my grandmother, and they married, starting a family that included my father.

Tragedy struck when my grandmother passed away from pneumonia when my father was only eleven years old. Despite this loss, my grandfather remained steadfast, never remarrying and tirelessly pursuing his aspirations. He ultimately achieved his goal, becoming a naturalized US citizen, a powerful demonstration of his perseverance. His career continued in the meatpacking industry, culminating in his retirement from Wilson's Packing House.

I am eternally grateful for the legacy he left, not just through his professional achievements, but through his personal stories and the invaluable life lessons he shared. One of the most impactful experiences was two trips to Mexico when I was about eleven, and another time with my two younger brothers. We traveled to Mexico City, where I met his brother Miguel, and further ventured into a rural village where extended family resided. This stark contrast between the affluent areas and the impoverished village provided an unforgettable lesson in socioeconomic disparity, instilling in me a deep appreciation for our own circumstances, despite our modest means in Omaha, Nebraska. The trip also included a visit to Acapulco, where witnessing the breathtaking cliff divers further broadened my perspective on the diverse ways people live.

My grandfather's life serves as a powerful example of resilience, hard work, and the pursuit of one's dreams. His influence continues to shape my life, and I carry his lessons of gratitude and understanding with me always.

Grandpa Lecuona's Mexican Food

There are some memories so rich, so steeped in warmth and flavor, that they transcend mere recollection and become a foundational part of who you are. For me, these memories invariably lead back to my Grandpa Lecuona and his kitchen, a place where culinary magic unfolded daily.

His Mexican food wasn't merely good; it was an experience, a symphony of tastes that truly felt divine. I can still vividly recall the masterpieces he'd lovingly prepare: his enchiladas, plump with savory fillings and drenched in rich mole sauce, the perfectly seasoned tacos, their crisp shells overflowing with tender meat; and the soulful tamales, each a miniature, steamed parcel of culinary art. The tostadas offered a satisfying crunch with every bite, while his frijoles, creamy and deeply flavorful, were elevated far beyond a simple side dish. He even made a refreshing salad using a hand-squeezed lemon dressing that was always a delightful counterpoint to the richer fare.

But the true cornerstone of every meal, the undisputed star, had to be his tortillas. Made entirely from scratch, each one was a soft, pliable marvel, still warm from the fire on the gas stove, carrying the faint, comforting scent of flowers. They weren't just an accompaniment; they were a foundational part of every meal and a testament to his dedication.

The moment we crossed the threshold into his home, a symphony of aromas would envelop us – the subtle spices, the earthy warmth of simmering chilies, the fresh zest of lime. It was a fragrance that didn't just whet the appetite; it promised a feast for the soul. My childhood friends, wise beyond their years when it came to good food, would ask me for an invitation.

Their constant refrain was, "When are we going back to your grandpas for Mexican food?" They knew, as we all did, that his table offered not just incomparable flavors but also boundless generosity, serving up as much as your heart (and/or stomach) desired.

I remember one time when my friend Steve Ray came with my brother and me to my grandpas to eat. Steve loved hot-tasting peppers and thought he could handle anything hot. Well, that night he met his match. My grandfather gave him some of his chili peppers, and Steve took a bite. We warned him not to do that, but he did it anyway. After that first bite, his eyes started to tear up and water, and his mouth started to burn. He grabbed a glass of water, and we told him that wouldn't work and to eat some tortillas to cool it down. We all had a good laugh at his expense.

Every dish was a testament to his unwavering dedication. He poured not just ingredients but genuine love and countless hours into his cooking, believing that good food was a direct expression of care. And his hospitality wasn't limited to food. He'd always offer us "pops, as we affectionately knew them as soda, a small gesture that spoke volumes about his generous spirit and desire to make everyone feel welcome and cherished. What a memory!

Grandpa's passion wasn't confined to his home kitchen. For a brief, shining period, he channeled his culinary genius into his own restaurant in South Omaha, which he proudly named "La Tapatía."

There, he extended his philosophy of abundance and quality, ensuring every customer walked away feeling they'd received not just a meal, but truly "their money's worth" a promise of authentic flavor and generous portions that few establishments could match. His legacy lives on, not just in my memories but in the enduring warmth those meals continue to bring to my heart.

My Grandfather Louis Scheschy

I want to share some cherished memories of my grandfather, Louis Scheschy. His life was a testament to the values of hard work, dedication, and self-reliance – qualities he instilled in my brothers and me.

Born to German parents, Grandpa was a skilled steam fitter, a profession he pursued with unwavering dedication. Beyond his trade, he actively participated in his community, serving as an elected official within the fitters' union, demonstrating his commitment to the well-being of his fellow workers. His service to his country during World War I further underscores his sense of duty and patriotism.

But Grandpa's contributions extended far beyond his professional life. He was a remarkably resourceful man, a builder who constructed several homes for his family, providing a tangible expression of his love and care. He cultivated a thriving two-acre farm, a vibrant testament to his connection with the land. The bounty of his labor – corn, potatoes, green beans, onions, radishes, peppers, tomatoes – filled our table with the freshest produce imaginable. The sweet taste of homegrown apples and cherries, and the rich flavor of his homemade wine, remain indelible memories. Grandma canned vegetables for use during the winter months, so they always had vegetables to eat with their dinners.

The harvest time was always a special occasion. Grandpa would enlist my brothers and me, and it was far more than just work; it was a significant part of our early education. We learned the value of honest labor, the satisfaction of seeing the fruits of our efforts, and the importance of self-sufficiency, lessons that have profoundly shaped my life. He taught us not only how to work hard, but also how to appreciate the rewards of hard work. His legacy continues to inspire me each day.

Grandpa and Grandma Scheschy's Food

There are certain memories, vibrant and cherished, that form the bedrock of my childhood, often drawing me back to the comforting embrace of my grandparents' home.

I can still recall the distinct, savory aroma of my Grandpa Scheschy's legendary Mulligan Stew. It wasn't merely a meal; it was a deeply ingrained ritual of love, a fragrant invitation that would invariably precede a phone call to my mother, summoning us for an impromptu family gathering. Each spoonful was a warm, satisfying balm, seemingly capable of dissolving any worry or chill.

Grandma often made spaghetti and meatballs with her famous Italian red sauce with fresh grated cheese. It was heaven. Alongside Grandpa's hearty creation, Grandma would orchestrate her own delightful culinary symphony. Her skilled hands, often dusted with flour, crafted the most exquisite homemade bread, its crust a golden-brown perfection, yielding to a tender, comforting crumb. And then came the sweet finales: bowls of creamy tapioca pudding, a childhood delight, or one of her renowned fruit pies – whether the tart burst of apple, the sweet tang of cherry, or the extremely delicate and light cloud of lemon meringue, each slice was a testament to her affection and culinary artistry.

Those unforgettable evenings often culminated in an overnight stay, a cherished adventure for us grandchildren. We'd nestle into the sunroom, a luminous haven on the south side of the house, filled with windows. When open, they welcomed a gentle, rhythmic cross-breeze, lulling us to sleep under what felt like a canopy of starlight, a perfect blend of outdoor freedom and indoor security.

Dawn, too, held its own magic. The tantalizing scent of sizzling pancakes would gently greet us, promising another breakfast feast. There, on the table, awaited stacks of golden perfection, ready to be drenched in thick, amber Karo syrup, poured generously from its iconic tin. Each sweet bite was an echo of family, warmth, and the simple, profound joy of those precious times. These aren't just recollections; they are foundational pillars of belonging and happiness that continue to warm my spirit.

Playing in the Back Yard on the Acreage

The sprawling landscape of Grandpa and Grandma's house wasn't just a patch of land; it was the vast, vibrant canvas of our childhood, where every acre held a promise of adventure.

Each morning presented a fresh slate of possibilities, igniting our imaginations and fueling endless explorations.

Our daily expeditions took us to the furthest reaches of their domain, tracing the whispering edges of the dense woods and venturing into the rustling, emerald labyrinth of the towering cornfield. Each journey transformed us into intrepid explorers, navigating untamed safaris or discovering fabled, distant lands hidden just beyond the next row of stalks. The thrill of discovery was constant, whether it was a hidden bird's nest or the tracks of a scurrying creature.

Grandpa's legendary pipe swing, a testament to his ingenuity and love, became our launching pad to the heavens. We'd pump our legs with a frantic joy, soaring ever higher, the wind roaring in our ears and the world momentarily shrinking below. The ultimate dare was to leap from its dizzying apex, convinced we could fly – until gravity asserted its undeniable claim with a satisfying thud onto the soft earth below. This daring ritual invariably drew Grandma to the back window, her voice cutting through the afternoon like a siren, a familiar refrain of "You're going to break an arm!" echoing across the yard, a warning we always heard but rarely heeded. When we took a break from playing, Grandma would make Kool- Aid for us. We watched as she would fill the clear glass pitcher with water, add a package of Kool-Aid, stir, then add sugar and stir as we watched it dissolve, and it's true, "Kool-Aid, Kool-Aid tastes great, Kool-Aid, Kool-Aid, Can't Wait".

The apple and cherry trees in the backyard were our forbidden castles, their sturdy branches, and irresistible invitations to ascend. Our clandestine climbs were often punctuated by Grandma's stern admonishments. Yet, a curious paradox unfolded each autumn: during harvest season, the very act that earned us a scolding suddenly became our duty. That seasonal shift from "get down!" to "go pick some fruit!" was a baffling logic that our young minds, despite much deliberation, could never quite reconcile.

And then, for those rare occasions when our boisterous spirits veered into true mischief, a specific threat would emerge from the dining room window, delivered with a formidable clarity: "You boys fetch me a switch off that willow tree so I can warm your backside!" The mere mention of that supple, stinging branch was usually enough to restore immediate, if temporary, decorum. Looking back, it wasn't the fear, but the sheer theatrics of Grandma's stern warnings, coupled with the underlying current of her boundless affection, that truly resonated. These vibrant echoes of childhood, filled with scrapes, laughter, and a grandmother's vigilant love, are memories I wouldn't trade for anything.

Lessons About the Great Depression from my Grandma Mary Scheschy

My grandmother, my mother's mother, was a fine and nurturing woman who possessed a remarkable resilience forged in the crucible of the Great Depression. Her life wasn't just a collection of hardships; it was a testament to resourcefulness and the profound value of making the most limited resources. She didn't merely survive; she thrived, teaching my mother, and subsequently me, invaluable lessons about frugality, resource management, and the art of finding joy and abundance even amidst scarcity. Her stories weren't simply tales of deprivation, but rather vibrant narratives illustrating ingenuity, community support, and the enduring strength of the human spirit during times of adversity. These lessons, the subtle art of stretching a dollar, the creative repurposing of everyday items, and the importance of prioritizing needs over wants, have shaped my perspective and continue to guide my approach to life, reminding me of the enduring legacy of her generation. I am forever grateful for her wisdom and the profound impact it has had on my life.

Therefore, cultivating this ability to apply common sense in unexpected environments is paramount. It's a skill honed through experience, self-awareness, and a constant willingness to learn and adapt.

The tapestry of our upbringing, woven from the threads of parental influence, forms the foundation of who we are. Understanding the lessons learned, both implicit and explicit, is a crucial step toward self-discovery and personal development. It allows us to appreciate the legacy they have imparted and, critically, to consciously choose to build upon or redefine these lessons in our own lives.

Experiencing Discrimination

My formative years in the 1950s provided an early, indelible lesson in the harsh realities of discrimination. I vividly recall the moments when my school classmate, through his words and actions, targeted not just me, but the very essence of my family. It was a stark introduction to prejudice, one that etched itself deeply into my consciousness.

However, it was against this backdrop that my parents truly shone. Hailing from rich Mexican and Italian heritages, they cultivated in me a profound and unshakeable belief: that all human beings are fundamentally equal, deserving of dignity and respect. They unequivocally taught me to stand firm against the insidious currents of prejudice, to never let it take root in my heart or actions.

This foundational value, instilled with such love and conviction, has proven to be an indispensable compass throughout my life's journey. It has not only shaped my personal integrity but has also fueled an enduring commitment to advocating for true equal opportunity, ensuring that every individual is judged by their character and contributions, not by superficial differences.

My First Car as a Tot

As I was wandering memory lane, a particular image from my childhood popped vividly into my mind. It was that little Champion convertible push pedal car my parents got me – my very first set of wheels! We lived on the boulevard, and I remember it so clearly, a gleaming light blue wonder, with thin black rubber tires that made it feel so real and important.

That car was my absolute pride and joy. I spent countless hours pedaling across every available surface, imagining myself as a seasoned driver on epic adventures. I'd navigate imaginary traffic, make pit stops for invisible fuel, and feel the thrill of speed (even if it was just my own toddler power). I drove that beloved machine with such unbridled enthusiasm that, in what felt like no time at all, I literally wore the rubber treads off its tires, right down to the metal rims beneath. The sheer determination I had to keep moving, even on those worn-down wheels, is something I can still vividly recall.

Looking back now, I truly believe that early, exhilarating taste of mobility and independence ignited a spark within me. It wasn't just a toy; it was the foundation of a lifelong fascination with automobiles. I'm convinced that the sheer joy and freedom I experienced behind the wheel of that little push pedal car set the trajectory for my enduring love of cars, shaping my journey through countless vehicles ever since. It's funny how such a small childhood memory can hold such a profound influence.

Christmas When I was Young

The essence of Christmas, for me, will forever be intertwined with the vivid tapestry of my childhood. Each passing year, as the festive season approaches, my mind drifts back to those magical days, largely shaped by my mother's heartfelt dedication. She didn't merely celebrate Christmas; she breathed life into its meaning, carefully nurturing our understanding of its deeper significance, far beyond the glitter and gifts.

The air on Christmas Eve was always thick with a feeling of almost unbearable excitement. My siblings and I, barely able to contain ourselves, would hum with anticipation, picturing the wonders that awaited us. Come Christmas morning, before a single present was touched, our family ritual unfolded. Lined up precisely according to age on the cool steps of our home, we'd squirm with impatience as Mom meticulously framed her shots with the 8mm movie camera and flash camera. These moments, capturing our wide-eyed wonder, were for posterity, a treasured record of our passage into the heart of Christmas.

Finally, the grand unveiling. Stepping into the living room was like entering a different world. A majestic, freshly cut green fir, standing proudly floor-to-ceiling, dominated the space. It was a beacon of light and scent, adorned with a multitude of colored bulbs that cast a warm, inviting glow, and shimmering tinsel that cascaded down its branches like frozen waterfalls.

The unforgettable aroma of real pine needles mingled with the anticipation, wrapping the entire house in a comforting, festive embrace.

Then came the presents! The sheer, unadulterated joy that erupted as my brothers, sister, and I delved into the brightly wrapped packages was something akin to winning the grand lottery. Our parents, despite their modest means during those years, possessed an incredible gift for making us feel like the richest children in the world. Each carefully chosen item, no matter how small, felt like a king's ransom, inspired by the immense love and sacrifice we were too young to fully comprehend. We played with our newfound toys, building Lincoln Log houses and Tinker toys that occupied us for hours. Santa, indeed, delivered year after year, and his sleigh was powered by our parents' tireless devotion.

Years later, a new chapter began in a new home. Our Christmas traditions evolved, subtly at first. We started with another grand green tree, but soon, a new, dazzling marvel graced our living room: a sleek, modern silver tree. And with it, the enchanting spectacle of a rotating color wheel. Oh, how sophisticated we felt! When the house lights dimmed, the silver branches caught the shifting hues, reds bleeding into greens, blues melting into purples, dancing and reflecting across the ceiling and walls. It was a mesmerizing display that cast a spell over our budding imaginations.

Even as we grew taller, shedding some of our childhood innocence, certain traditions remained the same. The annual lineup on the steps, the sound of the 8mm camera, the flash of the still camera, these acts of preservation continued, a testament to our parents' enduring desire to capture every fleeting moment of our shared joy. Those Christmases, steeped in the innocent wonder of youth and the boundless, unconditional love of our parents, forged memories that sparkle in my mind's eye to this very day, a truly magical legacy.

My Childhood with my Younger Brothers

My childhood in the 1950s was a tapestry woven with threads of boundless freedom and simple joys. It was a time defined not by screens, but by the sun-drenched landscapes of our imagination. Our days unfolded outdoors, a vibrant adventure fueled by creativity and the boundless energy of youth. We weren't passive consumers; we were active creators.

Cowboys and Indians, soldiers and explorers – our games transformed ordinary spaces into epic battlefields and fantastical frontiers. We built elaborate forts from scavenged materials; our constructions are limited only by our ingenuity. Toy soldiers, meticulously arranged within twig-and-leaf fortifications, became the protagonists in our ongoing dramas. Our world was large, yet our home always felt close, a reassuring beacon on the horizon.

I recall lying on the cool grass, gazing into the vast expanse of the sky, marveling at its endless expanse, and pondering the mysteries it held. Evenings brought the comforting glow of our television set, where we eagerly awaited beloved shows like "The Mickey Mouse Club," various cartoons, and the thrilling adventures of "The Lone Ranger," "Sky King," "Fury," "Superman," and "The Rifleman." These weren't just programs; they were moral compasses, each episode offering a potent message of courage, justice, and integrity. Mattel toys were the coveted prizes of our childhood, and Christmas mornings were filled with the anticipation of receiving the latest line of toy guns and holsters.

Even minor mishaps, like a bee sting or a muddy mishap, couldn't deter us from our outdoor adventures. The sting of the bee was quickly forgotten in the thrill of the game, the mud a small price to pay for uninterrupted play. Winter brought a different kind of magic: the construction of magnificent snow forts and igloos, epic snowball battles, and the painstaking creation of snowmen, each one a unique masterpiece. The thrill of sledding down steep hills provided an exhilarating rush, adding another layer to the richness of our outdoor experience.

That era, filled with unadulterated fun and the forging of strong bonds with friends and family, laid a solid foundation for my future. The lessons learned – creativity, resilience, resourcefulness, the importance of friendship and community – continue to shape my life today. It was a childhood imbued with a sense of freedom and wonder that remains a cherished memory, a timeless reminder of the simple joys and profound lessons of a bygone era.

Saint Cecilia's Catholic Church

Childhood memories often shimmer with a unique blend of nostalgia and sharp, formative lessons.

One such vivid memory unfurls within the hallowed, slightly musty halls of Saint Cecilia's school, where my two younger brothers and I attended catechism. Our instructor, a formidable nun, I swear that she floated across the floor in her nun's habit and whose very presence commanded an almost reverential silence, was a woman of unwavering discipline.

Her gaze, keen and unsparing, would sweep across the rows of fidgeting youngsters, detecting any lapse in attention or decorum. She held a particular disdain for youthful squirming, viewing it as a personal affront to the sanctity of the classroom.

My brothers, barely ten and nine at the time – I, a grand old eleven myself – were vibrant conduits of boundless energy, their minds far more attuned to the thrilling whispers of adventure than the solemn tenets being expounded. They found the confines of a classroom a severe impediment to their innate curiosity. Rather than grapple with their constant wiggling and hushed conspiratorial giggles, the good Sister frequently chose a more direct, and in my young mind, profoundly unjust path. She would hold "me" accountable for their behavior, punctuating her stern admonishments with the swift, stinging tap of a ruler against my knuckles – a clear, if painful, directive to "keep them in line."

Their inquisitive spirits, however, were not easily contained. One sunny afternoon, after catechism had concluded, a particularly audacious idea took root. The magnificent bell towers of Saint Cecilia's cathedral, soaring majestically into the sky, beckoned to their adventurous souls. Despite my fervent protests and dire warnings about the absolute prohibition against such an endeavor, the allure of the forbidden was too strong. They were convinced that climbing those ancient, winding stairs would reveal untold wonders. Left to my own devices, I reluctantly positioned myself outside the massive, ornate church doors, a self-appointed, albeit anxious, sentinel for their inevitable return.

A slow, creeping dread began to settle upon me as minutes stretched into an eternity. Then, a figure rounded the corner of the cathedral, his distinguished clerical attire rustling softly against the breeze. It was the Monsignor, the very embodiment of authority. His gentle, yet penetrating, gaze fell upon me. He inquired if I was alright, and I, mustering a shaky "I'm fine, thank you," braced myself for the inevitable follow-up. "What are you waiting for, son?" he asked, his voice kind but firm. A profound tremor shook me. I had been raised with an unwavering reverence for honesty, especially with figures of such moral standing. Yet, the unwritten, sacred code of brotherhood screamed louder. To betray my siblings, especially to a Monsignor, felt like an act of sacrilege itself. My mind raced, constructing a swift, convenient half-truth: "I'm just waiting for my brothers so we can walk home together." I felt an immediate, prickling guilt, already mentally composing fervent prayers for forgiveness.

As the Monsignor, seemingly satisfied, continued into the church, I dared to glance up. And there, framed perfectly within the ancient, arched openings of the bell tower, were two small, triumphant figures. My brothers, beaming with a mixture of exhilaration and youthful defiance, waved down at me. A wave of profound relief, tinged with exasperated annoyance, washed over me. I frantically motioned for them to come down.

The walk home, I delivered a lecture of formidable intensity, outlining in no uncertain terms the severe consequences should they ever repeat such a perilous stunt. "Next time," I declared with all the gravitas an eleven-year-old could muster, "I'm telling Mom and Dad." It was a moment that underscored the complex, often challenging, but ultimately unbreakable bond shared between brothers, forever etched into the annals of our shared childhood.

Walking to School

I found myself recently reminiscing about my early school days and how profoundly different the experience was for us. From the very first steps into kindergarten at Kellom Elementary, and then through the various chapters at Lothrop, Franklin, and Hartman Elementary schools, all the way to Monroe and Nathan Hale Junior Highs, our daily commute was an almost entirely foot-powered adventure.

It's remarkable to reflect upon it now, but each morning, we simply set off. There was an incredible sense of freedom and lack of urgency; we weren't consumed by the clock, nor did the concept of personal safety weigh heavily on our young minds. The only real exception to this steadfast routine was the much-appreciated lift from my neighborhood friend Steve Ray's mom when we transitioned to Benson High School.

Even then, the spirit of those independent walks remained a core part of our upbringing.

Looking back, those daily treks were far more than just a means to an end. They were integral, perhaps even unconscious, part of our development. This consistent physical activity was undeniably healthy, fostering a robust physical constitution and building an incredible amount of endurance that served us well in countless ways.

Beyond the physical, there was a quiet confidence and independence cultivated with every mile walked, every pathway discovered, and every moment spent navigating our neighborhood. It speaks to a bygone era, a time when our local communities felt incredibly safe and the world, perhaps, a little less rushed.

I was just reflecting on my school days recently, and one of the most indelible memories that consistently comes to mind is the morning tradition we all shared. Every single day, without fail, as the first bell signaled the start of classes, we would all stand, often with a hand over our hearts, and collectively recite the Pledge of Allegiance. It wasn't merely a routine; it was a foundational moment that set the tone for our entire day, fostering a shared sense of purpose and belonging among us.

Looking back, there was a palpable and sincere sense of pride and loyalty that permeated our school experience. This wasn't just a vague feeling; it was directed towards everyone and everything that made up our educational world.

We held immense respect for our teachers, who were more than just instructors; they were dedicated mentors who guided us through challenges and celebrated our successes.

The camaraderie we shared with our classmates was equally profound, creating a tight-knit community where friendships blossomed, and collective achievements were truly valued. And the school itself, with its halls, classrooms, and playing fields, felt like a second home, a place where we not only learned academics but also developed a strong sense of community, responsibility, and shared identity that truly shaped our formative years.

THE ZOO

Before Omaha proudly boasted about the incredible, world-class institution that is the Henry Doorly Zoo, there was a quieter, perhaps more intimate, place we knew as the Riverside Park Zoo. It truly held a unique charm.

I find myself reminiscing about those special occasions when Mom, with her characteristic thoughtfulness, would plan these wonderful outings for us. She'd meticulously pack everything we could possibly need for a day of adventure, always ensuring we were well- equipped for fun.

These weren't just simple trips; they were cherishing social gatherings, too. Mom would coordinate with her closest friends, and soon, the park would be alive with a whole gang of us kids.

The sheer joy of seeing all the kids knowing an entire day of exploration and play lay ahead was infectious. We'd be a blur of motion, dashing along the pathways, engaged in boisterous games of chase, our laughter echoing amidst the animal sounds. It felt like our own private kingdom where every corner held a new discovery.

And then, of course, came the highlight – our picnic lunch. Spread out on the picnic tables usually under a grand old tree, simple sandwiches, refreshing drinks, and those much- anticipated cookies tasted like the finest feast.

The easy chatter of the adults blended with our playful shouts, creating a vibrant, heartwarming atmosphere.

Those days at the Riverside Park Zoo, made so effortlessly memorable by Mom's love and planning, are truly some of the most precious and carefree moments of our childhood. What wonderful memories we share from that time.

Paper Airplanes

I was just swept away by a wave of nostalgia the other day, and a particularly vivid memory of Dad instantly came to mind. He always had a knack for turning everyday things into extraordinary lessons. Well, I vividly recall him teaching me the intricate art of crafting paper airplanes, emphasizing the ingenuity involved in each fold and cut.

He introduced me to two distinct types of airborne wonders. The first was a masterpiece of careful construction, requiring the use of scissors to meticulously shape the wings, body, and tail sections. I remember the satisfying snip of the paper and the careful alignment, resulting in a more robust model that, once launched, would often glide with a majestic, looping trajectory; its flight a slow dance across the air.

Then, there was the second, more streamlined design. This one was all about precision folding – no scissors required, just the deft manipulation of paper to create a sleek, aerodynamic jet. These were the speed of demons, capable of zipping across a room or a backyard with surprising velocity, a testament to the power of a perfectly executed crease.

Whether we were grounded indoors on a rainy afternoon or basking in the sunshine outside, those simple sheets of paper transformed into vessels of endless entertainment. We'd spend hours launching them, experimenting with different angles, and marveling at their flight paths. It wasn't just about the planes themselves; it was about the shared laughter, the quiet moments of concentration, and the invaluable time spent together, learning and creating.

Those moments, built on curiosity and the simple joy of making something with our hands, are truly cherished memories.

Hair Cuts

It's fascinating how certain childhood memories, seemingly simple, can carve such indelible marks on our lives, shaping our perspectives in unexpected ways. For me, one such series of recollections revolves around haircuts.

My father, a proud Marine, ingrained a sense of discipline and practicality into everything he did, and our haircuts were no exception. I vividly recall the ritual: my brothers and I would take turns on a sturdy, four-legged stool, becoming the willing (or sometimes not-so-willing) subjects of his "hair cutting prowess." He favored the no-nonsense "Butch" cut, high and tight, a style perfectly aligned with his military background. The distinct scent of "Butch wax" – that firm, clear pomade – often accompanied these sessions, used to slick back any remnant bangs, leaving us with a uniformly neat, almost helmet-like finish.

Those moments weren't just about grooming; they were lessons in precision, order, and perhaps, a quiet demonstration of his love and care, expressed through a clipper.

As we transitioned into our teenage years, the winds of cultural change, particularly the phenomenon of The Beatles, swept through our lives. Suddenly, the military precision of the "Butch" cut felt restrictive, and the desire for self-expression through longer hair became paramount. Our father's clippers were retired from active duty on our heads, marking a subtle but significant shift in our journey from childhood conformity to adolescent individuality.

It was during this era that I even found myself wielding the scissors and razor. My childhood friend, Steve Ray, often entrusted me with trimming his hair. We aimed for a look that was clean yet undeniably fashionable, reflecting the evolving trends of the time. It was an early, perhaps unconscious, exploration of personal style and the small ways we helped each other navigate the world of growing up.

Life continued its course, and after I married my wonderful wife, Diane, a new chapter in my personal grooming began. I asked her if she would be willing to take on the task of cutting my hair, a request born out of trust and affection. To my delight, she not only agreed but proved to be exceptionally skilled. What started as a thoughtful gesture quickly became an enduring tradition.

Her touch is precise; her understanding of what I like is intuitive, and the comfort of having my hair cut by the person who knows me best has made her my exclusive stylist ever since. It's a small, consistent act that speaks volumes about our partnership and the shared tapestry of our lives.

From my father's disciplined clippers to Diane's caring hands, these personal rituals of grooming have been threads woven through the fabric of my life, each moment a reflection of growth, change, and the enduring connections we make along the way.

Responsibility for my brothers and sister

I want to reflect on my upbringing as the eldest of four children in my family: myself, my brothers Ricardo ("Rick") and Ranaldo ("Randy"), and my sister Gina. My parents naturally placed certain expectations on me as the oldest, often implicitly casting me in the role of a role model. While I strived to live up to this, it wasn't without its difficulties. The dynamics of a large family, punctuated by the inevitable sibling rivalries, presented a unique set of challenges. Navigating these complexities – managing disagreements, mediating conflicts, and striving for a harmonious family environment – was a constant learning process. Looking back, I recognize the significant influence these experiences have had on shaping my ability to understand and manage interpersonal relationships, conflict resolution, and the ongoing work of maintaining healthy familial bonds. The lessons learned in mediating sibling squabbles and fostering cooperation within a diverse and often challenging family dynamic have proven invaluable in my personal and professional life.

My brothers and I, a trio I fondly dubbed "The Three Amigos," were a constant presence in my life. Growing up, I made a conscious effort to include them in my social circles, inviting them to hang out with my friends whenever possible. This wasn't just about fostering a sense of belonging for them; it was also a way for me to maintain a protective presence in their lives. I felt a strong responsibility for their well-being, and ensuring they were integrated into my social world allowed me to keep a close, albeit unobtrusive, watch over them. The dynamics were complex, balancing their independence with my need to ensure their safety. This experience taught me the importance of family unity and the subtle art of protective oversight, shaping my understanding of brotherhood and responsibility in profound ways.

My youngest brother, Randy, always said to me growing up that he appreciated being included and how my friends treated him like a brother. I had great and understanding friends.

When We Were Kids

I often find myself reminiscing about those sun-drenched afternoons of my youth, when the simplest joys held the greatest magic. Among them, the act of flying kites stands out vividly. Every now and then, our parents would surprise us with a new, brilliantly colored kite, a marvel of lightweight construction and aerodynamic design.

There was an unparalleled thrill in releasing it into the sky, feeling the taut string vibrate with the wind's energy, watching our vibrant creation ascend higher and higher, a tiny speck against the vast expanse of blue. Our shared ambition was always to send it as close to heaven as possible.

Yet, just as reliably as the wind would lift our spirits, it would inevitably falter. The once-strong currents would die down, and with a sense of quiet resignation, we'd watch our magnificent kites begin their slow, graceful descent, often culminating in a gentle, or sometimes not-so- gentle, crash back to earth.

Given that we couldn't perpetually ask for a fresh replacement for every mishap, we soon learned the art of resourcefulness.

With newspaper scraps, carefully selected twigs, and whatever string we could find, we'd set about constructing our own, often eccentric, flying machines. These homemade contraptions were rarely as elegant or efficient as their store-bought counterparts; they'd often wobble, struggle to gain altitude, and their flights were frequently cut short. But in the earnest effort, the shared laughter over our creations' peculiarities, and the sheer persistence of trying again, there was an immeasurable, enduring joy. It was in those imperfect, self-made moments that we truly discovered the essence of play and the satisfaction of bringing an idea, however flawed, to life.

YO-YO'S

The precise year may escape me, but the vivid sensation of receiving my very first yo-yo, somewhere within the nostalgic haze of my grade school years, remains remarkably clear.

That initial Duncan yo-yo wasn't merely a toy; it quickly transformed into a source of endless fascination and absorbed concentration. I recall spending countless hours, completely immersed in the rhythmic rise and fall, the satisfying hum, and the sheer delight of gradually mastering each new trick.

The satisfaction of executing a smooth "Walk the Dog," guiding the spinning disc across the floor, or launching it gracefully into the expansive arc of the "Cradle", or a "Around the World", "Rock the Baby", or the "Forward Pass", was truly immense. Each subtle flick of the wrist, every perfectly timed tug on the string, felt like a miniature triumph. As my skills and ambition grew, I distinctly remember transitioning to the Duncan Butterfly yo-yo. This felt like a significant upgrade; its wider body opening up a whole new universe of string tricks and longer, more elegant spins, thereby extending the joy and challenge of yo-yoing for many more unforgettable hours. Those were the days!

Feeling Safe Walking/Running to the Store

I often find myself drifting back to a time from my childhood, while living on 33rd & Blondo Street, a period imbued with a profound sense of community and security. I recall with perfect clarity the freedom we enjoyed, where navigating the familiar streets to the neighborhood grocery store, the bustling hardware shop, or even the local pharmacy was an effortless excursion, completely devoid of any apprehension for personal safety. The world felt open and welcoming then.

I can still picture those early mornings, the air crisp and quiet, as I'd eagerly race down the block, entrusted with the important task of fetching fresh cereal or milk to complete our breakfast. It was a small ritual that instilled a sense of responsibility and independence. And then there was the charming florist shop, just a stone's throw away, a treasure trove of color and scent. It was there, with a mix of earnest concentration and bubbling excitement, that I would carefully choose and purchase a single, beautiful flower for my mom on Mother's Day, a cherished memory of innocent love and thoughtful gestures. These moments, seemingly simple, form the bedrock of a precious past.

Pop Bottles

I vividly recall my elementary school years, a time when the siren song of sugary treats was almost irresistible. My young mind, driven by an insatiable craving for candy, quickly devised an ingenious, albeit humble, entrepreneurial scheme. My mission involved scouring the neighborhood; eyes peeled for discarded pop bottles – treasures waiting to be discovered.

Each bottle, once found, underwent a meticulous rinsing ritual before I embarked on my pilgrimage to George's corner drugstore.

George, a man of quiet demeanor behind the counter, would dutifully count my gleaming collection, each return earning a precious two cents. That handful of coins, earned through diligent effort, felt like a king's ransom. With my newfound wealth clutched tightly in my hand, I would then enter the hallowed aisles of his store, my gaze fixed on the vibrant array of confections.

The choice was always a delightful dilemma: the satisfying chew of gumballs, the mysterious allure of Sputniks, or the enduring challenge of a jawbreaker. Those simple transactions, from bottle collection to sweet indulgence, were not just about candy; they were my first lessons in resourcefulness and the sweet taste of earned reward.

Playing Mumblety Peg

Have you ever play a game of Humbly-peg? Well, let me tell you my story of playing the game with a neighbor and my brothers.

My first mistake was not wearing shoes.

We started the game, and it was going fine. After two of the four were eliminated during the game, it came down to my brother Rick and me.

Things were still going fine until my brother Rick threw the knife, and it stuck in my big toe.

Much to my surprise, it didn't hurt, but there it was, stuck in my toe, moving back and forth. My brother looked at the knife, then me, and took off running for fear that I would do something to him.

The rest of us just had a good belly laugh, and we still laugh today when the story is told.

Chapter Two

Riding Bikes

There was a unique chapter in my younger years, long before the freedom of a driver's license ever entered my mind, when independence truly rode on two wheels. My most steadfast companion and primary mode of transportation was, without question, my bicycle. It wasn't merely a vehicle; it was my passport to exploration, carrying me unwavering loyalty through countless sun-drenched afternoons and spirited neighborhood adventures.

That bicycle was the silent witness to every secret whispered, every daring shortcut discovered, and every grand plan hatched with friends.

I can still vividly recall the sheer ingenuity of our youthful endeavors to elevate the cycling experience. With a simple playing card and a trusty clothespin, we'd meticulously attach the card to the frame, perfectly angled to strike the spokes with each rotation. The resulting rhythmic "thwack-thwack-thwack" wasn't just noise; it was, in our vivid imaginations, the unmistakable, powerful rumble of a motorcycle's engine. This ingenious modification transformed an ordinary bike ride into an exhilarating, roaring journey.

That distinctive sound was our signature, our declaration of cool to the world. And in those days, when something truly resonated with us, something that blended cleverness with an undeniable sense of awe and excitement, there was only one fitting expression. We'd lean back, a knowing smile on our faces, and with absolute conviction, we'd pronounce it "far out!"

Phone/Bathroom/Television

Reflecting on my formative years, growing up in the 1950s and 60s, and the stark contrast between those times and our present-day realities is truly remarkable. We often speak of "simpler times," and while challenges certainly existed, the way we lived with and shared our resources was fundamentally different.

Imagine a household where a single bathroom served the entire family. Mornings were a meticulously orchestrated routine, a testament to patience, and the unspoken rule of "first come, first served" as we prepared for school.

Communication was similarly centralized; a solitary telephone was the lifeline to the outside world. As teenagers navigating the mid-to-late sixties, phone conversations were often subject to strict time limits, and the notion of personal privacy during a call was almost entirely foreign, given the constant potential for someone else to need the line. Even our entertainment was a shared communal experience, with one family television dictating our viewing schedules, its programming entirely at our parents' discretion.

My brothers and I also shared a single bedroom, learning the valuable lessons of compromise and camaraderie from a very early age.

It still brings a smile to my face when I recall telling people later in life that my father, in his own unique way, invented the remote control! His version involved me, patiently positioning myself directly in front of the television, holding the antenna in just the right spot to get a clearer picture, all while taking precise instructions from him: "a little to the left," "no, back a bit," or the triumphant "hold it right there!" It was an interactive, hands-on viewing experience, demanding a level of engagement and teamwork that today's seamless technology rarely requires.

A particularly cherished memory from my formative years revolves around a significant addition to our family home. It was a brand-new, all-in-one color television stereo console, an impressive piece of technology that seamlessly integrated with an AM/FM radio and a record player.

More than just an appliance, it was a magnificent piece of furniture, housed within a solid mahogany wood cabinet. Its rich, polished finish exuded warmth and sophistication, instantly becoming the focal point of our living room. But its beauty wasn't merely superficial; the audio experience it offered was truly exceptional. The stereo sound was nothing short of magnificent, filling the room with rich, resonant tones that transformed ordinary listening into an immersive auditory delight, whether we were tuning into our favorite radio stations or spinning records. This console wasn't just an entertainment system; it was a testament to the era's advancements, a cherished family possession that brought countless hours of joy and shared experiences, from watching television together to discovering new music on vinyl.

Looking back, these experiences fostered the importance of shared moments and cultivated a profound sense of patience and gratitude for what we had.

The world has transformed at an astonishing pace since then, offering unparalleled convenience and an abundance of personal devices that would have been unimaginable. Yet it's worth pausing to consider the quiet, invaluable lessons of those seemingly "limited" times imparted upon us.

I was just thinking about how dramatically different our world is now compared to the good old days. My mind wandered back to a time that felt so much simpler, especially when it came to television. I remember when local TV stations actually *signed off* for the night at midnight. It's almost impossible to imagine now, with countless channels and streaming services available 24/7.

Back then, our choices were delightfully limited to just three main channels: KETV, WOW, and KMTV. It meant we often watched the same things, and those shared experiences truly knit the community together. There wasn't this endless scroll of options, just those familiar voices and faces on our screens.

And what a ritual it was when the broadcast day concluded! Before the signal disappeared into static, they'd play the National Anthem. I can still vividly picture the American flag waving proudly in the breeze, often accompanied by a solemn orchestral rendition. It was a dignified, almost ceremonial way to end the evening. Right after that, we'd be greeted by that iconic "test pattern" – a curious, geometric design that signaled the end of entertainment until morning. It was a stark reminder that the world wasn't always on demand.

Of course, all this happened on our trusty black and white television sets. Colors were left to our imagination and tuning in often involved jiggling rabbit ears to get a clear picture, sometimes battling with static. It made every show feel a bit more precious, a little more magical, I think.

Those are such cherished memories. And let's be honest, managing to stay awake long enough to witness that entire sign-off sequence felt like a major accomplishment, a badge of honor for us kids! It truly was a different era, full of its own unique charm and quiet moments.

Sibling Rivalry

I was just reminiscing about a particular memory from my childhood home that came to mind, bringing a smile to my face. I recall those lively, sometimes tumultuous, dinner times when Rick and I were teenagers. There was often an undercurrent of brotherly friction, and it wasn't uncommon for our disagreements, unspoken through the meal, to manifest themselves in some rather unique ways.

I distinctly remember the subtle, yet undeniably firm, kick I'd sometimes receive under the table from Rick. Of course, my instinct was always reciprocating, escalating into a silent, clandestine battle of shins and ankles. Our father, with his uncanny ability to sense the unspoken tension, would eventually reach his breaking point. I can still hear the resounding slap of his hand on the dining table, followed by his booming, characteristic command: "Alright, you two, enough! Get the boxing gloves on and take it out to the backyard!

And so, we did. We'd tumble out into the yard, and for a few spirited minutes, we'd engage in a rough-and-tumble session – pushing, shoving, and wrestling out our frustrations. I'd usually get the upper hand, and my knowing laughter, more from the sheer absurdity and relief than malice, would often ignite a fresh wave of competitive fury in Rick. But once the energy was spent, it was truly over. No lingering grudges, no simmering resentment. Within minutes, we'd be off, playing together as if the conflict had never happened.

Looking back, it was an unconventional, yet profoundly effective lesson from Dad. He wasn't advocating violence, but rather teaching us to confront our differences directly, channel our youthful energy, and then, crucially, to let go. It taught us that disagreements are a part of life, but they don't have to define a relationship or lead to lasting animosity. We learned to clear the air, quite literally, and move forward without carrying the weight of unresolved conflict.

My Paper Route

The biting chill in the air this morning, registering a mere twenty degrees Fahrenheit before factoring in the wind, transported me instantly back to a specific time, the mid-1960s, my junior high years. It wasn't just the cold; it was the sharp, physical memory it triggered, a stark reminder of my days as a paperboy.

Back then, the sound of the thud of the morning paper hitting the porch was an essential part of daily life for countless families, including many on my paper route. Weekdays meant dashing through deliveries after school, but the true test of grit came on the weekends. We were out the door well before six a.m., rain or shine, snow or sweltering heat, or, like today, bone-numbing cold. The weather was simply irrelevant; the news "had" to reach its readers.

I lived on 69th and Parkview lane streets, and my distribution hub was conveniently located near 64th and Parkview lane. On those pre-dawn weekend mornings, right there on the corner, the painstaking process of preparing each paper began. During the week, every paper had to be tightly folded. Weekday morning editions were slender, but the largest paper was Sunday, laden with thick sections, advertisements, and entertainment guides, which demanded a heavy-duty rubber band. On those days, I had to bribe my two younger brothers to assist me; sometimes they would and other times they didn't. But I still had the responsibility to deliver. I remember one Sunday morning particularly, my brother Rick, after getting my dad involved to have him help me, reluctantly did so. We were on the corner, filling the bags with papers filled to the brim. I started out delivering papers and had the bag on. Rick, who didn't want to be there in the first place, decided he had enough and jumped on my back, throwing me to the ground. It was a struggle getting up, and I remember yelling, " Run, you better not let me catch you." Of course, I dealt with him after I was done delivering papers when I got home.

Collecting for the newspaper was the worst. Some of my customers would invite me in when it was extremely cold out, and some would make me stand outside until they returned with the money to pay their bill. I remember distinctly having to punch the ledger cards showing that they paid for the week. To do that, though, I had to take my gloves off, punch their card, and put my gloves back on, only to repeat the effort at the next house. I remember my hands were so cold, but it was part of the job. One winter, I was lucky enough to win a pocket hand warmer from the district office in Benson, and it helped, but I still froze. It was brutal.

The sheer responsibility was immense. People genuinely relied on us. Folding those papers invariably left my hands stained a deep, indelible gray from the ink, a badge of honor in its own way. My delivery bag, with large openings front and back, quickly became a burden of burden. You'd load both sides, and by the time it was half-full; it already weighed a ton. Sundays, with their colossal advertising supplements, were particularly brutal.

It was undeniably hard work. There were no convenient plastic sleeves if it rained. I had to place the paper in the door to ensure the subscriber received a pristine, un-soaked paper.

Sickness offered no reprieve; if you were ill, you still delivered. The paper route was an unceasing, unforgiving commitment.

The monetary compensation was modest, to be sure, but it felt like a king's ransom. It was "my" money, earned through my own sweat and effort. It funded my bike repairs, expanded my record collection, and afforded me an opportunity to start saving money. More profoundly, that grimy, ink-stained bag became a symbol of burgeoning self-reliance and deep-seated pride.

While nothing truly lasts forever, and a paper route was certainly never glamorous, those years taught me invaluable lessons. Responsibility, an unshakeable work ethic, and the profound satisfaction of earning something entirely on your own.

The Whistle

I often find my thoughts drifting back to the sun-drenched afternoons of my youth, spent with friends in our bustling neighborhood. We were an inseparable band of adventurers, convinced the day would never end, our laughter echoing down the streets as we chased each other through endless games of hide-and-seek or kick-the-can, basketball in the driveway, baseball in the vacant lot, riding our skateboards, or riding our bikes.

But there was always a clear, resounding signal that brought our glorious escapades to an abrupt, yet cherished, halt. The moment those first streetlights began to hum and glow, painting the twilight in an orange hue, my father's distinct whistle would cut through the evening air. It was a singular, powerful blast, carrying an undeniable command: "Time to come home, boys!" And without a second thought, a frantic scramble of bare feet and hurried goodbyes would ensue, as we sprinted towards the familiar comfort of our house. The unwritten rule was absolute; to linger was to face his quiet, formidable disapproval.

Our neighborhood friends even knew when they heard the whistle, and they would tell us, "Your dad's calling you, it's time for us to go home."

As the years unfolded and we grew from boisterous youngsters into slightly more independent teenagers, Dad relaxed his unwavering stance a little. The strict, immediate summons softened, allowing for a few extra moments of twilight camaraderie. Yet, even then, the whistle remained his chosen instrument of retrieval. It might have been a softer, more understanding call, a gentle reminder rather than an urgent decree, but its message was still clear, and our instinct to respond, to come running, never faded. It wasn't just a sound; it was a constant reminder of his watchful presence and the comforting, unwavering anchor of our home.

Watching the Wide World of Sports

"The thrill of victory, the agony of defeat, and the human drama of athletic competition".

Growing up, some of my most vivid and cherished memories revolved around the captivating world of boxing, a passion my father wholeheartedly embraced. Friday nights were sacred in our household; the television became a portal to a gladiatorial arena. On the weekends, we watched ABC Wide World of Sports, often narrated by the iconic voice of Jim McKay. The famous Howard Cosell, who brought every jab and cross to life with their insightful commentary, covered Muhammad Ali's fights.

But above all, one figure dominated our conversations and captured our imaginations: Muhammad Ali. My father, like countless others, held Ali in a reverence that bordered on awe. He wasn't just a boxer; he was, without a doubt, "the greatest of all time." We'd gather around, my eyes wide with wonder, as we watched him move with an unparalleled grace that truly embodied his legendary mantra, "float like a butterfly, sting like a bee." I recall the mesmerizing rhythm of his famous foot shuffle, a dance that confounded opponents and thrilled spectators. And then there were those unforgettable championship bouts where he ingeniously deployed the "rope-a-dope" strategy, a testament to his tactical brilliance and incredible resilience. Watching Ali was more than just a fight; it was a masterclass in athleticism, showmanship, and an unwavering spirit that inspired us all. Those shared moments with my father, witnessing the master in action, are memories I hold very dear.

Hide and Seek

As twilight descended, casting long shadows across our street, a different kind of energy would awaken in the neighborhood. It was the unofficial signal for us, the collective band of local kids, to emerge from our homes. Drawn by the magnetic pull of the cooling evening air and the promise of adventure, we'd converge under the streetlight at the bottom of our hill, an excited swarm ready to transform the familiar block into our personal playground.

The main event? An epic, high-stakes game of hide-and-seek under the stars. The air would buzz with anticipation as we meticulously divided ourselves into fiercely competitive teams, often after much good-natured debate and strategic alliances.

Once the boundaries were set and the 'seeker' began their booming count, the remaining players would scatter like dandelion seeds in the wind, each team member desperately seeking the ultimate, undiscoverable sanctuary.

Oh, the thrill of those moments! We'd squeeze into the densest rose bushes, flatten ourselves behind parked cars, or perch precariously in the branches of an old hedge, convinced we had found the ingenious spot no opposing team member would ever think to look.

The nervous giggles stifled behind cupped hands, the pounding hearts as footsteps drew near, the shared exhilaration of remaining undetected. It was a symphony of childhood joy and innocent strategy.

These weren't just games; they were nocturnal expeditions, binding us together in a shared secret world of shadows and whispers. The sheer joy of outsmarting our friends and the camaraderie born from those hidden moments made every single night an absolute, unforgettable blast.

Lionel Train Set

The rhythmic chug of a Lionel locomotive, the satisfying clickety-clack of the cars on the track – those sounds still resonate in my memory, as vivid as if I were a child again, hunched over that magnificent train set my parents gifted me. It wasn't just a toy; it was a portal. Each meticulously crafted piece, from the locomotive engine to the tiny cabooses, fueled my imagination, transforming our living room into a sprawling landscape of adventure. I wasn't just playing with a train; I was piloting a majestic iron horse across boundless prairies, scaling treacherous mountain passes, and hurtling through bustling cityscapes. My childhood journeys were epic in scope, limited only by the confines of the track and the boundless creativity of a young boy's mind. The sheer joy and wonder it instilled remain etched in my heart. Even now, years later, the carefully packed train set in my basement serves as a tangible reminder of those extraordinary voyages and the boundless gift of imagination. It's a treasure more precious than any monetary value could ever express.

Cub / Boy Scouts

I often find myself reflecting on those formative years spent in the Cub Scouts, a period rich with discovery and camaraderie. Each step of that journey, from achieving the initial Bobcat rank to proudly earning the Wolf, Bear, and ultimately the Lion badges, was a testament to dedication and learning.

The satisfaction of sewing on each chevron and year pin, witnessing my uniform to become a tapestry of my adventures, was immense. Our close-knit Den 7, part of the larger and spirited Pack 29, was more than just a group; it was a small band of explorers, learning essential life skills and the value of teamwork.

I vividly remember the crisp blue fabric of my uniform shirt, adorned with that vibrant yellow and blue scout scarf, each colorful badge a marker of a skill honed, an outdoor adventure experience, or a community service project completed.

Those early experiences instilled in me with a sense of accomplishment and belonging.

My experience in the Boy Scouts of America, beginning at a young age, profoundly shaped my character and instilled in me a strong work ethic and a deep appreciation for teamwork.

The program provided a unique environment for personal growth, far beyond simply earning merit badges. The rigorous process of achieving each badge demanded dedication, perseverance, and meticulous attention to detail, skills that have proven invaluable in my subsequent academic and professional endeavors. Beyond the individual achievements, however, the collaborative nature of many Scouting activities was equally formative. Working alongside my peers on projects ranging from wilderness survival exercises to community service initiatives taught me the importance of effective communication, conflict resolution, and the power of collective effort towards a common goal. These experiences fostered a sense of responsibility, leadership, and camaraderie that I carry with me to this day. The lessons learned in the Scouts extend far beyond the outdoor skills and technical knowledge; they instilled a fundamental understanding of self-reliance, resilience, and the value of contributing to something larger than oneself. I remain deeply grateful for the opportunities and mentorship provided by this incredible organization.

Tandy Leather Crafts

I was reminiscing the other day, and a particular set of childhood memories came flooding back – those precious few Saturday mornings that often smelled of freshly tooled leather. It always involved heading over to a friend's house, a fellow Scout, where we'd dive into the intricate world of Tandy leather crafts.

I can still vividly recall the workbench, scattered with swivel knives, an array of gleaming stamping tools, and the heavy mallet. My first major project, a humble billfold, felt like a monumental undertaking. The meticulous process of wetting the leather, carefully pressing the design stamps one by one with a deliberate tap of the hammer, aiming for perfect alignment, and then the delicate task of hand-sewing the binding together to secure it all.

The sense of triumph when it was finally completed was immense; in my young eyes, it was nothing short of a masterpiece. A short while later, a matching leather belt followed, each step in a mirror of the same painstaking, yet utterly rewarding, creative journey.

Looking back, these weren't merely craft sessions. They were profound lessons in patience, precision, and the sheer satisfaction of bringing something tangible to life with your own two hands. In a world increasingly dominated by screens, those hours spent shaping leather offered an invaluable connection to craftsmanship and enduring skill-building. They taught me the quiet discipline of focusing on a task until it reached its completion, a principle that has stayed with me ever since. It makes me wonder what other forgotten skills or hobbies from our youth still hold such a powerful resonance.

Safety Patrol

My path toward public service began surprisingly early. My fifth-grade election for safety patrol captain wasn't just a childish game; it ignited a spark within me. The responsibility of ensuring the safety of my classmates, symbolized by my meticulously folded belt and gleaming AAA blue-on-silver captain's badge, instilled in me a deep sense of pride and purpose. Controlling the traffic light at a busy intersection near our school, a key entrusted to a ten-year-old, was more than just a task; it was a profound experience in leadership and community responsibility. The weight of that responsibility, the trust placed in me, shaped my understanding of civic duty.

This commitment to service continued throughout high school, where I volunteered as a hall monitor. The role wasn't simply about maintaining order; it was about fostering a safe and secure environment for my peers, ensuring their well-being, and facilitating a positive learning atmosphere. Again, I approached this responsibility with the same seriousness and dedication that marked my early experiences as safety patrol captain.

My commitment to public service wasn't a fleeting childhood fancy; it's a core value that has guided my life choices. The lessons learned in those early roles – the importance of responsibility, leadership, and community engagement – were invaluable.

Cactus Candy

Remembering back to a truly cherished time in our childhood, a memory that vividly illustrates Grandpa's incredible spirit and the joy of shared experiences. That unforgettable journey to Mexico with him and my brothers wasn't merely a vacation; it was a profound voyage of discovery. I can still recall the vibrant colors, the melodic sounds, and the tantalizing aromas from the bustling markets, each scent weaving itself into the fabric of our understanding. Grandpa, who was born in Mexico, with his boundless wisdom and patient guidance, truly opened our eyes to a culture rich in history and warmth, transforming a simple trip into an invaluable lesson in life itself.

Among the many sensory delights, the discovery of the unique confectionery items was a particular highlight. And oh, that incredible cactus candy! Its distinct texture and subtly sweet, almost earthy flavor were unlike anything we'd ever tasted. A spark ignited in our young minds: wouldn't this be the most incredible, exotic treat to share with our friends back home at Hartman Elementary? We envisioned their wide eyes and delighted expressions, eager to share a piece of our adventure.

True to his generous nature and always keen to foster our budding sense of community and sharing, Grandpa Lecuona made sure we had an ample supply. He bought boxes of vibrant green and red confections, enough so that every single classmate and even our teachers could have a taste of our incredible journey.

The moment we returned to school, laden with our sugary treasures was electric. Sharing those exotic sweets became an event!

The excitement was palpable as we handed out the unique candies, watching our classmates and teachers alike savoring each piece, their curiosity piqued by our tales of Mexico.

The highlight, however, was when the Hartman Elementary newspaper decided to feature our trip and the delightful foreign treats.

Seeing our names and a story about our adventure, splashed across the school paper, filled us with an immense sense of pride and accomplishment. It wasn't just about the candy; it was about bringing a piece of our incredible journey back to share and seeing it celebrated.

It's a memory that still brings a warm smile to my face, a testament to Grandpa's enduring love and the simple, profound joy of sharing.

Competing for First Chair in Music Class

I competed for the first chair as a trumpet player in grade school and then as a drummer in the high school band. This wasn't just about securing a spot; it was about demonstrating the years of practice, the countless hours honing my technique, and the passion I pour into every beat. My goal was to contribute to the band's overall performance, bringing a dynamic and nuanced drumming style that would elevate the collective sound.

My approach to drumming wasn't simply about technical proficiency, although I was confident in my abilities there. I focused on creating a rhythmic foundation that's both supportive and innovative, allowing the other instruments to shine while adding my own unique layers of texture and energy.

Beyond technical skills, I believed in the importance of teamwork and collaboration within the band.

Nathan Hale Exercise Team

I often find myself reminiscing about a particularly formative chapter from my junior high school years. It was a time when I had the privilege of leading a dedicated 'Exercise Team,' an experience that deeply underscored the values of discipline, collaboration, and perseverance.

As captain, I bore witness to, and actively participated in, the immense dedication our team poured into perfecting our synchronized drills. Our practices were rigorous, demanding hours of precise movements and unwavering focus; all aimed at achieving a level of performance that bordered artistry. Each exercise was a coordinated sequence that was meticulously rehearsed, forging not just physical strength but an unbreakable bond among us.

At the heart of our journey was our remarkable Coach Jim Howard. He was more than an instructor; he was a visionary who painstakingly crafted our entire program. Coach Howard instilled in us a profound appreciation for physical fitness and an unyielding commitment to excellence. His quiet pride in our discipline and conditioning was a constant source of motivation.

One indelible memory stands out from my time at Nathan Hale Junior High. It was a vibrant holiday weekend in the mid-1960s, a period marked by a sense of burgeoning optimism and community spirit. Our team was scheduled to perform our intricate routine at the bustling Crossroads Mall.

As the anticipation grew, we launched into our routine, and the initial scattering of curious onlookers quickly transformed into a substantial, captivated audience. Shoppers paused, conversations ceased, and eyes turned towards our demonstration. The rhythmic precision of our movements, the sharp look of our school-colored uniforms, and the sheer energy we projected resonated deeply with the crowd. To our collective amazement and enormous pride, they responded with enthusiastic applause, a resounding affirmation of our concerted efforts.

Observing from the side, Coach Howard's face, usually set in thoughtful concentration, softened into a warm, satisfied smile. That look of profound contentment from him was the ultimate reward, a silent acknowledgment of all the sweat and dedication that had culminated in such a successful public display. It was a moment of pure triumph, cementing not just our coach's pleasure but also our shared sense of accomplishment.

Track & Field

I often find myself reflecting on those formative years in junior high school, a time brimming with youthful energy and burgeoning ambitions. It was then that my brothers and I, drawn by the allure of friendly competition and physical challenge, all ventured into the world of track and field. While I discovered a particular affinity for the rhythmic discipline and speed of running events, my brothers, with their unique blend of strength and precision, naturally gravitated towards the explosive power required for field events.

Our shared enthusiasm quickly transformed our humble backyard into an impromptu training ground. Driven by a blend of ingenuity and a sheer unwillingness to wait for official facilities, we embarked on constructing our very own high-jump pit. With scavenged two-by-fours forming the uprights, a flexible bamboo pole serving as our ever-challenging crossbar, and a generous pile of discarded foam scraps offering a surprisingly soft landing, our makeshift arena slowly took shape. It was a testament to our youthful resourcefulness; a project built with teamwork and boundless imagination.

But true magic, the indelible memory, lay in the act itself. The focused run-up, the powerful take-off, and then, that extraordinary, breathtaking fraction of a second: a perfect, exhilarating suspension in mid-air. As we cleared the bar, there was a profound, fleeting moment of absolute weightlessness, a sensation of defying gravity that was nothing short of euphoric. It wasn't just about clearing a certain height; it was about the sheer, unadulterated joy of flight, a temporary liberation that filled us with an incredible sense of accomplishment and freedom. That feeling, in those simple backyard jumps, was magnificent.

My Approach to Winning the Mile Run

As a track star, my approach to conquering a mile race isn't just about speed; it's a meticulously crafted strategy built on a foundation of consistent training, strategic pacing, and unwavering mental fortitude. This isn't a sprint; it's a carefully planned assault on the clock.

My training regimen is a multi-faceted approach designed to optimize both speed and endurance. It involves high-intensity interval training (HIIT) to build explosive power, tempo runs to enhance lactate threshold, and long, steady-state runs to bolster my aerobic base. Crucially, this plan incorporates rest and recovery days to prevent injury and allow for optimal muscle repair and growth. Specific workouts are adjusted based on ongoing performance data and any minor physical setbacks. I would run five miles per day and had a fresh quarter- miler on every lap to push me to the max.

Race day strategy revolves around intelligent pacing. I avoid the common mistake of starting too fast. Instead, I aim to find a comfortable pace within the first few hundred meters, strategically positioning myself within the leading pack without expending excessive energy early on. The middle portion of the race sees me maintaining a consistent, sustainable rhythm, carefully monitoring my breathing and heart rate. Finally, the final 400 meters represent a controlled surge, utilizing the remaining energy reserves to push for the finish line with maximum effort. This isn't a reckless all-out sprint, but a calculated and powerful finish.

Beyond the physical aspects, mental preparation is paramount. Visualization exercises help me mentally rehearse the race, anticipating potential challenges and developing strategies to overcome them. Maintaining focus and positive self-talk are essential to managing fatigue and maintaining motivation during those crucial moments of exertion. Race day nerves are acknowledged and managed, not allowed to dictate performance. My training includes methods for managing pressure and maintaining composure under pressure.

In essence, my approach to winning a mile race transcends simple physical training; it's a holistic strategy encompassing physical conditioning, intelligent pacing, and a strong mental game. It's a testament to disciplined planning, meticulous execution, and an unwavering commitment to success.

Remembering back the other day, revisiting a particular year – 1966, to be precise. It was track season, and for gym class, my footwear of choice, or rather, necessity, was a simple pair of US Keds tennis shoes. I distinctly remember the stark contrast with many of my peers, who proudly laced up actual running spiked shoes, purpose-built for the track.

Growing up, I was keenly aware of our family's financial situation. With four of us children to provide for, I understood the demands on Mom and Dad. It instilled in me a sense of quiet appreciation for what we had, and I never once entertained the thought of asking them for those specialized, and undoubtedly costly, track shoes.

My conviction was firm: the quality of one's shoes didn't define the runner; it was the athlete within their heart, their drive, their sheer will – that truly mattered.

As the weeks of practice wore on, those faithful Keds bore the brunt of every sprint and every lap.

By the time the track season reached its crescendo, culminating in the highly anticipated mile run, they were thoroughly worn, a visible testament to my effort. I recall it as if it were yesterday: crossing the finish line, victorious in the Mile Run, only to glance down and see a conspicuous hole right through the toe of one of my shoes.

That small detail, far from being a setback, has always been a powerful reminder. It never deterred me, and if anything, it solidified my belief that true strength comes not from external advantages but from an unwavering spirit. It taught me a valuable lesson that has stayed with me through the years.

As a result, I was able to win the Mile Run in four minutes. First place in the 880, 440, and the 220.

High School Years

I often find myself reminiscing about my high school years, a period dominated by an earnest desire to project an image of effortless sophistication and appeal. The pursuit of being impeccably neat, clean, and, perhaps most importantly, having an unforgettable scent became a genuine mission.

During those formative years, I dedicated considerable effort to curating what I believed was the pinnacle of masculine fragrances.

My treasured arsenal included renowned names like Jade East, which promised an air of exotic mystery; the undeniably classic and robust English Leather; and the bold, memorable character of Hy Karate. Each bottle wasn't just a fragrance; it was a carefully chosen accessory, a hopeful declaration of personal style and confidence, intended to make a lasting impression in the bustling hallways and social circles of adolescence. It's fascinating to look back and consider the sincere thought that went into those scent selections.

While reflecting on those days, my mind drifted back to my high school years. It's funny what details stick with you, isn't it? For me, a vivid memory is my personal 'uniform' from those days, and the meticulous effort I put into it.

My wardrobe was quite specific, almost a carefully curated collection. I practically lived in those incredibly soft mohair sweaters, always layered over a perfectly starched Oxford button-down shirt. Below that, it was invariably a pair of well-fitting corduroy slacks – I can still remember the texture and the subtle hum of the fabric. And to complete the ensemble, my trusty Penny loafers, polished to a gleam, often with a lucky penny tucked into the slit.

But it wasn't just "what" I wore; it was "how" it was presented. Every single item had to be impeccably clean and pressed, with sharp creases in the trousers and not a single wrinkle on the shirt. My shoes were always shining so brightly you could almost see your reflection, and my hair, without fail, was perfectly combed and in place.

Looking back, I realize that this commitment to appearance wasn't merely about vanity. For me, it was deeply ingrained – a sense of discipline, respect for myself, and a desire to make a strong, positive impression. It provided quiet confidence, knowing that I always looked my best when I walked out the door. It truly was an essential part of who I was during those formative years.

Spinning Records

Beyond the roar of the sports fields and the vibrant rehearsals with The Sound Effect, there's a particular chapter from my Benson High School days that remains remarkably vivid. The moment the final bell rang each afternoon wasn't just a signal for dismissal; it was the commencement of a cherished, simple ritual.

My brother and I, along with a small crew of friends, would embark on the short, familiar walk to Rick Burger's house. It was more than just a visit; it was our weekly pilgrimage to a sanctuary of sound. Rick's basement, for a few precious hours, transformed into our personal radio station, exclusively playing the latest and greatest hits on his 45-rpm record player.

The needle's distinct crackle would give way to the unmistakable opening notes of the era's defining anthems. We'd lose ourselves in the rich harmonies of The Mamas & Papas, the whimsical storytelling of Donovan, the revolutionary sounds of The Beatles, the sharp beats of the Dave Clark Five, and the sophisticated pop of Petula Clark. Each spin was a new adventure, a shared experience that bonded us. These afternoons weren't solely about the music, though. They were a symphony of simple pleasures: the satisfying crunch of potato chips, the refreshing, sugary fizz of Pepsis, and the absolute delight of fresh Dixie Cream doughnuts.

We'd sing along at the top of our lungs, often off-key but always with boundless enthusiasm, our voices blending with those of Rick's brother and sister, and our other friends. It was a time of uncomplicated joy, a pure connection fostered by shared tunes, laughter, and the simple, profound pleasure of each other's company. Those moments, steeped in music and camaraderie, forged memories that still resonate with warmth and happiness today.

Skateboarding

Looking back, a particular memory from my youth stands out vividly, painting a clear picture of how resourcefulness can spark true innovation. My best neighborhood friends' parents bought Steve a "Big Banana" skateboard, and in those days, a lack of financial means wasn't a barrier to fun, but rather a catalyst for our creativity. I recall the sheer joy and concentrated effort that went into constructing our own skateboards. Our 'materials' consisted of whatever we could find sturdy two-by-fours served as the basic deck, while my sister's well-used steel roller skates were meticulously (and probably irreversibly) dismantled to provide the vital wheels. Each nail driven in was a step towards our motorized dreams, a testament to youthful engineering. The grand finale, always performed with a flourish, was the paint job – a bold, almost audacious, spray coating of bright fluorescent orange. That vibrant hue wasn't just a color; it was a statement of our homemade pride, our ingenuity rolling down the pavement. Those makeshift boards, born from necessity, taught us a profound lesson about making the most of what you have, a lesson in inventiveness that still resonates with us today.

All-Star Wrestling at KETV 7

During the vibrant era of the mid-1960s, few spectacles commanded as much fervent attention in Omaha as the weekly All-Star Wrestling shows. These weren't merely athletic contests; they were theatrical events, rituals of strength and showmanship that drew passionate crowds to the KETV Channel 7 studios. I had the unique privilege of experiencing this world firsthand, thanks to my father, who served on security detail. His work offered me a fascinating, albeit sometimes chaotic, backstage pass, allowing me to witness the raw energy that unfolded both in front of and behind the cameras.

The roster was a legendary who's who of the squared circle. I vividly recall watching the stoic, technical genius of Verne Gagne, whose every grapple was a masterclass in precision. Then there was the menacing presence of Mad Dog Vachon, whose snarling intensity and unpredictable aggression could send shivers down your spine. The colorful Joe Sweiback added his own unique flavor, not just with his in-ring prowess but also famously hawking 'Gera Speed' to the roaring crowd – a testament to the era's blend of sport and grassroots marketing. And, of course, the legendary promoter

Joe Dusek, the architect of it all, was orchestrating the drama alongside formidable talents like Bob Orton, whose athleticism was undeniable.

Beyond the main events, the programming offered an intriguing variety, including specialty bouts featuring performers of diverse statures, a fascinating and popular element of the era wrestling landscape that added to the overall spectacle.

But perhaps the most indelible character outside the ring was a devoted fan, a woman who occupied the same front-row seat at every single show. Her passion was palpable; she would thunderously pound the ring mat with her fists, her voice raised in protest or adulation, whenever a referee's call went against her favored combatant. Her unbridled enthusiasm was a crucial, unscripted part of the spectacle, embodying the collective voice of the audience and adding an extra layer of raw authenticity to the carefully crafted drama. It was a captivating fusion of athletic competition and elaborate theatricality, where every roar, every controversial decision, and every over-the-top character was meticulously woven into the fabric of the show.

These pilgrimages to KETV Channel 7 forged an extraordinary childhood memory. They weren't just entertainment; they were a vibrant snapshot of a bygone era, a shared experience that bound a community, and for me, a cherished bond with my father. The sights, sounds, and sheer energy of those nights remain etched in my mind as a source of immense fun and enduring nostalgia.

Boxing Matches at the Civic

There's a particular vividness to my childhood memories of the boxing matches held at our local Civic Auditorium. They were far more than just sporting events; they were electric spectacles, often serving as the thrilling highlight of the night.

My father, a man of quiet strength and unwavering dedication, played a unique role during those evenings. He worked part-time security, his calm presence and imposing stature complementing the other law enforcement officers who ensured order. For me, these outings were less about the punches thrown in the ring and more about observing my dad in action. A steadfast guardian amidst the surging tides of human emotion.

The atmosphere within that auditorium was always charged, a volatile concoction of anticipation and raw passion. And then, sometimes without warning, the tension would invariably boil over. A contentious referee's call, a boastful shout from the stands, or simply too much adrenaline fueled by beer could ignite a powder keg in the crowd. Suddenly, the air would be thick with hurled chairs; voices would escalate into enraged roars, and what began as a spirited debate would rapidly descend into chaotic brawls. It felt as though the entire arena would hold its breath, only to explode into pandemonium moments later.

Watching from what I desperately hoped was a safe distance, my heart would invariably pound with a different kind of fear than the one gripping the rest of the spectators. While others focused on the unfolding melee, my gaze would be fixed solely on my father. He was never one to shy away from his responsibilities. With a resolute expression, he'd wade directly into the thick of it, his uniform a reassuring beacon of order; his mission clear: to quell the unrest and restore peace. Every single time, as he disappeared into the vortex of flailing limbs and enraged shouts, a cold, persistent knot would form in my stomach. The gnawing fear that he wouldn't emerge, or that he'd be seriously harmed, was a constant, unwelcome companion during those moments of stark anarchy.

Yet, with an almost uncanny consistency, he would re-emerge. Sometimes a little disheveled, perhaps, but always, unequivocally, whole. He possessed an innate ability to navigate the storm, to diffuse volatile situations not just with his authority, but with a quiet, unwavering resolve that commanded respect. Those evenings at the Civic Auditorium, fraught with both excitement and apprehension, taught me profound lessons about courage, about duty, and about the extraordinary, quiet strength of my father. They remain vibrant snapshots in my mind, etched with both the thrilling clang of the boxing bell and the profound relief of seeing my dad walk away, ready for whatever challenge came next.

An AM Transistor Radio

I can still vividly recall the pure wonder and excitement of receiving my very first transistor radio. It wasn't just a simple electronic device; it felt like a gateway to an entirely new world of sound, and a personal one at that. This was a classic A.M. model, encased in a sturdy plastic shell, a muted beige and brown typical of the era.

But the real magic, the element that truly set it apart and defined my early listening habits, was its unassuming earpiece. This wasn't a pair of sophisticated headphones; it was a small, often slightly uncomfortable, but utterly essential plastic bud designed for private listening. It transformed public broadcasts into private whispers, allowing me to tune into my favorite music late at night without disturbing anyone else in the house.

That tiny earpiece became my secret conduit to countless hours of entertainment and information, a testament to the quiet revolution portable electronics brought into our lives.

Watching American Bandstand

I often find myself transported back to those cherished Saturday mornings, a time when the world seemed to unfold with a unique rhythm and possibility. For many of us, a pivotal part of that weekly ritual was the captivating spectacle of Dick Clark's American Bandstand. It was far more than just a television show; it was a vibrant, living testament to the evolving heartbeat of American youth culture, a direct pipeline to the freshest sounds and movements shaping our generation.

Each episode was a true discovery. It served as our premier source for new music, often introducing us to chart-topping hits and emerging artists long before they dominated the airwaves.

Beyond the auditory delights, Bandstand was a veritable school of style and grace. The featured dancers, with their cutting-edge steps and effortless cool, were the trendsetters whose moves we eagerly practiced in our own homes.

And who could forget the invaluable, candid interviews with the biggest pop stars and up-coming talents? These segments offered a rare, intimate look behind the scenes, providing personal insights into the music and personalities that felt profoundly meaningful to a young audience.

Even today, decades later, the iconic opening theme song still resonates within me with an almost visceral clarity. It wasn't merely a jingle; it was the unmistakable fanfare announcing the commencement of excitement, discovery, and a shared cultural experience that helped define an entire era. That distinct sound continues to evoke the thrill of new rhythms, emerging fashion, and the undeniable, electric pulse of a time that etched itself deeply into our collective memory.

The Beatles Influence

My journey in music was profoundly shaped by a pivotal moment: watching The Beatles' debut on The Ed Sullivan Show with my family. The sheer impact of their performance – the electrifying energy, the innovative music – was transformative, not just for me, but for the entire world. It ignited a passion that would define my music life and beyond.

This experience fueled my ambition to create music. I first formed the Knight Watch, then The Red Devils, and later joined The Sound Effect, a rock band whose style was heavily influenced by the Fab Four.

Their music impacted everything from our hairstyles and clothing choices to our musical sensibilities. During my time with The Sound Effect, I was fortunate to play a variety of instruments – rhythm guitar, keyboards, bass, and even featured vocals. I even played a Hofner violin bass, just like Paul McCartney! The Beatles' music pushed me to strive for greater musical excellence.

Their legacy is undeniable. John, Paul, George, and Ringo's influence continue to resonate through generations. In fact, my own children have grown immersed in the Beatles' music; I played their albums constantly at home and in the car, and they now know every lyric.

Witnessing The Beatles' groundbreaking performance firsthand was an incredible privilege, a moment in history I will never forget. It's a memory that continues to inspire me to this day.

Local Talent Show on WOWT

The mid-1960s were a time of exhilarating change, and few phenomena captivated America quite like the arrival of The Beatles. Their groundbreaking music wasn't just a sound; it was a cultural earthquake, shaking every household, including ours. Amidst this whirlwind of Beatlemania, my ingenious mother hatched a truly delightful plan. She decided my brothers, my sister, and I would become our very own Fab Four for the local WOWT weekly talent show.

Her vision was both simple and brilliant. She transformed plain white sweatshirts into iconic stage wear using iron-on patches, each hand cut and each proudly emblazoned with "Beatles." My sister, the youngest and undeniably the cutest, received a special designation: "Beatle Baby."

The finishing touch, of course, was a quartet of those instantly recognizable mop-top wigs, transforming us instantly into mini-versions of John, Paul, George, and Ringo. With borrowed or toy instruments in hand, we were ready to take the stage, a family band prepared to lip- sync our hearts out to a beloved Beatles record.

Before we went on camera, the air backstage was electric, buzzing with a mixture of childlike nerves and immense excitement. When our moment arrived, the studio lights, blinding and thrilling, enveloped us. We mimed every chord and belted out every lyric with the passionate conviction only children can muster, lost in the magic of performing. The illusion was perfect, at least in our innocent eyes.

Then came the post-performance interview with the program host. He moved from one sibling to the next, asking charming questions, until he reached my sister. In an unscripted, utterly spontaneous moment that stole the show, she gleefully pulled off her wig, letting her long, beautiful hair cascade around her shoulders. It was her triumphant, adorable declaration to the world that the "Beatle Baby" was, in fact, a girl.

The host couldn't help but chuckle at her playful reveal.

We walked off that stage feeling like genuine superstars, basking in the glow of our momentary fame. That day remains a vibrant, cherished memory, a testament to a mother's creativity, a family's shared joy, and the indelible mark of The Beatles left on a generation – and on one little family's unforgettable talent show debut.

The First Guitar I Ever Bought

I had a memory flash back with such clarity it felt like yesterday. I could almost smell the department store as I walked into Sears at the Crossroads Mall back in 1963. That day marked the beginning of something truly special for me – the purchase of my very first guitar.

It was a Silvertone model 1448 single pickup electric guitar, a marvelous instrument with its amplifier ingeniously built right into the case! For a young, aspiring musician, it was nothing short of magic. I remember beaming with an excitement I hadn't known before, cradling that guitar, knowing it was my gateway to a whole new world of sound. It wasn't long after that initial thrill that, in 1965, I upgraded to a Silvertone model 1437 – 4 pickup electric guitar and a Silvertone 1484 twin speaker amplifier, which really made me feel like I was embarking on a serious musical journey.

Countless hours were spent in those early days, my fingers aching as I mastered chord progressions and painstakingly learned individual string picking. Every penny I earned from odd jobs felt like a direct investment into my passion. There was immense satisfaction in knowing that my dedication and hard work were literally fueling my dreams.

That humble beginning ignited a lifelong spark that propelled me directly into the vibrant pop music scene. What started as garage band dreams quickly evolved. From those first moments with The Nightwatch, to cutting our teeth with The Red Devils, and later, the exciting era of The Sound Effect – each step, each band, was a new chapter and a new opportunity. With every performance, every paid gig, I was able to invest back into my craft, upgrading equipment, and refining my sound.

Looking back, it's incredible to see how far that journey has taken me. Today, I'm fortunate to own a collection of instruments that are each a treasure in their own right: the iconic Rickenbacker 12-string, famous for its jangling harmonies, paired with a classic VOX amplifier; a versatile Fender Stratocaster that has seen countless riffs; and the smooth, unmistakable tone of my Hofner bass. Each one tells a story, but they all lead back to that wide-eyed boy in

Sears, forever grateful for that simple Silvertone and the path it opened.

The Birth of the Nightwatch and Red Devils Combos

Long before I joined the locally renowned "Sound Effect" rock band, my musical journey began with a group I formed, "The Nightwatch", then transitioned to "The Red Devils".

This band was a family and neighborhood affair, featuring my brothers Rick and Randy, and our incredibly talented friend Steve Ray.

Our early rehearsals were a chaotic blend of youthful energy and untamed ambition. We weren't technically proficient – our instruments were modest, reflecting our limited resources – but we played with a passion that transcended our skill level. Every practice session in my parents' basement was a thrilling adventure in creating music, a testament to the sheer joy of collaboration.

A highlight of our brief but memorable career was participating in a battle of the bands at Nathan Hale Junior High during my eighth-grade year. This presented a unique challenge: my sixth-grade brother, Randy, was eager to join us. Securing his release from school required parental intervention, but thankfully, they granted their permission. Determined to make a lasting impression, I rented a Farfisa organ for a show-stopping rendition of "96 Tears," adding a touch of professional flair to our performance. To elevate Randy's drum setup, I collaborated with a classmate who crafted a custom riser in exchange for assistance in sanding his Model T hot rod project. The riser was a triumph of ingenuity, adding visual pizzazz to our stage presence, even though his car remained a work in progress.

The competition itself was fraught with excitement and a few unexpected hiccups. During one particularly energetic performance, our bass player's guitar strap snapped. With remarkable composure,

Steve salvaged the situation by holding the instrument close, ensuring a seamless continuation of our set. Despite the mishap, our performance resonated with the audience, and we were thrilled to be declared the winners. The experience solidified the profound bonds we forged through shared musical passion and remains a treasured memory of our early days making music. The entire experience taught me invaluable lessons about teamwork, resourcefulness, and the power of shared passion. It truly was the best of times at that age.

My Time in "The Sound Effect" Rock and Roll Band in the late 60s

My time in "The Sound Effect" rock and roll band during the vibrant 1960s remains a defining experience, profoundly shaping my lifelong passion for music. It was an exhilarating period of creative exploration and collaborative energy of Ned Gray, Dave Gausden and Rod Griffith and beyond simply playing, I was fortunate to contribute across multiple instruments, handling guitar, bass, keyboards, and drums on a few numbers and even taking the lead vocals on several tracks. This multifaceted role allowed me to delve deeply into the performance. The camaraderie, the electrifying energy of live shows, and the sheer joy of making music with talented individuals are memories I cherish deeply.

The experience fostered a profound appreciation for the collaborative nature of music-making and a deep love for music. During our time together, we won several band battle competitions and capped it by winning the coveted "Battle of the Bands" competition sponsored by the KOIL radio station at the Omaha Civic Auditorium in 1969.

While in the Sound Effect, we played such venues as Sandy's Escape, Elkhorn Lanes, Bellevue Chieftain, Merits Beach, The Barn, St. Luke's, Peony Park, the Crossroads, the Southroads Mall, the Omaha Civic Center, and the Douglas County Fair.

Song Writing

My songwriting musical journey began in the mid-1970s, a time of vibrant creativity and self-discovery. I embarked on a songwriting adventure, crafting six heartfelt ballads, each lyric meticulously chosen to convey deep emotion. The process was deeply personal, a testament to the power of music to express the inexpressible. Remember those old reel-to-reel recordings? I still cherish those early attempts, capturing the raw energy and unbridled enthusiasm of a young musician finding his voice. They're a fascinating snapshot of a pivotal period in my life.

The experience wasn't simply about songwriting; it was about connecting with something profound. Music, as you know, transcends language, reaching into the soul and stirring emotions that words alone can't capture. It's a gift, a passion, and an enduring part of me that I've carried throughout the years. That passion led to opportunities performing at weddings during that era. Each performance is a thrilling reminder of the joy and fulfillment I found in sharing music with others. It was a continuation of my band days, a chance to connect with audiences and let the music speak for itself. The songs I wrote were entitled, "Let Me Tell Ya", "Wanted by The One You Love", "Once When I Was Young", "One Day I Found My Love", "I want to Tell You", "Let Me into Your Heart", "Let Me Take you by the Hand", and "Because You Are Mine".

These experiences, both the quiet moments of songwriting and the electrifying performances, shaped my understanding of music's transformative power. It is a part of who I am.

Watching My Youngest Brother

I remember those moments that truly define sibling bonds, and one memory always stands out vividly. It involves my youngest brother, Randy, and a pivotal afternoon from our childhood.

Randy, with all the boundless enthusiasm of youth, was gearing up for tryouts for the local Pop Warner midget football team. This wasn't just another activity for him; it was a deeply held aspiration, a chance to be part of something meaningful. The challenge? The tryouts were scheduled for a late afternoon, a good few miles from our home, and our parents were still at work, leaving us without a ride.

Seeing the earnest hope in his eyes and understanding the profound significance this opportunity held for him, I didn't hesitate.

I remember looking at my bicycle, our most reliable mode of transport at the time, and instantly knew what I had to do. With Randy either perched precariously on the crossbar or clinging tightly to the back, I embarked on what felt like a marathon journey for a young boy on two wheels. Every pedal stroke was fueled by a sense of duty and the desire to see my brother's dreams take flight.

It wasn't just about getting him there; it was about ensuring he had every chance to pursue something he loved. That ride, with the wind in our faces and the destination looming, solidified an unspoken understanding between us.

It was a simple act of brotherly support, but Randy meant the world. To this day, he recounts that afternoon with a warmth that never diminishes, frequently reminding me how much he appreciated that effort, that ride, and that belief in his young ambitions. It's a testament to how small gestures can leave an indelible mark on the heart.

I am so proud of my youngest brother, Randy, who possessed an extraordinary athletic talent that spanned multiple disciplines. He excelled not only as a wrestler, but also as a gifted football player, gymnast, diver in swimming, and track & field athlete. Watching him compete, I was consistently impressed by his unwavering dedication, ferocious drive, and relentless work ethic – a masterclass in perseverance that profoundly impacted me. His exceptional achievements culminated in a truly remarkable accolade: he was crowned "King of Sports" at Omaha Benson High School, a testament to his exceptional skill and tireless training. He lettered 11 times in 3 years.

This recognition, however, is only a small reflection of the larger lesson we taught each other about the power of hard work and the importance of striving for excellence. His commitment to his athletic pursuits validated my strong work ethic that continues to shape my approach to all aspects of my life. The memory of his dedication serves as a constant inspiration.

What I Learned from My Sister about Art

I would like to share my profound admiration for my sister, Gina, and her remarkable artistic talent. Gina possesses a truly God-given gift, evident in the stunning artwork she creates. I've been fortunate enough to have copies of some of her pieces, and each one is a testament to her dedication and skill.

Her discipline is truly inspiring. She approaches her art with an unwavering focus, meticulously crafting each detail with a precision that is both captivating and humbling. Whether wielding a paintbrush or a pencil, her work displays a masterful understanding of color and composition.

Watching Gina's creative process has had a significant impact on me. It opened my eyes to the beauty inherent in color palettes and the power of artistic expression. Her work not only showcases technical proficiency but also a deep emotional resonance, a capacity to evoke feelings and spark imagination within the viewer. I find myself constantly marveling at her ability to translate her vision into tangible works of art.

My Love of Architecture

My passion for architecture was ignited during high school. It wasn't just about the aesthetics, though the artistry of drawing plans for homes certainly captivated me. I remember the thrill of seeing my first set of blueprints, a tangible representation of my ideas, printed out, and a copy of which I still cherish. That initial experience was far more than just sketching lines on paper; it was a deep dive into understanding the intricacies of design and construction. I immersed myself in learning building codes, foundational principles, material properties, and the seemingly mundane yet crucial placement of electrical outlets. The sheer prospect of transforming those drawings into a physical structure was incredibly inspiring.

This hands-on experience, the process of translating vision into reality, proved invaluable. It fostered a problem-solving mindset and a meticulous attention to detail that has served me well throughout my career. The analytical skills homed in understanding complex blueprints, deciphering symbols, interpreting dimensions, and visualizing spatial relationships have become essential tools in my professional success. My high school's foray into architecture wasn't just the beginning of a hobby; it was the foundation upon which I built a successful career, demonstrating the power of translating passion into practical skill.

The Value of Close Personal Friendships

This section deals with exploring the profound and often underestimated impact of close personal friendships on our lives. In my case, I have three close friends, Rick Burger (deceased), Steve Ray, and Russ Kennedy (deceased). The value extends far beyond simple companionship; it touches upon our emotional, mental, and even physical well-being in significant ways.

Consider the emotional support provided by true friends. They are the individuals who celebrate our triumphs with genuine joy and offer unwavering comfort during times of hardship. This emotional resilience, fostered by strong bonds, equips us to navigate life's inevitable challenges with greater strength and perspective. Their empathy and understanding provide a safe space for vulnerability, allowing us to process difficult emotions and avoid feeling isolated during stressful periods.

Beyond emotional support, close friendships often contribute significantly to our mental health. Research consistently demonstrates a strong correlation between strong social connections and reduced rates of depression and anxiety. Friends challenge us to grow, encouraging us to pursue our goals and offering constructive criticism when needed. This constant intellectual and emotional stimulation can lead to increased self-awareness and personal growth.

Furthermore, the influence of close friends can extend our physical health. Studies show that individuals with strong social networks tend to live longer, healthier lives. Friends can encourage healthy habits, provide accountability for fitness goals, and simply offer the kind of positive influence that reduces stress and its associated health risks. The simple act of shared laughter and enjoyable activities with close friends can be a powerful antidote to the pressures of daily life.

In conclusion, the value of close personal friendships is immeasurable. It's a dynamic and reciprocal relationship that enriches our lives in countless ways, impacting our emotional resilience, mental health, and even physical well-being. Nurturing and maintaining these precious connections is an investment in our overall happiness and fulfillment.

Steve Ray

From sixth grade on, my best friend Steve Ray and I were inseparable. A year older but in the same grade, our childhood was a whirlwind of imaginative games. We commanded armies of neighborhood kids, staging elaborate battles with painstakingly crafted strategies. I recall one particularly memorable "army" game where Steve, perched high in a tree as our sniper, took an unexpected tumble when a branch broke after my brother Rick playfully pretended to shoot him. The laughter that followed was as loud as the crash. Though shaken, Steve thankfully went home unscathed.

Our friendship evolved as we entered junior high. We formed a band, "The Red Devils," a chaotic mix of youthful energy and untamed talent. I handled rhythm and lead guitar, Steve played bass and saxophone, Randy (my brother) pounded the drums, and Rick added tambourine and vocals. We were convinced we were the next big thing!

High school brought new adventures. We were inseparable, sharing lockers and conquering the sprawling hallways of Benson High. We became track teammates and ball players; our bond deepened with each shared experience. Once Steve got his license, Friday and Saturday nights were spent cruising in his family's Buick LeSabre. His passion for driving was legendary, resulting in more than one memorable "cookie spin" session in empty school parking lots, a testament to our youthful exuberance. We'd also spend countless hours cruising down Dodge Street near 72nd, engaging in the somewhat reckless but ultimately harmless fun of "Chinese fire drills" at stoplights.

Our social life was equally vibrant. Double dates to movies and concerts were commonplace. One date stands out: Steve and Ann (a friend of Diane's) had a particularly lengthy goodbye on her porch swing. Upon returning to the car, his explanation for the delay, "I was just a-swinging'," still makes me laugh.

Those years were filled with laughter, shared dreams, and an unbreakable bond forged in the crucible of childhood and adolescence. The memories, from epic battles to spontaneous car stunts and everything in between, remain some of the most cherished moments of my life.

Steve and I grew up together, sharing experiences that shaped who we are today.

When Diane and I decided to get married, we asked Steve to be in the wedding, and when Steve and Karen got married, they asked us to be theirs. True friends forever.

Ned Gray

My memories of Ned stretch back to when he was just fourteen, a vibrant young man whose passion for music mirrored my own. It feels like only yesterday we were conceptualizing "The Sound Effect," searching for a drummer who could truly ignite our sound. Ned possessed that rare spark and an energy that was palpable. He wasn't just 'a drummer'; he *was* the heartbeat we needed. His raw talent for crafting an infectious backbeat was simply unparalleled among his peers; he had an instinctive rhythm that propelled our music forward.

From the moment our sticks and strings first harmonized, an undeniable bond formed. I quickly came to see Ned not just as a bandmate, but as a cherished younger brother. On those early stages, amidst the exhilarating chaos of gigs, I often found myself watching over him, gently guiding his youthful exuberance and channeling his boundless curiosity into our shared musical passion.

Beyond the music, another remarkable soul touched our journey: Ned's mother, Dorothy. She was a truly wonderful woman, whose quiet strength and unwavering support were a constant source of encouragement. After our energetic performances, I cherished our conversations; she was more than just a listener – a thoughtful confidante and a fantastic sounding board, offering wisdom and perspective. Our mutual respect formed a deep, unspoken bond.

Even after our chapter with "The Sound Effect" drew to a close, Ned's musical journey was far from over. He continued to carve out an impressive path, gracing stages and studios with several other notable groups, constantly pushing the boundaries of his artistry. To call him merely a 'musician' feels an understatement; he blossomed into a truly exceptional singer, songwriter, and recording artist. Witnessing his fulfilling and celebrated career has filled me with immense pride. His passion has taken him to corners of the globe, sharing his extraordinary talent with audiences worldwide.

Through all the years, the distance, and the separate paths our lives took, our connection never faltered. The enduring strength of our brotherhood was truly put to the test, and reaffirmed, a few years ago when we mourned the passing of his beloved mother, Dorothy. Diane and I made the journey to her funeral, and in a deeply moving tribute, Ned and I once again stood side-by-side. Guitars in hand, we offered a heartfelt song in her memory, a bittersweet moment that honored her spirit and our shared history.

Today, Ned and his wonderful wife, Tina, call Australia home. While continents may separate us, the marvels of modern technology allow us to bridge that gap with ease, keeping our conversations flowing and our bond vibrant. The years may have passed, but the spirit of "The Sound Effect" and the profound kinship forged in those formative years endure. He remains, unequivocally, my brother.

Rick Burger

I'd like to share a story about a truly exceptional person, my best friend, Rick Burger. Our friendship began unexpectedly during tenth grade at Benson High. I was a long-distance runner, and Rick, a larger-than-life kid, was diligent, though perhaps not swiftly, tackling the mile run during gym class. His determination struck me; I slowed my pace to run alongside him, offering encouragement. That simple act of support blossomed into a lifelong bond.

Our conversations that day revealed a shared love for Dixie Cream Doughnuts, a local Omaha favorite that had been a treat for my family and, unbeknownst to me then, Rick's as well. That chance encounter led to Friday afternoon's record spins at his house in Benson, after school filled with laughter, singing, and, of course, more doughnuts.

As our friendship deepened, we discovered a surprising number of shared interests and values. Our families connected, forging a strong and enduring bond that extended beyond ourselves. Rick became an integral part of my family, attending our wedding (where he served as an usher), celebrating the births of our children, and sharing all our milestones.

My children knew him simply as "Uncle Rick," or affectionately, "Booger," a testament to the love and warmth he brought into our lives.

Rick possessed a remarkable array of talents: a gifted artist, a gourmet chef whose dinners were legendary, and a connoisseur of fine wines who held management positions at several five-star restaurants. Yet, beyond his professional achievements, it was his spirit that truly shone. He was the heart of countless gatherings, from our annual family trips to the pumpkin patch – complete with campsite meals, park explorations, and evenings around the campfire under the stars – to his unforgettable Halloween parties.

Rick was the Master of Games, his car trunk perpetually overflowing with board games (much to the chagrin of anyone looking for the spare tire!). His playful nature and easygoing style effortlessly drew people in. His parties were legendary, particularly his Halloween celebrations, where costumes were mandatory, and a keenly anticipated prize awaited the winning couple. The evenings always featured his "Name That Tune" game, played to the soundtrack of his beloved 45s, testing our knowledge of both the A-sides and, more challengingly, the B-sides. His playful pronouncements of "I can't believe you don't know this one!" were as much a part of the game as the music itself. He was a truly generous and gracious host. To this day, my children invoke "Rick's Rules" before starting any game, a lasting tribute to his influence.

In 2014, we lost Rick, and the void he left remains deeply felt. This isn't merely a recounting of events; it's a heartfelt tribute to a remarkable friendship, a testament to a man whose kindness, generosity, and unwavering spirit touched the lives of everyone he knew. His memory continues to inspire us, reminding us to cherish the simple moments, to celebrate life's joys, and to always play by "Rick's Rules."

Chapter Three

Russ & Peg Kennedy

I'm writing to share some cherished memories of Russ Kennedy, a truly exceptional man and a dear friend. Russ, who was married to my friend Rick's sister, Peggy Burger (a wonderful and generous woman), Russ was more than just an acquaintance; he was a pivotal figure in my life. His entrepreneurial spirit, evident in his successful nationwide trucking company, was inspiring. Beyond his business acumen, Russ possessed a remarkable wit and a genuine warmth that touched everyone he knew. His profound kindness and unwavering love for his family and friends were truly unmatched.

Our friendship extended beyond casual acquaintances. For years, Peggy and Russ lived just outside Des Moines, and we'd regularly make the trip for long weekend visits, Rick, Diane, and I. These weekends were legendary. We'd play cards, board games, and share laughter and libations late into the night (Russ and I shared love for Captain Morgan). After a few precious hours of sleep, we'd wake up to a hearty breakfast of eggs, potatoes, sausage, toast, and huge amounts of coffee, reliving on the previous night's escapades. One Pictionary game stands out. Diane, attempting to illustrate "Me and My Shadow," used Russ, a large man, as her prop while standing behind him. The ensuing confusion, culminating in Rick's uproarious laughter and tumble from his chair, is a moment I'll never forget.

Our bond deepened over time. Russ and I would occasionally talk on the phone, sharing life updates and insights. One particularly memorable gathering was Russ's Toga party. Peggy's surprise element, combined with our togas, Mason jar wine, and stogies, created a hilariously unforgettable evening. Even a quick trip to the local convenience store for milk for the next morning in our toga attire resulted in amused glances and a shared laugh, a perfect encapsulation of our spontaneous joy.

Russ's passing in 2020 left a void in our lives that can never be truly filled. Our gatherings just aren't the same without him and Rick. The memories we shared, however, remain vibrant and serve as a testament to the profound impact they had on our lives. Their absence is deeply felt, but the joy and laughter they brought will forever be cherished.

Bill and Winnie Champenoy

Diane and I want to take a moment to express our deepest affection for Bill and Winnie Champenoy. As close friends, we've shared countless wonderful memories with them over the years – a friendship spanning nearly as long as Diane and I have been together. Winnie, of course, is Rick and Peggy's sister, and the connection through them has only strengthened our bonds.

We cherish the times we've spent together, filled with laughter, shared stories, and joyous occasions. I especially remember the sing-alongs at Rick's parties! Belting out "Hair" by the Cowsills, with such a lively group, remains a treasured highlight. Those were truly some of the best times, emblematic of the warmth and camaraderie we've always shared.

Bill and Winnie are a remarkable couple, deeply loved and admired by us. Their enduring relationship is an inspiration, and their presence in our lives is a constant source of joy and happiness. We feel incredibly fortunate to call our friends.

After High School Graduation

My upbringing instilled in me a deep appreciation for hard work and perseverance. I come from a large, close-knit family – I'm the eldest of four children – where resources are always limited. My parents, deeply religious and incredibly hardworking individuals, prioritized providing for us, even if it meant sacrificing their own desires.

The question of college loomed large as I neared high school graduation. My mother, ever supportive, offered to find a way to finance my education. While profoundly grateful for her generous offer, I recognized the significant financial strain it would place on our family, with three younger siblings still needing support. My decision to forgo college wasn't one taken lightly. I understood the value of higher education but felt a stronger responsibility to contribute to our family's well-being immediately.

Instead of pursuing a traditional academic path, I channeled my ambition into seizing every opportunity that presented itself. This self-driven approach, coupled with the added responsibility of starting a family at twenty, fueled my unwavering determination to succeed.

The challenges I faced became the foundation upon which I built a strong work ethic and a resilient spirit. It taught me invaluable lessons about resourcefulness, strategic planning, and the power of personal commitment. These experiences have shaped my perspective and continue to guide my actions today.

Be the Best

My father instilled in me a profound work ethic, emphasizing excellence in every endeavor. His philosophy transcended the specific task; it was about approaching all challenges with dedication, striving for mastery, and finding fulfillment in a job well done, regardless of its perceived importance or prestige. This principle has guided my career and continues to shape my approach to problem-solving and collaboration.

My Fascination with Space

My lifelong fascination with space began in childhood, fueled by countless hours watching

'Star Trek' with my father. The show ignited a sense of wonder, a yearning to explore the uncharted territories of the cosmos and the myriad possibilities they held. While my faith provides a framework for understanding the universe, it doesn't diminish the profound awe I feel contemplating the vastness of space and the potential for life beyond Earth.

The Apollo moon landing remains a pivotal moment in my life. The grainy black and white images of Earth rising above the lunar landscape profoundly impacted my perception of our planet's fragility and interconnectedness. Subsequent space shuttle missions and the establishment of the International Space Station further solidified my fascination, showcasing humanity's remarkable capacity for innovation and collaboration in the pursuit of exploration.

Elon Musk's ambitious endeavors, particularly his efforts to establish a human presence on Mars, represent a bold and inspiring chapter in our ongoing cosmic journey. The challenges are immense, the risks substantial, yet the potential rewards, the expansion of humankind's reach and understanding, are simply breathtaking.

Imagining life on the Moon or Mars is to embark on a fantastic voyage of the mind. To contemplate the unique challenges and opportunities presented by these alien environments, the adaptation of human physiology, the development of sustainable habitats, the very nature of existence under different gravitational forces, is to grapple with fundamental questions about our place in the universe and our future as a species. This constant exploration, this persistent questioning, is what continues to fuel my enduring passion for space.

My First New Car

My automotive journey began inauspiciously, yet memorably, with a 1965 Ford Galaxy 500 4-door automatic with a 390 engine. Eighteen years old and brimming with newfound freedom, I proudly purchased this classic for $500 – a testament to diligent saving and youthful ambition. The Galaxy served me faithfully (although the car used more oil than it did gas) until a motorcycle accident sidelined me.

My brother Rick, ever the resourceful body and paint man, lovingly resurrected the car with a complete restoration: fresh paint, a new hard top, and stylish new wheels. It emerged transformed, looking practically showroom new.

Unfortunately, this automotive fairytale took an unexpected turn. My youngest brother, Randy, borrowed the Galaxy for his prom night. A tragic accident involving a tree sadly resulted in the car being totaled. The experience was profoundly disheartening, but it didn't extinguish my passion for automobiles.

After a year of recovery from my motorcycle accident, a year later, I achieved a significant personal milestone: the purchase of my first brand-new car, a 1971 Ford Mustang Mach 1.

This wasn't just any Mustang; it boasted a powerful 351 Cleveland engine, a thrilling Hurst 4- speed shifter, and a stunning Jade Green metallic flake paint job. It was, without a doubt, the most beautiful car I had ever owned, a source of immense pride. This purchase was made possible with the generous support of my future father-in-law, whom I repaid in full within eighteen months, demonstrating my commitment and gratitude. The Mach 1 represented more than just a car; it symbolized the culmination of hard work, perseverance, and the unwavering support of family.

A&W

The other day, I was reminiscing about childhood, and a particular memory surfaced with incredible clarity: our first trip to the A&W drive-in with our parents. I can still practically taste that root beer float – the creamy texture, the fizzy sweetness, the perfect balance of cold and refreshing. It felt like such a special treat, a luxurious indulgence in a simpler time. We probably both wished for a second, maybe even a third, but one was all we got – a testament to the more frugal times, perhaps, but it certainly didn't diminish the joy of the experience.

The atmosphere of that A&W remains vividly etched in my memory. I recall the warm summer evening, the low hum of conversation from other families enjoying their own treats, the aroma of burgers and fries mingling with the distinct scent of root beer. Everything about that night felt perfect – a harmonious blend of family, simple pleasures, and the magic of childhood memories. It's a moment I cherish, a small piece of happiness that still brings a smile to my face whenever I think about it.

Kings & Shakey's Pizza

Some of my fondest memories of high school center around two iconic establishments: Kings and Shakey's. The anticipation for Friday nights at Kings was palpable. All week, Steve Ray and I diligently saved portions of our lunch money, a small sacrifice for the culinary reward that awaited. The culmination of our efforts was always a delicious cheeseburger, crispy onion rings, a rich chocolate shake, and the pièce de résistance, a decadent brownie sundae. Every bite was pure bliss, a perfect end to a long school week, whether we were heading home directly or celebrating after a football game.

Weekends often found us at Shakey's Pizza Parlor, a vibrant hub of activity. The aroma of pizza filled the air, complemented by the lively sounds of a banjo and piano duo providing a soundtrack to the evening. Old black and white movies played silently on the walls, creating a unique and nostalgic ambiance. It wasn't just the pizza and sodas; it was the atmosphere, the shared laughter, and the sense of community that made Shakey's so special. In fact, during my dating years, Shakey's became the quintessential spot for a memorable date, a testament to its enduring charm and appeal. Those were truly golden years, shaped by simple pleasures and shared experiences with a good friend.

Bowling & Drive-in Movies

My fondest memories of my youth are inextricably linked to the simple pleasures of bowling and drive-in movies on a Friday or Saturday night. The thrill of the game, the satisfying swoosh of the ball down the lane, and the camaraderie with friends at Ames Bowl and Kelly's North Bowl – those were golden days. My friends even gave me the unforgettable nickname, "Rocket Pocket," a testament to my (perhaps slightly exaggerated) bowling prowess.

The magic of the drive-in experience is something I'll always cherish. Summer nights spent at The Sky View, Q Twin, and Golden Spike, watching the latest releases under a blanket of stars, created an unparalleled sense of romance and adventure. Eating popcorn that my mom made and canned pop she packed. The vibrant energy of "The Beatles – A Hard Day's Night" at The Sky View remains vivid in my memory; it was truly an unforgettable experience.

I remember one evening at the Sky View drive-in when Diane and I had a date and drove to the movie in her '69 Mercury Cougar convertible. We found our strategic spot to watch the movie and settled in our seats. Much to my chagrin, my brother Randy and my sister Gina came up from behind and jumped into the back seat of Diane's car. I didn't realize that my mom and dad came to the drive-in that night and brought them along. We could not get rid of them even though I pleaded with them. I apologized to Diane as it ruined our date, but she was very forgiving. From that moment on, I never told them which drive-in theater we were going to go to.

Even the long, sometimes sleepy, winter evenings at the Indian Hills Movie Theater, enjoying the immersive surround sound while watching classics like "Gone with the Wind," (though I admit, I may have nodded off a time or two during that epic!), and all of the James Bond Movies. These experiences weren't just about the films or the scores; they were about shared laughter, friendship, and the creation of lasting memories. They represent a simpler time, filled with carefree fun and the joy of shared experiences.

Sky View Drive-in Theater

I was thinking about those long, sun-drenched summers of my youth, and a particular memory popped into my head – one of our earliest, most ingenious schemes for entertainment. It involved my brothers and our intrepid neighborhood accomplice, Steve Ray, and our clandestine cinematic adventures.

We'd make our way up the quiet, dead-end of Ogden Street, where the world seemed to drop away, revealing the magnificent, glowing spectacle of the Sky View drive-in theater below.

From that vantage point, the anticipation would build as we carefully picked our way down a steep, treacherous dirt incline, the loose earth scattering under our sneakers. Our destination? A pre-dug slightly expanded 'hole in the wall' – more of a strategic breach, really – It was our secret gateway, carved out with boyish determination and a few pilfered garden shovels.

Once through our portal, we'd scramble silently onto the hallowed ground of the parking lot. Our mission wouldn't be complete, of course, without our crucial sound upgrade. We'd discreetly creep to the back two rows, the ones closest to our hidden nook, and meticulously adjust the sound poles, turning up the volume just enough for our viewing and hearing pleasure. Then, nestled comfortably within our cozy, dirt-floored hideaway – a clandestine box seat with an unparalleled view – we'd watch the silver screen come alive.

Those Saturday nights, and sometimes even a dull Friday, transformed into magical cinematic journeys under the vast, starry summer sky. The flickering images, the muffled sounds amplified just for us, the shared popcorn (or whatever meager snacks we'd scrounge up) – it was pure, unadulterated youthful bliss.

It might sound like a mischievous caper now, and perhaps it was, but in our defense, it felt entirely justified. We were just four teenagers, full of boundless energy but empty pockets, without the luxury of car keys or admission fees.

This ingenious workaround became our cherished ritual, our escape from the mundane, providing unforgettable entertainment on those endless summer evenings when boredom was a real threat.

Thinking back, it was more than just watching movies; it was about shared adventure, ingenuity, and the simple joy of discovery. A time when a 'hole in the wall' offered the grandest of memories.

Fourth of July's

Some of my fondest childhood memories are linked to the Fourth of July celebrations on North 69th Street in Omaha. Our neighborhood transformed into a vibrant, albeit somewhat chaotic, spectacle of pyrotechnics. The air crackled with anticipation as the evening progressed, a symphony of explosions punctuating the twilight. From the humble Black Cats and Bottle Rockets to the dramatic Roman Candles, each firework painted a fleeting masterpiece across the night sky.

Then there was Dennis. He wasn't just any neighbor's kid; he was our neighborhood resident pyrotechnician, a self-proclaimed expert who always managed to acquire the coveted M-80s, adding a thrilling, and slightly terrifying, element to the festivities. Our youthful ingenuity led us to devise makeshift rocket launchers from drainpipes, turning simple bottle rockets into surprisingly powerful projectiles. We engaged in playful, albeit reckless, "battles," the smoke from countless explosions swirling under the streetlights, creating an eerie, almost war-like atmosphere.

Looking back, I'm struck by the sheer audacity of our actions. The risks we took were considerable, and the fact that we escaped without injury or property damage is nothing short of miraculous. Yet, these seemingly dangerous escapades forged indelible memories, moments of uninhibited joy that I continue to cherish. The Fourth of July on North 69th Street wasn't just a holiday; it was where childhood dreams, youthful exuberance, and a healthy dose of mischief collided, creating a tapestry of unforgettable experiences.

Summer Swimming/Boating

I vividly recall a truly special summer project that brought our family closer together: the meticulous restoration of a classic wood-frame boat. This wasn't merely a task; it was a shared endeavor intended to create lasting memories of leisure and exhilaration on the water.

The process itself was an odyssey of dedication, spanning several arduous weeks. My father, my brothers, my mom, and I committed countless hours, painstakingly sanding down every inch of the hull until its surface was smooth as silk. It was a labor of love that left our hands aching but filled our spirits with quiet determination. Following this exhaustive preparation, we carefully applied multiple layers of sealer and a robust protective coating, transforming the weathered vessel into a gleaming, resilient craft, ready to withstand the elements once more.

The final, triumphant piece of our puzzle arrived when my dad, with a gleam of excitement in his eyes, located a formidable 35-horsepower Johnson outboard motor in Plattsmouth, Nebraska. This powerful engine was the vital heart our boat needed, a promise of exhilarating adventures to come. Once mounted and meticulously checked, she was truly complete, and the anticipation for her inaugural launch became almost unbearable.

The eagerly awaited day for our maiden voyage finally dawned. With life vests neatly stowed and our shining water skis eagerly awaiting their turn, we packed the car and embarked on the journey to Carter Lake. The air buzzed with an infectious sense of excitement as we trailered our beautifully restored vessel towards the glistening expanse of water that would soon become our playground.

Launching the boat into the cool waters of Carter Lake felt like a true rebirth. It transcended being just a boat; it was a tangible symbol of our collective effort and shared dreams. We began by simply cruising, feeling the gentle sway of the waves and the invigorating spray on our faces.

But the true magic, the highlight of the day, undeniably began with water skiing. The thrill of gliding effortlessly across the lake's surface, the wind whipping through our hair, and our laughter echoing across the water created indelible memories.

Each turn and every splash brought pure, unadulterated joy. Those sun-drenched hours spent on the water, bound by the shared excitement of our newly restored boat, were truly unforgettable. It was more than just summer leisure; it was an extraordinary family adventure that forged deeper bonds and painted vivid, joyous pictures in the album of our lives.

My fondest childhood memories are inextricably linked to water. Merit's Beach holds a special place in my heart; I recall countless sunny days spent splashing in the water and building elaborate sandcastles with my family. Occasionally, we'd venture to the slightly more secluded LinOma Beach, relishing the quieter atmosphere and the joy of shared family time.

As I grew older, my brothers and I discovered new aquatic adventures. The Country Club pool and Hartman Pool became our regular haunts, often accompanied by our close friend, Steve Ray (whom we affectionately nicknamed "Mr. Nose-plugs"). Our shared passion for swimming led to some memorable, albeit mischievous, escapades.

We had a rather… enthusiastic approach to diving. Our repeated "splash dives," while intended as playful pranks, unfortunately resulted in us being temporarily banished from both pools on several occasions. It became a sort of playful game of cat and mouse – expelled from one pool; we'd head to the other, only to repeat the cycle. Our interactions with the lifeguards were always light-hearted, a blend of innocent flirting and playful banter. The high dive at the Country Club became our stage for perfecting our splash dives, much to the amusement (and occasional chagrin) of the lifeguards. Their frustrated whistles and temporary suspensions only served to add to the thrill of our youthful exploits.

Looking back, those days represent a time of carefree laughter, sibling camaraderie, and the unforgettable thrill of youthful rebellion – all seasoned with the refreshing chill of a perfectly executed splash dive. These are memories I cherish dearly.

Wintertime Fun

When the chill of winter settled in, blanketing our world in white, my fondest memories weren't just of spirited snowball skirmishes or the intricate architecture of snow forts, nor even the graceful glides across Benson Park's frozen lagoon. No, my mind invariably drifts to the exhilarating adventures we concocted with our trusty sleds and toboggans.

Our neighborhood's winter magnet was undoubtedly the sprawling hill behind Hartman School, merely a block and a half from home. It was a natural amphitheater of snow, culminating in a perfect, snow-packed berm at its base – a ramp seemingly designed by nature itself to launch us into glorious, albeit brief, flights through the crisp, cold night air.

One winter, an audacious idea sparked among us: how could we make our descent even faster, even more thrilling? The answer came in five-gallon buckets and sheer determination.

Over several frigid evenings, we tirelessly hauled water, sloshing through the deepening snow, meticulously pouring it onto the chosen sledding path. The mercury plunged, and by morning, our makeshift ice track gleamed, promising unprecedented speeds.

The moment of truth arrived. Piling four of us, me, my two brothers, and friend Steve Ray onto a single, robust rung sled – a relic built for shared exuberance – we braced ourselves at the summit. With a collective push, we launched. The world blurred into a white streak as we tore down the glassy incline, the wind whipping past our faces, each gasp swallowed by the rush. The berm loomed, then we hit it. A glorious moment of weightlessness as we soared, suspended against the starry, winter sky.

The landing, as you might imagine, was more about physics than finesse. With a resounding thud, the impact reverberated through us.

Our beloved sled, a vessel of pure joy, bore the brunt; its sturdy metal rungs splayed outwards, permanently bent into new, quirky angles. But instead of disappointment, a tidal wave of unadulterated laughter erupted, echoing across the frozen landscape, bubbling forth for what felt like an eternity.

It was a moment of pure, uninhibited childhood joy, a memory so vivid it still brings a smile to my face, a story I cherish and often recount.

Starting the Old Family Car in the Winter

I remember those biting Lecuona winters and how, without fail, our old family car would stage its annual protest the biting cold. It seemed like every single time the temperatures plummeted and the wind howled; the engine would stubbornly refuse to turn over.

And their dad would be, ever the determined engineer, already bundled up and disappearing under the hood. A cloud of frosty breath his only companion. My crucial, albeit shivering, assignment was always the same: flashlight bearer. The piercing chill of the night air would seep right into my bones, making me shiver uncontrollably, a full-body tremor that felt impossible to suppress. Consequently, the beam of light, meant to illuminate his intricate work on the carburetor or whatever component he was wrestling with, would dance and waver like a frantic firefly.

"For crying out loud, hold it still!" his voice, laced with an exasperated sigh, would cut through the frigid air. I swear, my teeth were chattering so violently, I couldn't even manage a steady grip, let alone process whatever invaluable automotive lesson he was attempting to impart.

My brain, much like the engine itself, just seemed to freeze up, utterly incapable of retaining any mechanical wisdom.

Yet, through sheer persistence and, I suspect, a few choice words aimed directly at the stubborn machinery. He always managed to coax that old engine back to life. That first sputtering cough, then the triumphant, roaring surge – it was truly the sound of salvation.

We'd tumble back into the blessed warmth of the house, a little numb but incredibly relieved, alive to tell the tale of another conquered cold winter night. It's funny how some memories just stick with you.

Camping

Thinking back to my high school days evokes a flood of cherished memories, particularly those spent with my closest friends. Steve Ray, my next-door neighbor and confidante, along with my brothers, Rick and Randy, and I embarked on numerous summer adventures. Our expeditions typically centered around the serene beauty of Fremont Lakes and the meandering Elkhorn River.

Steve's father's trusty Ford Bronco served as our chariot, transporting our camping gear – a motley collection of tents, fishing rods, and enough provisions to sustain a small army (or at least four hungry teenagers!). Our simple fare – hot dogs, canned tuna, saltines, beans, and an abundance of water and sugary drinks – somehow tasted infinitely better under the open sky. The four of us squeezed comfortably into our tents; the nights filled with the crackling of our carefully tended campfire.

Our days were a delightful tapestry of activities: casting lines in the hope of catching the day's supper, taking refreshing dips in the cool lake waters, lazily drifting along on an inflatable raft, and, shall we say, engaging in some unauthorized off-road adventures in the Bronco (don't tell Steve's dad!). The evenings were equally captivating, filled with the shared laughter and camaraderie that only true friendship can forge. We spun endless yarns, traded jokes, and often laughed so hard our sides ached.

These expeditions weren't merely camping trips; they were rites of passage, forging bonds that time cannot easily erode. The memories of those carefree days remain vibrant, a constant reminder of the simple joys of friendship, adventure, and the unadulterated fun of youth. To this day, they rank among the most treasured experiences of my life.

Fishing with My Brothers

I was recently reflecting on some of my cherished family memories, and a particular fishing trip with my brothers, Rick and Randy, immediately came to mind. It's a story I often recount, not just for its humorous outcome, but for the glimpse it offers into our sibling dynamics.

Rick, bless his heart, was the quintessential outdoorsman of our family. His connection to the water ran deep; it was his sanctuary, a place of profound tranquility. He wasn't just a fisherman; he was an artisan of the craft, meticulously hand-making his own lures, each one a testament to his patience and passion. He always had a supply of live bait, too, ensuring no opportunity was missed. Randy, ever the loyal companion, often joined him on these aquatic escapades, forming a duo that was as comfortable on the water as on land.

Now, I, on the other hand, never quite shared their enthusiasm for the sport. The idea of sitting patiently by the water, waiting for a bite, didn't hold the same allure for me. Yet, their persistent invitations, bordering on earnest pleas, eventually wore down my resistance. After what felt like an eternity of cajoling, I finally relented, agreeing to accompany them on one of their fabled outings.

Our chosen destination was Fremont Lakes, a place that held many fun memories. The drive itself was filled with anticipation – for them, of the catch; for me, of… well, merely surviving the experience. Upon arrival, we set about establishing our base camp. Tents were pitched, the cooler stocked, and the fishing gear – an arsenal of poles and tackle boxes – was meticulously organized. Then, the procession began, down the path leading to the water's edge.

This is where my conditions came into play. I made it abundantly clear that if I were to participate, certain amenities would be non-negotiable. First, a prime viewing spot had to be meticulously cleared of any unwieldy weeds. Second, my throne – a comfortable lawn chair – needed to be strategically positioned. And third, a steady stream of refreshments was to be on standby. My brothers, with an amused resignation, obliged my royal demands.

Once settled, a peculiar division of labor emerged. Rick, with the expert touch of a seasoned angler, would meticulously bait my hook, ensuring everything was perfect. Randy, ever the sidekick, was assigned the task of de-hooking any fish I might, against all odds, catch. I honestly didn't harbor any expectations; my complete lack of experience led me to believe I'd spend the day simply observing.

To my utter astonishment, the day unfolded in the most unexpected way. Despite my amateur status, the fish seemed to have a particular affinity for my line. One after another, I reeled them in, much to the growing disbelief and, I suspect, slight frustration of my seasoned fishing companions. As the sun began to dip below the horizon, casting a warm glow across the lake, we continued to fish. I distinctly recall the magic of that twilight hour, with a glow stick tied to my line, its light bobbing and weaving on the water's surface – a truly captivating sight.

As darkness fully embraced us, we packed up our gear, heading back to camp with a surprisingly bountiful catch, all thanks to yours truly. My brothers, with a mix of good-natured grumbling and genuine admiration, cleaned my haul. Soon, the tantalizing aroma of fresh fish sizzling over an open flame filled the air. That fish fried dinner, under the starlit sky, was one of the most memorable meals of my life.

I couldn't resist it. Between bites of perfectly cooked fish, I leaned back, a satisfied grin spreading across my face, and declared, with an air of mock triumph, "Now *that's* how you catch fish!" I'm certain, by that point, they were seriously contemplating whether a gentle toss into the lake would be an appropriate response to my newfound, albeit undeserved, expertise. It was a day filled with laughter, sibling rivalry, and the creation of a truly unforgettable memory.

School of Hard Knocks

While my path to professional success didn't involve a traditional college education, my journey has been a rich and rewarding one. I opted to enter the workforce directly after high school, focusing on building a family and establishing a career. This hands-on approach provided an invaluable experience and a unique perspective. Rather than the structured learning environment of a university, my education has been shaped by the challenges and triumphs of real-world experiences – a rigorous curriculum indeed. Each day presented new opportunities for learning, adaptation, and growth, fostering a resilience and practical problem-solving skillset that I believe was exceptionally valuable. This practical experience, coupled with a strong work ethic and a constant pursuit of knowledge, has allowed me to achieve significant success in government administration. I was always confident that my skills and experience were a valuable asset, and I was always eager to contribute to the employers I worked for. Working for the citizens of the Great State of Nebraska was a dream come true.

Success without College

The idea that a college education is a prerequisite for success is a pervasive myth, one that often overshadows the diverse paths to achievement. While a college degree can undoubtedly provide valuable skills, knowledge, and networking opportunities, it's far from the only route to a fulfilling and prosperous life.

Many incredibly successful individuals have achieved remarkable things without ever setting foot on a college campus. Their success stems from a combination of factors, including innate talent, unwavering dedication, entrepreneurial spirit, strong work ethic, and, perhaps most importantly, identifying and capitalizing on opportunities. Think of the countless self-taught programmers, visionary entrepreneurs, and skilled artisans who have built thriving businesses and made significant contributions to society without formal higher education.

The path to success is incredibly personal and diverse. It's less about the specific route taken and more about the passion, perseverance, and adaptability demonstrated along the way.

Focusing solely on a college degree as the "only" benchmark for success can limit one's perspective and potentially hinder the exploration of alternative, equally valid, and potentially more fulfilling avenues. Ultimately, the definition of success is subjective and should be defined by individual aspirations and accomplishments.

American Flag

The American flag, for me, is far more than just a piece of fabric adorned with stars and stripes. It stands as a profound and enduring symbol, deeply interwoven with the very essence of our nation's history, its ongoing struggles, and its unwavering aspirations.

When I see the Stars and Stripes unfurl, it evokes a powerful sense of connection to the generations who have contributed to the grand American experiment. It represents the sacrifices made for freedom, the courage displayed in the face of adversity, and the relentless pursuit of a more just and perfect union. Each star and stripe tells a story of innovation, resilience, and the relentless quest for opportunity that has defined our country from its inception.

Ultimately, it serves as a constant reminder of the fundamental ideals we hold dear: liberty, justice, and equality for all. It's a beacon of hope, inspiring us to uphold our shared responsibilities as citizens and to continue striving towards a future where these principles are fully realized for every individual. It signifies our collective identity, uniting diverse voices under one banner with a shared vision for a brighter tomorrow.

We installed a flagpole in our front yard. For us, the American flag represents more than just patriotism; it's a symbol of the freedoms and opportunities this nation has provided, and continues to strive towards, for all its citizens.

Displaying the flag is a way for us to express our gratitude and unwavering commitment to the principles upon which this country was founded. We hope that our flag serves as a visible reminder of those values and inspires a sense of community pride in our neighborhood.

Patriotism Growing Up Then and Now

Growing up, patriotism was woven into the fabric of my daily life, a complex tapestry of experiences and lessons. It was the quiet pride in my community's resilience, in seeing neighbors help neighbors during tough times, the spirit of collective action that solved problems large and small. It was the unwavering belief in the potential of our nation, even when confronted with its imperfections. Patriotism, for me, wasn't blind to adherence to tradition but a continuous striving for a better future, rooted in a deep understanding of our history – both its glories and its failings. My dad put USMC green military blankets on our beds to teach us about military service. It was the responsibility to be a contributing member of society, to uphold justice and fairness, and to work towards a more equitable and inclusive nation. It's a constant process of learning, reflecting, and engaging with the ongoing story of my country, one that I am privileged and proud to be a part of. It's a journey, not a destination.

Motorcycle Accident

My life took an unexpected turn at eighteen. Earlier that year, I bought a brand-new Honda CB 450 motorcycle. I loved that bike.

Unfortunately, a serious motorcycle accident left me with a cascade of injuries: twelve broken ribs, a punctured lung, ninety-eight stitches in my head, and an extensive road rash. Reflecting on that pivotal moment in my life, a conversation I believe was divinely guided, profoundly shaped my perspective. I recall vividly a prayer, a desperate plea for understanding amidst challenging circumstances, vividly. My question to God was simple yet profound: Why me? Why was I spared? The answer, while enigmatic, resonated deeply. The divine message, "when you get to the fork in the road, take it," wasn't a literal instruction about geographical paths. It was, I believe, a metaphor for the countless choices we face in life.

I interpreted this message as a call to action, a challenge to embrace the uncertainties of life's journey and choose the path of righteousness and compassion. The "fork in the road" represents the constant decision points where we must choose between self-interest and altruism, between ease and responsibility. My understanding led me to dedicate myself to serving others, to seek opportunities to extend kindness and generosity whenever possible, however small the act may seem. This commitment to positive action has become the guiding principle of my life.

The year of recovery that followed was undeniably challenging, a period of intense emotional introspection. Confined to my bed and then slowly regaining mobility, I was forced to confront my mortality and re-evaluate my life trajectory. This unforeseen circumstance, though devastating at the time, ultimately proved to be a catalyst for profound personal growth and a renewed sense of purpose. The experience profoundly shaped my perspective, leading me to reassess my priorities and charting a new course for my future.

Reflecting on a pivotal moment in my life, a conversation I believe was divinely guided, profoundly shaped my perspective. I recall vividly a prayer, a desperate plea for understanding amidst challenging circumstances, vividly. My question to God was simple yet profound: Why me? Why was I spared? The answer, while enigmatic, resonated deeply. The divine message, "when you get to the fork in the road, take it," wasn't a literal instruction about geographical paths. It was, I believe, a metaphor for the countless choices we face in life.

I interpreted this message as a call to action, a challenge to embrace the uncertainties of life's journey and choose the path of righteousness and compassion. The "fork in the road" represents the constant decision points where we must choose between self-interest and altruism, between ease and responsibility. My understanding led me to dedicate myself to serving others, to seek opportunities to extend kindness and generosity whenever possible, however small the act may seem. This commitment to positive action has become the guiding principle of my life.

The Military Draft

In the tapestry of life, certain threads stand out, often those woven with unexpected challenges and profound revelations. For me, one such thread began to unravel in 1970, a year that beckoned with the solemn call of national service. As a young man, deeply moved by the spirit of patriotism and a family legacy rooted in military service, particularly the proud tradition of the U.S. Marine Corps, I had already committed my future. My intention was clear: to answer the draft summons and join the ranks of the Marines, pending the final induction physical.

The path, however, took an unforeseen turn. Just weeks before that critical physical, a motorcycle accident left its indelible mark, a shadow hanging over my aspirations. I still reported to the induction center, filled with a mixture of apprehension and resolve, spending three long days navigating the bureaucratic maze and the medical assessments. On that final, decisive day, a medical captain delivered the news that would forever alter my trajectory. He informed me, with a clinical detachment that couldn't soften the blow, that I had not met the physical standards. The belief was that I wouldn't withstand the rigors of boot camp, leading to a "4-F" medical deferment.

To say I was simply "disheartened" would be a profound understatement. For a young man who had always prided himself on physical fitness, whose identity was inextricably linked to strength and capability, this pronouncement felt like a crushing defeat. Tears welled up, not merely from sadness, but from a profound sense of shattered purpose. The dream of following in the footsteps of my Marine Corps father and serving my country in the most direct way I knew seemed irrevocably lost.

Returning home to my parents, my heart heavy with unspoken grief, was one of the hardest moments. Explaining why I couldn't fulfill what I felt was my duty, why I had been declared unfit, was agonizing. Yet their quiet understanding offered a profound solace. My father, a former Marine himself, looked at me with wisdom in his eyes and simply affirmed that everything would, in time, work out. He respected my fervent desire to serve, even if the path I envisioned was now closed.

That disappointment, that ache of unfulfilled duty, has remained a persistent, quiet echo throughout my life. It never truly fades. However, life, in its infinite wisdom, often opens new doors when others close. While the uniform of a Marine was not to be mine, the call to serve my nation remained. This led me to a different, yet equally meaningful, form of public service: an appointment to the United States Selective Service System years later, where I served for two decades, I dedicated myself to this organization, finding a profound sense of purpose and contributing to the security and functioning of our nation in a capacity I never initially imagined. It was a testament to the enduring belief that true patriotism finds many expressions, and while my early dream was denied, my commitment to service ultimately found its fulfillment.

My Only Regret

It is with a deeply reflective heart that I often ponder my connection to this extraordinary nation. My profound love for the United States, and especially for the iconic symbolism of our flag, has always been a guiding force. It is precisely this fervor that leads to a singular, abiding regret: the inability to have served our country directly within the ranks of the United States Marine Corps, a path I envisioned with great pride. A medical deferment, an unforeseen barrier, prevented me from realizing this cherished ambition, and with it, the solemn honor of having the beautiful and patriotic American flag draped over my final resting place, an honor so profoundly deserved by those who have given their service.

The sight of the Red, White, and blue stirs within me an unparalleled sense of pride and reverence. It represents not just a piece of fabric, but the very essence of our shared values, our history, and the indomitable spirit of liberty that defines us. My admiration for our armed forces, and particularly for the Marine Corps, is boundless, recognizing their immense sacrifices and unwavering dedication.

May this glorious banner continue to fly high, perpetually symbolizing the enduring strength and freedom of our beloved America.

My Commitment to Our Country's Readiness

My lifelong aspiration to serve my country began in 1970, amidst the turbulence of the

Vietnam War. The call to duty, echoing the legacy of my father's service in WWII and the Korean War, resonated deeply within me. Receiving my draft notice filled me with patriotic fervor, and I eagerly prepared to enlist in the Marine Corps. Fate, however, intervened in the form of a devastating motorcycle accident. The resulting severe injuries, including a collapsed lung, forced a medical deferment, leaving me profoundly disappointed and frustrated. The dream of immediate service was shattered.

This setback, however, did not extinguish my unwavering commitment to national defense. Instead, it fueled a relentless search for alternative ways to contribute. Years later, the opportunity arose to serve my nation through a volunteer position with the United States Selective Service System. This appointment marked a pivotal moment, transforming unfulfilled ambition into meaningful action.

For two decades, I dedicated myself to supporting military readiness, finding immense satisfaction in this role. A highlight of my service involved developing and implementing impactful outreach programs within Douglas County, a responsibility I approached with dedication and a genuine desire to improve community engagement with national defense. My contributions culminated in the honor of serving as Vice-Chair for our jurisdiction.

This experience transcended mere duty; it fulfilled a deeply personal yearning to contribute to my country's security. The journey from aspiring Marine to a dedicated volunteer with the Selective Service System has been a profound one, teaching me resilience, adaptability, and the enduring power of commitment. I am immensely proud of the contributions I made during these two decades and deeply grateful for the opportunity to have served in this capacity.

A Tribute to My Brother Rick

I want to share a deep personal experience that has profoundly impacted my perspective on disability and inclusion. My younger brother, Rick (now deceased), was involved in a devastating motor vehicle accident that resulted in a spinal cord injury, leaving him quadriplegic and reliant on an electric wheelchair for mobility. He is now deceased, but during his life, he taught me a valuable lesson. He was a proud, honorably discharged Marine.

The initial shock and grief were immense, but what followed was an even more profound journey of learning and understanding. Witnessing Rick's unwavering spirit and resilience in the face of such adversity has reshaped my understanding of what it means to live with a disability. He didn't just navigate the challenges of daily life; he demonstrated incredible strength, creativity, and adaptability in overcoming obstacles that most people would find insurmountable.

Through Rick's eyes, I gained a firsthand appreciation for the unique perspectives and talents that individuals with disabilities bring to the workplace and to society. His experiences have illuminated the systemic barriers that exist, and the urgent need for greater inclusion and accessibility. What he taught me isn't just about physical limitations, but about the power of the human spirit, the importance of empathy, and the richness that diversity brings to our shared human experience. His journey was a powerful lesson in unwavering determination and the resilience of the human spirit.

Picking Your Life Partner

The question about recognizing the right life partner is a profound one, and there's no single, easy answer. It's not a checklist you can tick off, but rather a feeling, a culmination of experiences, and a deep understanding built over time.

While initial sparks and intense attraction are exciting, lasting love requires more. Consider these aspects: Do you feel comfortable being your authentic self around this person, vulnerabilities and all? Do you share core values and life goals, or at least possess mutual respect for differing perspectives? Is there a genuine sense of mutual support and encouragement, even during challenging times? Do you communicate openly and honestly, resolving conflicts constructively? Do you genuinely enjoy spending time together, even in quiet moments of simple companionship?

The "knowing" isn't a sudden epiphany, but a gradual realization that this individual enhances your life, complements your strengths, and helps you grow as a person. It's about feeling a deep sense of peace and contentment within the relationship, a feeling of being truly seen and understood. It's a journey of shared experiences, mutual growth, and unwavering support.

Consider exploring your own values and desires in a relationship before assessing your current situation. Ultimately, finding the right person is as much about self-discovery as it is about finding someone else.

I knew the moment I met Diane, and I fell head over heels in love with her, and over the next couple of years following, we fell deeper in love with each other than I knew for sure.

My Wonderful Wife Diane Samson-Lecuona

It's an extraordinary privilege to speak of a woman who stands as the undisputed center of my universe, the very heart of my existence. For me, that woman is Diane.

She is far more than just a wife; she is my truest confidante and dearest friend, the one person with whom I've shared every triumph and whispered every fear. Her counsel has been my steady compass, guiding me through life's most complex decisions. As a mother, grandmother, and now even a great-grandmother, she has not only nurtured generations but has also, through her boundless love and unwavering commitment, instilled in each of us the deepest and most profound understanding of what family truly means.

For over five and a half decades, through life's unpredictable currents – the joyous highs and the challenging lows, the moments of prosperity and the times of adversity – her steadfast spirit has been my unwavering anchor. Her strength has been my refuge, her wisdom, my guide, and her compassionate presence as a constant source of comfort and reassurance. I cherish and respect her beyond measure, not just for the incredible roles she fulfills, but for the resilient soul and loving heart she possesses.

Diane is not merely an 'emotional support mechanism'; she is the very pulse of my emotional well-being, the irreplaceable fabric of my daily life. The thought of navigating this journey without her by my side is, quite simply, unimaginable. Her presence is a profound blessing that continues to enrich every single day.

Reflecting on the remarkable journey, Diane and I have shared, my mind often drifts to the rich tapestry of our travels. It all began with our enchanting honeymoon in Rapid City, South Dakota, a cherished memory that truly set the stage for a lifetime of exploration.

As the years unfolded, our passports filled with stamps and our hearts with treasured experiences. We ventured across borders, from the vibrant energy of Juarez, Mexico, and the expansive landscapes of Dallas and El Paso, Texas, to the breathtaking fjords of Norway, the serene lakes of Finland, and the historical depths of Germany. Our domestic adventures were equally diverse, taking us from the iconic monuments of Washington D.C. and the genteel charm of Atlanta and Savannah, Georgia, to the beauty of Seattle,

Washington, the resilient spirit of Oklahoma City, Oklahoma, the majestic vistas of Salt Lake City, Utah, the coastal allure of Rhode Island, and the academic grandeur of Boston, Massachusetts, to name but a few.

While many of these later expeditions were primarily tied to my professional endeavors, they always presented wonderful duality. As I attended meetings and conferences, Diane, with her boundless curiosity and independent spirit, would often join other spouses on captivating excursions. They immersed themselves in local history, explored vibrant cultural sites, and discovered hidden gems, returning with stories and insights that illuminated our evenings.

Our time together, once my commitments concluded, was always a highlight. We savored quiet dinners, explored new neighborhoods on foot, and simply absorbed the unique atmosphere of each destination. These shared moments, whether a gourmet meal or a stroll through an ancient market, forged indelible memories.

Each journey, each new encounter, contributed to a profound education for us both. These weren't merely trips; they were unforgettable adventures that broadened our horizons, deepened our appreciation for diverse cultures, and, most importantly, strengthened the incredible bond Diane and I share. The memories created on these roads less traveled remain etched in our hearts, forming an invaluable part of our grand life together.

There are moments, countless moments really, when I find myself simply marveling at the vibrant heart that Diane breathes into our family's world. She has always kept an immaculate home, and her presence is an immeasurable blessing, woven into the very fabric of our home through the extraordinary warmth and unwavering devotion she pours into every detail. It stands as a luminous testament to her boundless dedication and the truly generous spirit that radiates from within her. The inexhaustible energy she channels into cultivating our home is nothing short of inspiring, an artistic endeavor that transcends mere arrangement and truly becomes a continuous, palpable expression of her profound love.

Indeed, she is our home's visionary curator, a maestro of ambiance who orchestrates a seamless ballet of seasonal transformation.

Every holiday, no matter its scale, receives her meticulous, celebratory touch.

But, amidst this year-long symphony of domestic artistry, it is the Christmas season that unmistakably ignites the very essence of her creative brilliance. As December approaches, her passion finds its ultimate expression, channeling every ounce of its vibrant energy into crafting an exquisite, immersive tapestry of festive joy. She transcends mere decoration; she conjures a veritable, breathtaking winter wonderland, metamorphosing our entire dwelling into a luminous, warm, and utterly enchanting sanctuary.

The very air seems to hum with anticipation as December arrives; our home meticulously poised to embrace the holiday spirit. Our two magnificent Christmas trees become not just focal points but living narratives. Upstairs, the majestic, snow-dusted beauty stands as a sentinel of classic elegance, draped in timeless ruby spheres and a celestial cascade of delicate, shimmering lights. Yet it is the downstairs tree that truly serves as a poignant repository of our shared history, glowing softly with a constellation of lights and a cherished collection of ornaments. Each one is a silent storyteller, a relic from our journey, especially those tenderly shaped by our children's innocent fingers years ago, now holding within them the indelible echoes of laughter and pure, unadulterated wonder.

Diane's discerning touch ensures that jovial Santa figurines gleam from unexpected corners, while sumptuous, festive pillows transform every sofa and armchair into an irresistible haven of warmth and repose. The very atmosphere within our walls becomes incandescent, suffused with countless lights and the rich embrace of dark green garlands. They are artfully woven along the venerable fireplace mantle, spiral gracefully on the staircase banister, and even grace the steadfast grandfather clock, infusing it with a touch of days gone by.

This elaborate symphony of decor transcends simple ornamentation; it is a wholly immersive experience, bathing every corner of our lives in a profound, almost sacred sense of warmth, boundless joy, and the quintessential, transformative spirit of Christmas. This truly is the pinnacle of her year, her most vibrant and expressive season. To witness her conjure this magic, year after year, fills my heart with an immeasurable depth of admiration and gratitude.

She does not merely decorate our spaces; she meticulously sculpts an entire culture, a cherished sentiment, forging a sanctuary that profoundly embodies the very essence of 'home' and the eternal, radiant spirit of the festive season.

I want to express my deepest gratitude for the incredible woman who has been my partner for 54 years and counting, my wife, Diane. Her contributions to my life and the success we've shared are immeasurable. It's not merely a matter of supporting my career; her role has been foundational to the happiness and stability of our entire family.

Throughout my professional life, her dedication to our children was unwavering. She created a loving and nurturing home environment, ensuring they received the care and attention they needed to thrive, even as I pursued my ambitions. This allowed me to focus on my work, knowing our family was in the safest and most supportive hands imaginable.

Once our children were in school, she seamlessly transitioned into a full-time career while continuing her tireless support of our family. This dual commitment highlights her incredible strength, resilience, and unwavering dedication to providing us all. She's not just my wife; she's my partner in every sense of the word.

Together, we raised three children, instilling in them the values of responsibility, respect, love, and faith. The strong family unit we've built is a direct testament to her incredible influence and guidance. I couldn't have achieved any of this without her.

Now, in our retirement, we are blessed to enjoy the fruits of our labor and the company of our children, grandchildren, and even great-grandchildren. Every day is a celebration of a life well-lived, a life enriched immeasurably by her constant love and companionship. She truly is my best friend and the love of my life.

Chapter Four

My Commitment to My Wife Diane and My Family

I've been incredibly fortunate in life. In 1971, at the young age of twenty, I married the love of my life, Diane. Our commitment to one another has been the bedrock of my life, a constant source of strength and inspiration. This journey has been enriched immeasurably by the arrival of our three wonderful children, Leslie, Nikki, and Fred. Their unwavering love, support, and encouragement have been instrumental in my professional endeavors. Their belief in me propelled me forward, allowing me to pursue my career with passion and determination. I am eternally grateful for their presence in my life and for the beautiful family we've built together. The strength of our family unit has been a gift that continues to shape and bless me every single day.

Now that I am retired, my family has grown by two sons in laws, Chad Fleming, Jeff Elwood, and a daughter in law, Nikki Gorges-Lecuona, seven grandchildren Trent and Brittany Fleming, Cade and Kelly Elwood, Maddie, JR, and Izzy Lecuona, and two great grandchildren, Beau and Cooper Fleming and at the time of this writing, our granddaughter Brittany is pregnant and we are now expecting a great granddaughter Olivia in March of 2026. Our family has expanded by the addition of two grand son-in-law's, Jon Van Beek married to Brittany, and RJ (Roy) Robles married to Kelly. We have truly been blessed.

The Support of My In-Laws

My deepest gratitude goes to my parents-in-law, Don and Jeanne Samson. Their unwavering love and support have been instrumental in my life from the moment I married their daughter to navigating my career path. Their acceptance and encouragement have created a strong and loving family unit, a foundation that has undeniably contributed to my achievements and overall well-being. The strength and unity of our extended family have been a constant source of strength and inspiration, shaping me into the person I am today. I am eternally grateful for their belief in me and for the positive impact they've had on my life.

My Father-in-Law, Don Samson

I want to share my experience working for my father-in-law, Don Samson, at his sewer contracting business, S&S Trenching. My journey began even before my marriage to his daughter, Diane, and it proved to be a formative period of my professional life. Our relationship quickly evolved beyond that of son-in-law and employer; Don became a mentor, guiding me through the intricacies of the trade.

My initial tasks involved the hands-on aspects of trenching – from mastering the precise placement of batter boards and grade stakes to the meticulous installation of sewer lines, manholes, storm drains, and water mains. I developed a keen eye for detail and maintained comprehensive job logs, documenting every aspect of each project. This meticulous record- keeping became a crucial asset.

However, my ambition extended beyond the physical labor. I expressed a desire to fully understand the business's operational aspects – the critical elements that distinguished success from failure. Don generously took me under his wing, imparting his extensive knowledge of project bidding and business management. Gradually, he entrusted me with increasingly significant responsibilities, including bidding on projects to maintain our crew's workload. This provided invaluable real-world experience in strategic business decision- making. I was also involved in bookkeeping, further solidifying my understanding of the financial aspects of the operation.

My high school training in blueprint reading proved exceptionally useful, providing a head start in understanding project specifications and plans. This, combined with Don's guidance, laid a solid foundation for my career. This experience shaped my approach to business and project management, impacting my work significantly.

My Mother-in-Law Jeanne Samson

I wanted to share a cherished memory, a story of love, family, and the profound impact one remarkable woman had on my life. My mother-in-law, Jeanne Samson, possesses a gentle spirit and a warmth that embraces everyone she ever met. From the very beginning, she welcomed me into her family with open arms, her acceptance laying a solid foundation for Diane and me. I recall countless Sundays spent at their home, surrounded by laughter, love, and the aroma of her incredible fried chicken, a culinary masterpiece that remains unmatched to this day!

Those Sunday dinners were just the beginning. After my band's weekend performances, Diane and I would often return to Don and Jeanne's house, sharing popcorn and sodas with her younger brothers. It was a time of youthful joy and carefree companionship.

Looking back, I realize how deeply rooted in tradition my proposal to Diane was. I felt strongly about seeking her parents' blessing, a gesture that spoke volumes about the importance I placed on their daughter's happiness and their role in her life. Their gracious consent, their visible pride and joy, filled me with an overwhelming sense of happiness and solidified my commitment to Diane. That moment, receiving their blessing, stands out as one of the most significant and cherished moments of my life.

A year later, in August of 1971, Diane and I exchanged vows, embarking on a journey filled with love and shared memories. To this day, I remain eternally grateful for Jeanne's kindness, support, and the indelible mark she has on our lives. Her kindness serves as a constant reminder of the importance of family, love, and the simple joys of life.

Proud of My Children's Career Paths and Success

From my background in the construction and building trades, I've developed a profound respect for the dedication and expertise required of skilled craftsmen. This firsthand experience shaped my own parenting philosophy. My wife and I instilled in our children the belief that education, in its broadest sense, is paramount to achieving their full potential. We committed to supporting their individual educational journeys, regardless of the path they chose.

Our eldest daughter pursued a four-year college degree, a path that led her to her current success. Our second daughter discovered her strengths through the community college system, gaining valuable skills and knowledge that perfectly aligned with her aspirations. Our son, taking a different route altogether, thrived in two rigorous apprenticeship programs, mastering a highly specialized trade.

What unites their distinct journeys is not just their individual achievements but their unwavering mutual support. Each child celebrated the others' successes, fostering a strong familial bond built on shared values and understanding. Their diverse educational experiences highlight the importance of individual pathways to success and the power of collective encouragement. We are immensely proud of their accomplishments and the individuals they have become. Their stories are a testament to the importance of personalized education and the enduring strength of family support.

Sports and Our Grandchildren

Diane and I both were athletes and played sports in high school. Diane was a Captain on her volleyball team, and I wrestled and was a track and cross-country runner, where I was a 1st place Champion in the Mile Run.

Our children and their spouses were athletes in football, wrestling, gymnastics, softball, rugby, and golf. Our grandchildren didn't fall far from the tree. It was with great pride that we watched our grandchildren play sports. Our oldest grandson, Trent Fleming, was a high school wrestler, baseball and football player at Millard West, and his sister, Brittany, was a volleyball player in high school at Omaha Gross and received a scholarship to play in college at Morningside College. Cade Elwood, our second-oldest grandson, played high school football and baseball at Millard North as a quarterback for 4 years and a Nebraska State Champion. His sister, Kelly, played soccer at Millard North for 4 years and is also a Nebraska State Champion. Received a scholarship to play soccer at Missouri Western University. Our granddaughter Maddie Lecuona played soccer at Millard West High School for 4 years and is a Nebraska State Champion and received a scholarship to play college soccer at the University of Nebraska-Kearney. Her brother, JR Lecuona, wrestled, played baseball (State Champions), and played football for Millard South High School, where he earned Super State, All-State, All Metro honors for playing defensive end. He even received academic letters each of his 4 years. He earned a scholarship to play football at South Dakota State, then transferred to Washington State University to play defensive end for the Cougars in the PAC 12. His little sister, Izzy Lecuona (still in middle school), is very involved with cheer competition and competes on an Elite Cheer Squad that travels to competitions, and her squad has won several first-place awards in National competitions in Florida.

Diane and I have sat in the bleachers for every game and completion from their early days getting into their sport and all the way through high school and college, and we couldn't be prouder of them. We were so happy that we were able to attend their activities and show our love and support. They have brought much joy and great memories to our lives. Being a bit of a photography buff, I was able to take hundreds and hundreds of pictures of them playing sports. The education they received and are receiving, and the education from playing team sports, will serve them well. They are all leaders in their own right. We know that they will all be successful in their chosen fields and professions.

Coaching Youth Football

My time as head coach of the KWAA Pee Wee Packers was an incredibly rewarding chapter of my life. I became a certified coach through the National Youth Sports Coaches Association.

More than just teaching football fundamentals, conditioning, and strategy, my focus was on fostering a genuine love for the game, building strong teamwork, and ensuring every player had fun. For many of these young athletes, this was their only experience with contact sports, and I was committed to making it positive and memorable.

I strived to be a motivating force, encouraging the boys at every practice and game. To facilitate learning and improve team cohesion, I developed comprehensive playbooks covering offense, defense, and special teams, ensuring each player understood their individual roles and how they contributed to the overall team strategy. The privilege of coaching 25 young people each season was immense. My wife, Diane, played an invaluable role, meticulously videotaping our games so we could analyze our performance and continually improve. Our consistent winning record wasn't just luck; it was a testament to the dedication of the entire team. Our team concluded each season with an exceptional record, securing the most victories of any team within the league every year for seven consecutive years.

Our success was a collaborative effort. The unwavering support of the parents, from fundraising and concession sales to hosting end-of-season banquets, was crucial. But above all, our winning seasons year after year were a direct result of the incredible coaching staff: Joe Gotsch, Guy Peters, Roger Petersen, Jerry Deming, Mic Flynn, Randy Lecuona, Shawn McDonna, and our team manager, Steve Timmons. Their commitment and expertise were instrumental to our success. To emphasize our unity, I ensured we all wore matching apparel.

My coaching philosophy centered on the idea that "we practice five quarters to play four," pushing our players to develop the stamina and resilience to outlast our opponents—a strategy that consistently paid off.

To further strengthen team bonds and reinforce lessons learned on the field, I regularly invited the coaches and players to my home to review game film, watch NFL highlight films, and enjoy snacks provided by Diane. The parents were incredibly supportive and embraced my coaching approach, creating a positive and encouraging team environment. It's deeply gratifying to have stayed in touch with some former players and hear about their continued success in high school and college football. These stories are truly rewarding moments.

The culmination of years of dedication, countless hours invested in the team and organization, led to my nomination and induction into the Packers Youth Sports Football Program Hall of Fame—an honor I am deeply proud of and cherish. In 1991, the Peewee Packers won the first KWAA Invitational Super Bowl.

Packers Youth Football Hall of Fame Award

I wanted to share a cherished memory that remains a cornerstone of my journey and a source of immense pride: my induction into the Packers Youth Football Hall of Fame back in 1991.

The moment was an absolute surprise, unfolding amidst the camaraderie of the annual Packers Youth Football banquet. It was our esteemed general manager, Steve Timmons, who delivered the unexpected news, transforming an ordinary evening into an unforgettable milestone in my coaching career.

As Steve unveiled the award, the words etched onto the plaque brought a wave of profound emotion: "To Coach Butch Lecuona (1985-1991)." This recognition, marking an induction into the Packer Football Hall of Fame for outstanding coaching achievement, honored my "unselfish dedication and outstanding performance" as a coach for the Kingswood Peewee Packers. It was a testament to the years spent building our peewee program, striving to mold not just athletes, but young individuals of character and sportsmanship. The plaque further acknowledged how my "leadership and ethical approach to teaching football" had been instrumental in developing the program into the thriving entity it is today, ensuring its principles would be "forever etched in Packer Football history."

Receiving this recognition was, and remains, an immense honor. It reinforced a belief I've always held close, a creed that guided my time on the field and continues to define my spirit: "Once a Packer, always a Packer."

Our Favorite College Football Teams

For years, Diane and I have been dedicated Nebraska Husker fans, attending countless games and proudly displaying our Husker flag on game days. It's a tradition we cherish and a part of our identity. When our grandson JR went to play for the Jackrabbits of South Dakota State, we enjoyed showing our support and pride flying the Jackrabbits school flag. This year, however, something wonderful has added a new dimension to our college football enthusiasm.

Our grandson is now playing football for Washington State University, and his games often coincide with Nebraska's schedule.

This presents a delightful dilemma! While our Husker pride remains strong and unwavering, we've found ourselves enthusiastically embracing the Cougars as well. We've added a WSU flag to our game day display, a testament to our expanded fandom and our immense pride in our grandson's accomplishments.

It's a thrilling experience to cheer for two teams, each holding a special place in our hearts. The shared excitement and the joy of supporting both the Huskers and the Cougars have enriched our game day experiences beyond measure. We look forward to many more years of passionate cheering, experiencing the thrill of victory and the agony of defeat (hopefully less of the latter!) with both teams. We are incredibly proud of our grandson and all the players on both teams. Go Huskers! Go Cougars!

Outstanding Young Omahan Award

I still vividly recall the immense pride and inspiration I felt in 1986 when I was named one of the ten recipients of the prestigious Outstanding Young Omahan Award by the Omaha Jaycees. This wasn't merely an accolade; it was a profound affirmation of a commitment to community that continues to shape my endeavors today.

The "Ten Outstanding Young Omahan" (TOYO) program stands as a beacon, recognizing individuals between the ages of 21 and 40 who exemplify selfless dedication to improving our beloved community, all while excelling remarkably in their professional careers. It celebrates those who actively weave acts of kindness and impactful service into the fabric of daily life, driving positive change from within.

For an extraordinary 88 years, the Omaha Jaycees have meticulously sought out and honored these incredible individuals across Greater Omaha. It's a testament to their vision that many of our amazing fellow Omahan, first recognized locally, have gone on to achieve national and even international acclaim, all stemming from their foundational work right here in our community. This program consistently highlights how local engagement can pave the way for broader influence and recognition.

What makes the TOYO award truly distinctive is its rigorous and comprehensive vetting process. Each year, individuals under the age of 40, residing and working in Omaha and its connected suburban areas, are nominated by their peers. The judging transcends specific industries or areas of impact, instead focusing on the holistic essence of each nominee. It's about evaluating the depth of their character, the authenticity of their contributions, and the tangible value they bring to our community. A dedicated team of judges meticulously reviews hundreds of exceptional applicants annually, ensuring that only the most deserving ten are chosen to be celebrated at their annual banquet.

To have been selected from such a competitive and esteemed pool of candidates remains a deep honor for me. It underscored the importance of community involvement and instilled a renewed sense of responsibility and purpose. This recognition continues to be a driving force, reminding me of the profound impact each of us can have when we dedicate ourselves to the betterment of our shared home.

Benson High School - Hall of Fame Award

I wanted to take a moment to share a profoundly meaningful personal reflection with you all. A truly humbling and inspiring milestone occurred in 2010 when I received the incredible news of my selection for induction into my beloved alma mater, Benson High School, as a distinguished alumnus.

The induction ceremony itself was an unforgettable and deeply emotional experience. To stand on that stage, acknowledging the journey that began within those very halls, and to be recognized for my efforts, filled me with an immense sense of pride and gratitude. The presence of my family, witnessing this significant moment, made the occasion even more poignant and special, adding an immeasurable layer of joy to the celebration.

The honor specifically acknowledged my dedicated contributions within the critical fields of workforce development and education. It was truly validating to have my work, focused on empowering individuals and fostering progressive change, recognized for its impact. My efforts, both in developing innovative programs and advocating for improved access, have been fortunate enough to resonate and contribute at various levels—from local initiatives within our city and state, to broader national conversations, and even on international platforms. This recognition underscores the importance of continuous service and dedication to these vital areas.

This milestone continues to serve as a powerful source of inspiration, reinforcing the foundational values and lessons imparted during my formative years at Benson High. It strengthens my resolve to continue championing causes that drive positive societal and professional advancement.

Reaching Your Full Potential

I often find myself pondering a fundamental question that shapes our journeys of growth and achievement: What genuinely holds us back from actualizing the vast, inherent potential residing within each of us?

It's a query that delves beyond superficial challenges, inviting us to examine the deeper factors – be they internal hesitations, external circumstances, learned limitations, or even the comfort of the familiar – that might be inadvertently constraining our path. Recognizing these potential anchors is the crucial first step toward truly understanding ourselves and our capabilities.

I encourage you to take a moment for thoughtful introspection on this very point. What are the specific barriers, visible or invisible, that you perceive as standing between your current reality and the fullest expression of your unique talents and ambitions?

Identifying these impediments isn't merely about overcoming them; it's about gaining clarity, charting a more deliberate course, and ultimately unlocking the unparalleled heights you are capable of reaching.

Worth Doing

When confronted with an endeavor that truly merits our dedication and passion, one that holds the promise of significant impact or profound personal growth, our response must transcend passive acknowledgement. It demands a proactive and spirited embrace. We are called to marshal our capabilities, ignite our resolve, and engage with unwavering enthusiasm. Let us not merely meet the moment, but rather, charge into it with all our might, fully prepared to contribute our utmost and shape its outcome with purposeful action.

Private Ventures of Entrepreneurship: Magic Mirror and Le-Ward Cleaning

The mid-1980s marked a pivotal moment in our lives, a time of bold ambition and entrepreneurial spirit. Diane and I independently launched our own ventures, reflecting our diverse skills and passions. Diane established MM Figure Salons, a pioneering women-only salon that quickly gained a loyal following, renowned for its exceptional service and welcoming atmosphere. Diane also served as an aerobics instructor and held several classes each day.

Simultaneously, I founded Le-Ward Cleaning Co., a commercial office cleaning company dedicated to providing meticulous and reliable cleaning services for businesses in the area.

For several years, we poured our hearts and souls into building these companies, navigating the exhilarating and often challenging landscape of entrepreneurship. The experience was a profound learning curve, teaching us invaluable lessons about business management, client relations, and the importance of adaptability. We cherished the relationships we built with our clientele; their satisfaction was, and remains, a source of great pride.

Ultimately, the demands of raising our children and managing our respective professional commitments proved to be a significant undertaking, more than we could comfortably manage at that time. The decision to close both businesses was not made lightly, and we deeply regret disappointing our valued clients, many of whom expressed their sadness at our departure. The memories of those years, however, remain a testament to our shared ambition and entrepreneurial drive.

Serving on Community Boards

My involvement on multiple community boards has been incredibly rewarding. These experiences have provided me with invaluable opportunities to contribute to the betterment of my community while simultaneously building a robust professional network spanning diverse fields. The collaborative nature of these boards has allowed me to hone my skills in strategic planning, consensus-building, and effective communication, working alongside individuals possessing a wealth of expertise in areas such as finance, education, healthcare, and environmental sustainability. I've not only learned from these diverse perspectives but also made significant contributions. I served on the following Boards of Directors: Labor United, Consumer Credit Counseling Services, United Way of the Midlands, C.H.A.D (Combined Health Agencies Drive), American Red Cross, Omaha Area Food Bank, Federal Post Office Credit Union, KingsWood Athletic Association, and Septemberfest, Inc., a Salute to Labor. These experiences have broadened my understanding of community needs and strengthened my commitment to public service.

Travels Around the World

My career in employment securities, unemployment insurance, and workforce training at the local, state, and national levels has afforded me incredible opportunities for international collaboration. I've had the privilege of representing the United States in discussions with counterparts in Norway, Finland, Germany, and Taipei, Taiwan, sharing insights into our employment security system and exploring potential models for other nations.

These experiences have been profoundly enriching. Beyond the technical aspects of employment policy, I discovered a powerful common thread uniting leaders from diverse cultures: a shared vision for their children's futures. This universal desire for quality education, skilled employment opportunities, comfortable living standards, peace, and longevity transcends geographical boundaries and political differences.

These international exchanges highlighted not only the nuances of various national approaches to workforce development but also the fundamental human aspirations that bind us together. The conversations I participated in underscored the potential for global cooperation to achieve shared goals, confirming my deep belief in the power of dialogue and collaboration to foster international understanding and peace. The pursuit of a more peaceful and prosperous world requires ongoing engagement and a commitment to open communication, and I remain deeply grateful for the experiences that have reinforced this conviction.

9/11/2001 in Washington

I was on Capitol Hill on 9/11/2001 when terrorists flew planes into the New York Twin Towers, and a plane was downed in a field in Pennsylvania, and one hit the Pentagon. I was only a few blocks away in the Hall of States building for a meeting I had scheduled with the U.S. Department of Labor. Because I was president of the National Association of State Workforce Associations at that time, I went to their office early before the meeting, where I was watching the news and could not believe my eyes as I watched it unfold on television. Obviously, my meeting with USDOL was canceled as D.C. was shut down. That day had a profound effect on me. I remember thinking, how could this happen in our country, and a real sense of uncertainty.

Because I had already checked out of my room at the hotel, I was stranded in D.C. for a few days. No communications out (no way to contact my family), all rental car companies had no cars available, no trains, buses, or planes out of D.C., and you could feel the uncertainty in the air.

It was heartwarming to see a coming together in this country of people helping people, supporting one another, opening up their homes for people like me for a place to stay, along with other colleagues, where I will be eternally grateful.

I was finally able to hitch a ride with colleagues from Chicago who were able to secure a rental car, and I dropped them off in Chicago and continued on to my home in Omaha, Nebraska.

To this day, the visions of that day will be forever ingrained in my mind.

Climbing the Stairs to Heaven

The phrase "Climbing the stairs to heaven" evokes such a powerful image, doesn't it? It speaks to the arduous journey of life, the challenges we face, and the ultimate aspiration towards something greater than ourselves. After my motorcycle accident, while lying in bed recovering, I reflected on the various ways we interpret the "stairs" and the "heaven" they lead to.

For some, the stairs might represent the struggles of pursuing a cherished dream, the obstacles encountered along the path to personal fulfillment. Each step could symbolize a small victory, a lesson learned, a moment of growth. The "heaven" at the top is then the realization of that dream, the achievement of a goal, the sense of profound satisfaction.

For others, the metaphor could depict a spiritual journey, the steps representing acts of faith, moments of introspection, and the overcoming of personal demons. In this context, "heaven" might be enlightenment, peace, or a deeper understanding of one's place in the world.

Regardless of the specific interpretation, the underlying theme is one of perseverance, hope, and the unwavering belief in a brighter future. It's a reminder that while the climb may be challenging, the view from the top is worth the effort.

As I've journeyed through life, my understanding of spirituality and being of

The Catholic faith has deepened considerably. The path to enlightenment and the concepts of heaven and the afterlife are subjects I've been reflecting on with increasing intensity. It's a complex and personal exploration, and I find myself grappling with many questions about the nature of existence and our place within the larger cosmic scheme.

I've been engaged with reading the Bible, engaging in discussions with my mother and my wife; these discussions have been profoundly enriching and have offered diverse perspectives that challenge and broaden my own beliefs.

I'm sure that there is an afterlife in heaven, and the process of seeking understanding is in itself a deeply rewarding journey. It's a continuous conversation with myself, and with God.

And in the End

My journey through life, from the innocent wonder of childhood to the quiet reflection of retirement, has been a rich tapestry woven from countless experiences and relationships. I've been fortunate to learn invaluable lessons from a remarkable cast of characters: the unwavering wisdom of my parents and grandparents, the playful camaraderie of my siblings, the enduring bonds of friendship, the unwavering love of my wife and children, the joyous chaos of my grandchildren, and the profound spiritual guidance of my faith.

This journey has shaped my perspective, highlighting the inherent beauty in the diversity of human experience and the multitude of ways we find meaning in life. While our individual paths may diverge, the common thread that binds us is the power of connection. The love we share, the support we offer, and the empathy we extend—these are the threads that create the rich fabric of our lives.

In Conclusion

As I draw this particular section to a close, I wanted to leave you with a thought that I find incredibly profound and essential for a truly fulfilling life. I believe that our journey is perpetually enriched when we actively embrace every single opportunity to learn something new, each and every day. It's more than just accumulating facts; it's about nurturing our innate curiosity, challenging our established perspectives, and allowing ourselves to be constantly surprised by the world around us.

Whether it's a small insight from a casual conversation, a new skill attempted, or a deeper understanding gleaned from a book, these moments of discovery keep our minds agile, our spirits vibrant, and our lives endlessly expanding.

This continuous quest for knowledge is, in my eyes, the true secret to perpetual growth and joy.

Within the pages of this book, I've endeavored to weave a narrative that, at its heart, is a profound homage to the extraordinary individuals who have journeyed alongside me. Their unwavering presence, the invaluable wisdom they imparted, and the boundless love they generously shared have not only enriched my existence beyond measure but have also intricately shaped the very essence of the person I am today.

This work stands as a deeply personal expression of gratitude, a testament to the myriad interactions – both fleeting and enduring – that have served as pivotal crucibles in my growth and understanding. Each challenge overcome, every insight gained, and indeed, every joyful moment celebrated, bears the indelible imprint of these cherished connections.

It is a truth that reverberates with profound clarity, echoing the timeless sentiment so beautifully articulated by The Beatles: "And in the end, the love you take, is equal to the love you make." This lyrical wisdom serves as a guiding principle, affirming that the ultimate measure of a life truly well-lived transcends mere accomplishments or individual triumphs.

Instead, it is found in the intricate and enduring tapestry of relationships cultivated, the genuine bonds forged, and the depth and breadth of human connection fostered along the way. This book, then, is as much theirs as it is mine.

Part Two of Hour Glass

This part of the book delves into the significant cultural shift I spearheaded during my time leading the Nebraska Department of Labor. This section provides an insightful look at the strategies, challenges, and ultimate successes of implementing transformative change within a large-scale public organization. I've included specific examples and lessons learned that are applicable to a wide range of leadership contexts. My hope is that this section will serve as a valuable resource for anyone striving to create a more positive and productive work environment. You will find recurring themes in this part of the book, but it's important to reemphasize their importance as it ties the themes together.

Acknowledgements

I would be remiss if I didn't recognize the contributions to my success as the Commissioner of Labor. This group of folks believed in me and supported the vision I had for the Department of Labor. They include: John Albin, Daphne Airan, Allan Amsberry, Leesa Anderson, Bill Hetzler, Terri Johnston, Vicki Leech, Kay Marti, Joan Modrell, Nan Merrill, and Bonnie Smith.

My Circle of Influence

My influence circle included the teachings of the Bible, my good friends and mentors, Alan D. Simon CEO of Omaha Steaks, Lou Tice of The Pacific Institute, Sandra Hastings of Sandra Hastings Associates, Hans Zobel of Festo Corp., Doug Pauley Central Community College, and Emily DeRocco, Kate Cashen, Rich Hobbie, who all served as NASWA Executive Director during my tenure. It's true, "you are only as good as the people you surround yourself with."

Easy Read for State Agency Heads

This isn't just a book; it's a roadmap that I created for my success at the Nebraska Department of Labor. Consider it your strategic guide to transforming your state agency's culture. Within these pages, you'll find a comprehensive framework for fostering efficiency, enhancing accountability, and cultivating exceptional leadership. We're not talking about superficial changes; this is about building a sustainable, high-performing organization.

The book delves into practical strategies for overcoming common obstacles in organizational transformation, including resistance to change, communication breakdowns, and resource constraints. You'll learn how to identify key stakeholders, build consensus, and effectively communicate your vision for a more efficient and accountable agency. Further, it explores methods for developing strong leadership at all levels, from frontline supervisors to executive management. This includes cultivating a culture of collaboration, empowerment, and continuous improvement.

Think of this as an investment in your agency's future. By utilizing the tools and strategies outlined in this book, you can build a culture of excellence that will benefit not only your agency but the citizens of the state it serves. I encourage you to approach this as a journey, not a destination; consistent implementation and adaptation will be key to success.

As you delve into this particular segment of my journey, you will undoubtedly observe the deliberate recurrence of several overarching conceptual threads. These are not merely incidental repetitions, but rather foundational distinctions each meticulously integrated to serve as a critical analytical lens. Their consistent presence is designed not only unify the diverse subjects explored but also to profoundly deepen and solidify your comprehension of every discrete topic addressed within these forthcoming sections.

Hour Glass

Hourglass offers a unique insider's perspective on the realities of working within a state government. Drawing on my extensive experience as a former high-ranking state administrator, "Hourglass" provides a nuanced and detailed account of the challenges, triumphs, and often-overlooked aspects of public service. It promises to be a fascinating read for anyone interested in the inner workings of government, the complexities of policy-making, and the human stories behind the headlines. The book delves into the bureaucratic hurdles faced, the ethical dilemmas encountered, the personal sacrifices made. I believe this book will resonate particularly with administrative staff, students of public administration, those working in government, anyone interested in political science.

I applied this "hourglass" theory to the management of government as a business. The traditional hourglass, with its narrow constriction in the middle, represents a process of refinement and bottleneck. In the context of government, we can envision this in several ways.

The upper portion of the hourglass could represent the broad spectrum of citizen needs and demands – a wide array of ideas, suggestions, and concerns flowing in. This stage involves extensive public engagement, data collection, and the formulation of various policy proposals.

The narrow constriction represents the critical decision-making process within the government. This is where rigorous analysis, prioritization, and resource allocation occur. This phase necessitates careful consideration of budget constraints, logistical feasibility, and potential societal impact. The efficient management of this phase is crucial to the overall success of the system. A bottleneck here leads to inefficiency, delays, and potentially, public discontent.

The lower portion of the hourglass represents the implementation of policies and the delivery of services to the citizens. This stage involves the execution of approved projects, monitoring their progress, and evaluating their effectiveness. It requires clear communication, coordination among various government agencies, and robust feedback mechanisms to ensure accountability. Ideally, this should be a broader outflow of positive results benefiting the populace.

However, the analogy is not without its limitations. Unlike the physical hourglass, where the flow is purely mechanical, the government's processes are complex and influenced by political dynamics, bureaucratic inertia, and often unpredictable external factors. The challenge lies in designing a system that efficiently manages the flow through the bottleneck while remaining responsive and adaptable to changing circumstances.

This analogy, while a simplification, offers a useful framework for examining the effectiveness and efficiency of government operations.

Chapter Five

Sports Analogy

I've been reflecting on the challenges of leading a government agency, and a compelling analogy emerged—that of coaching a sports team. The parallels are surprisingly profound.

Consider the similarities: both require building a high-performing team, fostering collaboration and communication, setting clear goals and objectives, and adapting strategies in response to changing circumstances.

A successful sports team isn't just about individual talent; it's about synergy, strategic alignment, and effective resource management. Similarly, a thriving government agency necessitates clear roles and responsibilities, effective delegation, and the skillful utilization of resources—both human and financial. Just as a coach motivates players, a leader needs to inspire employees through clear vision, open communication, and recognition of individual contributions. Dealing with challenging deadlines and unexpected setbacks is commonplace in both scenarios, demanding resilience, adaptability, and problem-solving skills.

Crucially, the analogy extends to the need for regular performance reviews and continuous improvement. A winning team constantly analyzes its performance, identifies weaknesses, and implements corrective strategies. A high-performing agency should operate similarly, seeking feedback from stakeholders, evaluating its efficiency, and refining its processes to deliver better results for citizens.

Moreover, effective communication is crucial in both contexts. Clear communication of goals, strategies, and performance expectations is vital for both motivating teams and ensuring alignment with the agency's overall mission.

My Beginnings

My career journey began early, forging a foundation in dedication and customer service. At fourteen, I navigated the demanding schedule of a paperboy for the Omaha World-Herald, managing a substantial route of 250 customers, seven days a week. This experience instilled in me a deep understanding of consistent delivery and the importance of meeting client expectations under pressure.

This early foray into the workforce transitioned into physically demanding roles. At eighteen, I gained valuable experience as a construction laborer on a high-rise project, followed by work with a sewer contractor. These experiences provided a practical understanding of hard work, teamwork, and the complexities of large-scale projects.

At the age of twenty, I took a significant entrepreneurial leap, becoming an owner-operator of a sewer construction company. The challenges and rewards of building and managing a business proved invaluable, providing a strong foundation for future leadership roles.

My entrepreneurial journey eventually led me to a shift in focus toward workforce development. I transitioned to a role as an administrator for a laborer's training program, directly impacting the lives of individuals seeking employment in the construction trades. This experience sparked a passion for providing opportunities and improving the lives of others through meaningful employment.

Laborers Training Program

Following a dedicated period engaged in direct construction roles, my career path evolved to an administrative leadership position within the Construction Laborers Multi-Skilled Training Program. I had a team of six skilled craftsman journeymen from each craft. This innovative program was meticulously designed to equip aspiring professionals with a comprehensive suite of foundational and versatile skills, enabling them to confidently transition into entry- level skilled tradesperson roles across diverse construction projects.

The curriculum we offered was robust and hands-on, encompassing a broad spectrum of essential construction disciplines. Participants gained practical experience and theoretical knowledge in areas such as carpentry, electrical systems, carpet and tile installation, painting techniques, heavy equipment maintenance, and pipe laying.

The program also ingrained vital principles of job site preparation, efficient cleanup, and an unwavering commitment to safety and health protocols. This holistic approach was paramount in fostering well-rounded, competent individuals ready for the demands of the industry.

I genuinely believe this initiative served as a pivotal gateway, not merely an opportunity, but a transformative door opener for countless individuals eager to forge sustainable and rewarding careers in the construction industry. It effectively demystified complex trades and provided accessible, structured pathways into a sector often perceived as difficult to enter without prior specialized experience.

During my tenure as administrator, I had the distinct privilege of overseeing the successful training and mentorship of hundreds of aspiring professionals. This collective effort not only reshaped individual career trajectories by providing tangible skills and employment readiness but also significantly contributed a vital pipeline of skilled, adaptable, and safety-conscious talent to the broader construction sector.

Working for Organized Labor

This passion led me to the Omaha Federation of Labor, where I served as a program director, later moving on to the Nebraska State

AFL-CIO, where I developed and administered a statewide Job Assistance Program for Dislocated Workers. These roles further honed my abilities in program management, stakeholder relations, and advocacy for workers' rights.

The culmination of my experience in workforce development culminated in my appointment as Director of the Omaha Office of Employment Resources, a Comprehensive Employment Training Agency for the City of Omaha. This position served as a critical stepping stone, providing invaluable experience that ultimately prepared me for the significant responsibility of becoming the Commissioner of Labor for the State of Nebraska.

Observation About the Subjective Nature of Public Service Responsiveness

Observations about the subjective nature of public service responsiveness are insightful. It's true that what constitutes "gladness" or satisfactory service is highly individual and dependent on various factors. However, public agencies can actively work towards a more objective and measurable understanding of customer satisfaction. This goes beyond simply registering whether a citizen feels "glad." A more robust approach would involve analyzing specific metrics. For example, agencies could track response times to inquiries, citizen feedback scores on specific services, and the clarity and effectiveness of their communication channels.

By collecting and analyzing this data, agencies can identify areas for improvement and implement targeted changes. This systematic approach allows for continuous improvement and a more data-driven understanding of customer needs, moving beyond the subjective "gladness" to a more quantifiable and actionable measure of success. Furthermore, incorporating diverse feedback mechanisms, including surveys, focus groups, and social media monitoring, can provide a more comprehensive picture of the public's perception and expectations.

The Needs of the Many

This statement, "The needs of the many outweigh the needs of the few, or the one," while concise and impactful, warrants further consideration. It speaks to a fundamental principle of societal organization – the prioritization of collective well-being over individual interests.

However, the simplicity of the truth masks the inherent complexities and ethical dilemmas it presents.

While prioritizing the collective good is often necessary for a functioning society – think of public workforce initiatives or infrastructure development – a critical analysis reveals that the line between "many" and "few" can be fluid and subjective. Defining "needs" itself presents another challenge. What constitutes a genuine need versus a want? What methods are ethically justifiable for achieving the collective good? Does it necessitate sacrificing individual rights or liberties?

History is filled with examples where the pursuit of the collective good has led to oppression and injustice. The suppression of individual dissent in the name of social harmony, or the prioritization of economic growth at the expense of environmental sustainability, serves as a stark reminder of the potential pitfalls of this principle. A truly just society requires a nuanced approach – one that values both individual rights and the collective well-being, while constantly engaging in a dialogue about what constitutes a fair and equitable distribution of resources and opportunities.

Before You Start, Take a Deep Breath

This isn't about a simple fix; it's about a fundamental shift in how we approach service delivery. Are you ready to embrace a challenging, yet ultimately rewarding, transformation?

Success requires commitment, a willingness to adapt, and a dedication to sustained effort. You are facing the opportunity to significantly improve your service delivery system, and that means investing the time and resources necessary to achieve lasting positive change.

I believe we possess the collective expertise and resilience to accomplish this. However, it demands a shared vision and a robust commitment from every member of the team. This initiative will require careful planning, rigorous execution, and a proactive approach to addressing challenges as they present themselves.

Do You Believe You Can Make a Difference?

Reflecting on a career in public service, I considered the profound impact we can have on the well-being of our community. The question of whether we can truly make a difference is paramount. I believe that through dedicated service and strategic initiatives, we possess the potential to significantly improve the lives of citizens. However, achieving meaningful change requires a comprehensive understanding of the challenges we face, as well as a commitment to collaborative efforts and innovative solutions. This calls for a careful evaluation of our capabilities and a commitment to continuous learning and improvement.

Be Honest with Yourself

Reflect on your commitment to the ongoing cultural transformation within the organization.

This isn't a simple yes or no question; it requires honest self-assessment. Consider your actions, behaviors, and contributions over the past few months, quarter, year. Have you actively embraced the new values and principles? Are you consistently modeling the desired behaviors? If not, what obstacles are preventing you from fully engaging? Identifying those roadblocks is crucial to making meaningful progress. We're all on this journey together, and your participation is vital to your collective success. Schedule some time for introspection, and consider journaling or discussing this with a trusted colleague or mentor to gain further clarity. Your honest reflection will not only benefit you but also contribute to the overall effectiveness of our cultural change initiative.

Attitude

For too long, the phrase "I'm from the government, and I'm here to help" has carried a connotation of skepticism and distrust. This perception undermines the vital relationship between public servants and the community we are privileged to serve. It's time for a fundamental shift in approach; a paradigm change that moves beyond mere words to a demonstrable commitment to action.

We believe the guiding principle of our service should be, unequivocally, "We are here to serve you." This isn't just a slogan; it's a mandate that requires a conscious and sustained effort from every member of our organization. It necessitates transparency in our actions, responsiveness to your needs, and a relentless pursuit of excellence in the delivery of public services.

Building public trust is not a simple task. It requires consistent effort, a commitment to integrity, and a proactive approach to addressing your concerns. We understand that regaining your confidence requires more than words; it demands tangible improvements in efficiency, communication, and the overall quality of our services. We are actively working towards these improvements and invite their feedback, suggestions, and collaboration as we strive to better serve them.

What Draws People to Public Service

What draws people to public service is a fascinating question, and there's no single answer. It's a complex interplay of motivations, often deeply personal and varied from individual to individual.

Some are driven by a profound sense of civic duty, a belief in contributing to the common good, and making a tangible difference in their communities and beyond. They see public service as a calling, a responsibility to use their skills and talents to improve the lives of others.

Others are motivated by a desire for social justice, seeking to address systemic inequalities and advocate for marginalized groups. They may be driven by a personal experience of injustice or a deep-seated commitment to creating a more equitable and inclusive society.

Still others are drawn to the intellectual challenge and the opportunity to shape policy and contribute to the development of effective governance. The ability to influence decisions that impact millions, to solve complex problems, and to leave a lasting legacy can be a powerful motivator.

Finally, some individuals are attracted to the diverse and dynamic nature of public service itself, the chance to collaborate with colleagues from diverse backgrounds, and engage in meaningful work that has a direct impact on people's lives. The opportunity for continuous learning and professional growth is also a significant factor for many.

Understanding these varied motivations is crucial to attracting and retaining talented individuals in the public sector. It's a field requiring dedication, resilience, and a strong commitment to service – qualities driven by a wide spectrum of individual aspirations and beliefs.

My Calling to Public Service

The phrase "a calling for public service" resonates deeply, but it feels somewhat incomplete, doesn't it? It's a powerful sentiment, implying a profound sense of duty and a desire to contribute meaningfully to the well-being of our community and country.

However, it lacks the specificity to truly capture the weight and complexity of such a commitment.

What specific aspects of public service are drawing you? Is it the challenge of crafting effective policy, the satisfaction of directly helping individuals in need, or perhaps the opportunity to shape a more just and equitable society? Reflecting on these questions will help you define this "calling" more precisely.

Consider exploring different avenues for public service. This isn't limited to elected office. It could encompass volunteer work with local organizations, advocacy for specific causes, participation in community initiatives, or even pursuing a career in a public sector agency.

Each path offers unique challenges and rewards, and a deeper exploration of your personal strengths and passions will illuminate the best fit for you.

This journey of self-discovery will also clarify the sacrifices and commitments inherent in public service. It demands dedication, resilience, and a willingness to navigate complex political and social landscapes. Understanding these aspects upfront is crucial for making an informed and sustainable commitment.

Ultimately, the "calling for public service" should not be viewed as a mere aspiration, but rather as the beginning of a long, fulfilling, and potentially transformative journey. I encourage you to delve further into your motivations, explore various options, and develop a concrete plan for how you envision contributing your talents to the betterment of the world.

Why Pursue and Accept a Political Appointment

The pursuit of a political appointment from a governor presents a complex decision with significant implications, demanding careful consideration of both potential benefits and drawbacks. Let's explore the motivations behind such an ambition and the factors influencing this choice.

On one hand, a gubernatorial appointment offers access to considerable power and influence within the state's political landscape. It provides a platform to implement policy changes, advocate for specific causes, and potentially affect the lives of numerous citizens. The prestige associated with such a role can also enhance one's professional reputation and open doors to future opportunities. Furthermore, the appointment might offer financial benefits, depending on the specific position and responsibilities involved. Finally, for individuals deeply invested in the political process, it represents a significant opportunity to contribute directly to shaping the state's future.

However, it's equally crucial to acknowledge the potential downsides. The political environment can be highly competitive and demanding, often requiring navigating complex interpersonal relationships and managing potentially conflicting priorities. The role may also involve considerable public scrutiny, exposure to criticism, and the need to maintain a consistently positive public image. Furthermore, the appointment might involve compromises on personal beliefs or values, necessitating difficult ethical considerations. The job security associated with such appointments can also be precarious, subject to the changing political tides and the governor's priorities. Finally, the potential for burnout and the strain on personal life cannot be underestimated.

Therefore, a thorough assessment of one's own aspirations, capabilities, and risk tolerance is paramount. A careful analysis of the specific appointment's responsibilities, the governor's administration, and the potential impact on one's personal and professional life is essential before making this significant decision. Weighing the potential rewards against the potential risks will clarify the most suitable course of action.

Skills Required

The key lies in understanding and adapting to differing governing philosophies while maintaining professionalism and a commitment to effective public service.

Success in such a bipartisan role demands a highly nuanced skillset. Here are some key areas to consider:

Exceptional Communication and Interpersonal Skills: The ability to build rapport, actively listen, and communicate complex information clearly and concisely to diverse audiences is paramount. This includes tailoring your communication style to resonate with individuals across the political spectrum.

Political Acumen and Strategic Thinking: Understanding the nuances of both Democratic and Republican platforms, legislative processes, and political strategies is critical. This requires deep awareness of current events and the ability to anticipate potential challenges and opportunities.

Adaptability and Flexibility: Governors from different parties will have varying management styles, priorities, and policy agendas. The capacity to adapt quickly and seamlessly to changing priorities and work styles is essential.

Strong Analytical and Problem-Solving Skills: The ability to analyze complex information, identify key issues, and develop effective solutions that can gain bipartisan support is crucial. This often involves finding common ground and compromising to achieve results.

Impeccable Ethical Conduct and Discretion: Maintaining confidentiality and acting with the utmost professionalism and integrity is non-negotiable. Trust is fundamental, especially in a high-stakes environment where political sensitivities are prevalent.

Deep Understanding of Policy and Governance: A strong foundation in public policy, governmental processes, and relevant legal frameworks will allow you to navigate the complexities of serving different administrations effectively.

Further research into the specific policy areas and governing styles of individual governors within each party will significantly enhance your understanding and preparation. This detailed approach will ensure you can successfully adapt your approach and skills to effectively serve under various leadership styles.

The Privilege of Being Appointed

This is a significant honor and responsibility. Your appointment by the governor to lead a state government agency represents a profound vote of confidence in your capabilities and experience. It signifies not only your personal achievements but also the potential for positive impact on the lives of citizens within your state.

This leadership role demands a comprehensive understanding of the agency's mission, its strategic goals, and the challenges it faces. It also requires effective communication, collaboration, and resource management to ensure the agency operates efficiently and effectively. Your ability to inspire and motivate your team will be crucial in achieving the agency's objectives and in fostering a positive and productive work environment.

Consider this appointment not simply as a privilege, but as an opportunity to contribute significantly to the well-being of your state and to leave a lasting legacy of positive change. The weight of this responsibility is substantial, but the potential rewards are equally great. I wish you every success in this important endeavor.

The Opportunity to Serve

The opportunity to lead a state government agency is a significant undertaking, demanding a considerable commitment of time, energy, and dedication. It's not merely a title, but a responsibility to serve the public effectively and efficiently. Therefore, the question of willingness to dedicate the necessary time isn't simply a matter of "yes" or "no."

Before accepting such a role, I believe a thorough self-assessment is critical. This involves honestly evaluating your existing commitments, assessing your capacity to manage the demands of the position without compromising your effectiveness or well-being, and critically examining your vision for the agency's future and how you plan to achieve it.

A successful leader in this context needs to possess not only strong leadership skills and a deep understanding of public policy, but also a resilient work ethic and an unwavering commitment to serving the public good. The time commitment is extensive, encompassing long hours, often involving weekends and evenings, and a constant need for responsiveness to evolving situations.

This is not to deter potential candidates, but rather to underscore the seriousness of the responsibility. If, after careful consideration and thorough self-assessment, are you confident that you can dedicate the time, energy, and expertise necessary to excel in the role and truly serve the people of your state, take the leap!

Political Appointment Life

Reflecting on my eighteen years leading a state department under three governors from diverse political backgrounds, I've gained a profound appreciation for the cyclical nature of political appointments. While the privilege of serving the public in such a capacity is immense, its inherent temporality necessitates proactive planning for the future. This isn't merely about securing a "next job," but rather thoughtfully considering how to leverage the skills and experience gained in public service for a fulfilling and impactful future career. The lessons learned – navigating complex political landscapes, managing budgets responsibly, building consensus amongst diverse stakeholders, and leading a large organization – are transferable and highly valuable. This transition period presents a unique opportunity for strategic career exploration. You should actively investigate potential avenues, exploring both public and private sector options, networking with former colleagues and mentors, and perhaps even pursuing advanced training or education that builds upon my expertise. The goal is to transition smoothly and confidently into a role that continues to utilize my abilities while offering new challenges and opportunities for growth. Develop potential strategies and a concrete action plan.

Attending Governor's Cabinet Meetings

This part serves as a reminder regarding the Governor's Cabinet meetings. To ensure a smooth and efficient process, please anticipate the possibility of needing to provide specific dates and detailed information in response to questions that may arise. Thoroughly reviewing the relevant materials and preparing comprehensive answers to commonly asked questions will significantly enhance your experience.

Consider creating a concise yet thorough summary of pertinent dates and details. This will allow you to quickly and accurately respond to inquiries, ensuring all information is readily available and presented clearly. Anticipating potential questions will not only save time but also demonstrate preparedness and professionalism.

Demanding

It's crucial to remember that effective action starts with clear thinking. Before diving into your to-do list, allow yourself dedicated time for reflection and prioritization. This isn't about procrastination; it's about strategic planning. Consider breaking down large tasks into smaller, more manageable steps. Identify your most important priorities and focus your energy there, leaving less urgent items for later. Taking the time for mindful processing will ultimately enhance your efficiency and reduce stress, leading to better outcomes. Schedule this reflection time just as you would any other important meeting—treat it as an essential appointment with yourself. Remember, you are your most valuable resource, and taking care of yourself is a key component of success. Let's discuss this further if you feel you need support in prioritizing tasks.

Balancing Home Life

The demands of a political appointment often present unique challenges to maintaining a fulfilling and balanced home life. The long hours, intense pressure, and frequent travel inherent in such roles can strain relationships and disrupt established routines. Successfully navigating this requires proactive strategies and a conscious effort to prioritize both professional responsibilities and personal well-being.

My experience as a political appointee has highlighted the importance of clear communication with family members. Openly discussing the workload, anticipated absences, and potential stresses allows for shared understanding and collaborative problem-solving.

Finding ways to maintain regular family time, even if it's just brief moments throughout the day or scheduled activities on weekends, is crucial for fostering connection and preventing feelings of isolation.

Furthermore, setting firm boundaries between work and personal life is essential. This may involve establishing specific work hours, resisting the temptation to check emails constantly after hours, and utilizing technology strategically to manage communications effectively.

Delegation of tasks, when possible, allows for more efficient use of time and reduces overall stress levels.

Finally, self-care practices are paramount. Making time for physical activity, relaxation techniques, or pursuing personal hobbies helps to manage stress and maintain a sense of equilibrium. Recognizing the limitations of one's own time and energy, and accepting the need to prioritize, are vital aspects of achieving a sustainable balance. This is an ongoing process of adaptation and adjustment that requires continuous self-reflection and a commitment to nurturing both professional and personal aspects of life.

Dress for Success

The way we present ourselves significantly impacts how others perceive us, and more importantly, how we perceive ourselves. Dressing for success isn't merely about conforming to a specific dress code; it's a strategic approach to self-expression and projecting confidence. It's about choosing attire that aligns with your professional goals, reflects your personal brand, and fosters a sense of self-assuredness. This respect for your appearance translates directly into respect for your position and the responsibilities that come with it.

Consider the message you want to communicate: competence, authority, trustworthiness, creativity? Your clothing choices should be a conscious reflection of these aspirations, allowing you to embody your professional persona effectively. It's an investment in yourself and your success. Thoughtful consideration of your attire extends beyond simply adhering to a dress code; it's about crafting a visual narrative that supports your ambitions.

Managing your Beliefs

This encourages a moment of personal reflection. Over the coming weeks, I'd like you to consider the multifaceted influences shaping your perspectives and approaches to your work.

This includes examining the role of your personal beliefs – be they religious, spiritual, or secular – in how we interact with each other and serve the public. Furthermore, let's explore how our family lives and commitments impact our professional lives, and acknowledge the diverse experiences and perspectives within your agency. Ultimately, understanding these interwoven factors will foster a stronger, more empathetic, and collaborative work environment. I encourage open and honest self-reflection, as this is not a judgment but rather an opportunity for growth and understanding.

Religious Beliefs

Regarding the intersection of faith and public service merits further consideration. While the separation of church and state is a cornerstone of our legal framework, preventing the government from establishing or endorsing a religion, it doesn't preclude individuals holding deeply held religious beliefs from serving the public good. Indeed, many find that their faith informs their values and motivates their commitment to compassionate leadership.

However, it's crucial to distinguish between personal faith and the performance of public duties. Compassionate leadership in a state agency necessitates a multifaceted approach. It requires empathy, strong decision-making skills, effective communication, and a commitment to ethical governance—attributes not exclusively linked to any particular religious belief.

While a deep faith might inspire these qualities in some individuals, others may find similar motivation in secular values like humanism or a dedication to social justice. The focus should remain on demonstrably effective leadership, ensuring all citizens are served equitably and impartially, regardless of their religious beliefs or lack thereof. Our mission to serve the people demands objectivity and inclusivity, ensuring that our actions reflect the needs and rights of everyone within our community, not just those who share our beliefs. Therefore, while personal faith can be a powerful source of motivation, it's essential to ensure public service remains inclusive and governed by principles of equality and justice.

Develop Personal Affirmations for Yourself

I'd like to share some thoughts on cultivating a positive mindset through the consistent practice of personal affirmations. Simply stating "Develop personal affirmations for yourself daily" is a good starting point, but the real power lies in understanding "how" to effectively integrate affirmations into your life.

Instead of merely generating affirmations, focus on crafting them thoughtfully and intentionally. Consider what areas of your life you want to improve – be it confidence, productivity, health, or relationships. Then, formulate positive statements that reflect your desired outcomes. These should be phrased in the present tense, as if they are already true, and should evoke strong feelings of belief and certainty. For example, instead of "I will be more confident," try" I am confident and capable." Or instead of "I will lose weight," try "I am healthy and energetic."

Remember, consistency is key. The impact of affirmations comes from repeated exposure and genuine belief. Integrate your affirmations into your daily routine – perhaps recite them first thing in the morning, before bedtime, or even throughout the day during moments of self-reflection. Experiment with different methods to find what works best for you: writing them down, saying them aloud, or even recording them and listening back.

Beyond simple recitation, consider the emotional connection. Infuse your affirmations with genuine emotion. Feel the truth of the words as you speak them. The more conviction you bring, the more effective your affirmations will be.

Finally, be patient and persistent. Developing a positive mindset is a journey, not a destination. Don't get discouraged if you don't see immediate results. Keep practicing, and over time, you'll begin to notice a shift in your perspective and a greater sense of self-belief.

Here's my example of a personal affirmation:

How I started my day. Every morning when I was getting ready for work, I would look in the mirror and ask myself this question: "What will I do today that will make a positive difference in someone's life? All day long, I searched for the answer. At night, when I was getting ready for bed, I would look in the mirror and answer the question, and no matter how big or small the result, I found a way to make a positive difference."

Circle of Influence

Cultivating a strong and supportive circle of influence requires a strategic and multifaceted approach. It's not merely about accumulating contacts, but about forging genuine connections based on mutual respect, shared values, and reciprocal benefit. This process can be broken down into several key phases:

1. Self-Assessment and Goal Definition: Before reaching out to others, understand your own strengths, weaknesses, aspirations, and the type of influence you wish to cultivate. What specific goals do you hope to achieve through networking? Defining these objectives will help you target your efforts effectively.

2. Identifying Potential Influencers: This involves identifying individuals who possess the knowledge, skills, resources, or connections that align with your goals. This might include mentors, industry experts, peers, or community leaders. Consider both direct and indirect influences – individuals who might not directly impact your immediate goals but who can open doors to others who can.

3. Strategic Relationship Building: Networking is not about self-promotion; it's about building genuine relationships.

Engage in thoughtful conversations, listen actively, and offer value to others. Provide assistance where you can, share your expertise generously, and show genuine interest in their work and perspectives. Attend industry events, join relevant professional organizations, and leverage online platforms to expand your network.

4. Maintaining and Nurturing Connections: Once you've built relationships, nurture them consistently. Stay in touch, share relevant information, offer support, and celebrate each other's successes. Regular communication, even brief check-ins, can make a significant difference in maintaining strong connections.

5. Reciprocity and Giving Back: A strong circle of influence is built on reciprocity. Be willing to give back to your network by offering your time, skills, or resources to others. This fosters trust and strengthens the bonds within your circle.

6. Continuous Growth and Adaptation: The dynamics of your circle of influence will evolve over time. Be open to new connections, adapt your strategies as your goals change, and continuously cultivate your relationships to ensure long-term success. Regularly assess your network, identifying areas where you can strengthen existing ties or expand into new areas.

By following these steps, you can develop a powerful and supportive circle of influence that will enhance your personal and professional growth. Remember that building genuine relationships takes time and consistent effort.

Notes and Diaries

Effective meeting management is crucial for productivity and success. Taking meticulous notes isn't just about remembering what was discussed; it's about creating a readily accessible record for future reference, facilitating informed decision-making, and tracking progress on action items. Consider your notes a living document, not merely a transcription of the conversation. Beyond recording key decisions and assigned tasks, incorporate context: who was present, the overall objective of the meeting, and any significant points of contention or agreement. This detailed approach allows you to synthesize information more effectively later.

While a daily personal journal can be beneficial for self-reflection and stress management, it serves a different purpose than meeting notes. However, integrating key insights from your meetings into a personal journal, reflecting on your performance and contributions, can be a valuable tool for professional development. This dual approach—detailed meeting notes for record-keeping and personal reflection for self-improvement—enhances organizational efficiency and personal growth. Experiment with different note-taking methods to discover what best suits your style and needs. Consider using digital tools for easier searchability and organization. Remember, the goal is to create a system that works for you, maximizing productivity and self-awareness.

Leadership

I'd like to discuss the critical distinction between leadership as a title and leadership as a practice. The assertion that "Leadership is action, not a position" highlights a fundamental truth often overlooked. Holding a leadership position confers certain responsibilities and authority, but true leadership stems from demonstrable actions that inspire, motivate, and guide others toward shared goals. This active engagement involves proactive decision-making, effective communication, fostering collaboration, and taking ownership of both successes and challenges. It's through consistent and impactful actions that individuals truly embody the essence of leadership, regardless of their formal title or hierarchical placement within an organization. This principle is crucial for effective organizational performance and achieving collective success.

Commitment to Professional Development

My commitment to continuous professional development is a cornerstone of my approach to work and life. I believe in the importance of ongoing learning and self-improvement, not just for achieving immediate goals, but also for fostering long-term growth and adaptability in a constantly evolving environment. This commitment manifests in several ways, including actively seeking opportunities for skill enhancement through training, mentoring, and pursuing advanced certifications. I also consistently seek feedback, both formal and informal, to identify areas for refinement and leverage this insight to optimize performance and effectiveness. My dedication to this continuous improvement process reflects my desire to not only excel in my current role but also enhance my capacity for future contributions and leadership. A Commitment to Public Service

A deep and unwavering commitment to public service forms the cornerstone of effective and ethical leadership. This commitment transcends mere duty; it demands a profound understanding of the needs and aspirations of the community, coupled with a relentless dedication to addressing those needs. It requires not only the diligent execution of responsibilities but also a proactive approach to identifying and resolving challenges before they escalate. Furthermore, a commitment to public service necessitates transparency, accountability, and a willingness to engage in open and honest dialogue with the people we serve. It's a continuous process of learning, adapting, and striving to consistently improve the quality of life for everyone within our sphere of influence. This commitment requires selflessness, empathy, and a genuine desire to make a positive impact on the world around us. Ultimately, the success of public service is measured not solely by actions taken, but by the positive and lasting impact those actions have on the lives of others.

My Time in City Government

Reflecting on my career, I'm deeply grateful for the formative experience of serving as the appointed head of Omaha's Office of Employment and Training Resources under four different Mayors. This role, funded by federal grants, provided invaluable insight into the complexities of workforce development and the crucial role it plays in a thriving community.

Managing these federally funded employment and training programs gave me a practical, hands-on education, far exceeding any theoretical understanding. I learned to navigate the intricacies of budget management, program development, and community outreach within a constantly evolving political landscape. The challenges and successes I encountered during this period solidified my commitment to public service and laid the groundwork for my future career aspirations. It was within this dynamic environment that I honed my skills in leadership, strategic planning, and collaboration, skills that I continue to utilize and refine today. This experience was truly foundational, not just in terms of my career progression but also in shaping my deep-seated desire to contribute to the betterment of others' lives.

Serving in City Government

This outlines a collaborative initiative aimed at optimizing the delivery of essential municipal services to our community. My overarching goal was to create a streamlined and integrated system that ensures efficient and equitable access for all citizens. This project involved close collaboration with the mayor's office, the city council, and relevant state agencies. I needed to identify key areas for improvement, analyze existing infrastructure and processes, and develop a comprehensive plan that incorporated technological advancements, efficient resource allocation, and robust community engagement.

This plan required a phased approach, commencing with a thorough needs assessment to pinpoint the most pressing challenges and opportunities. Subsequently, we will develop specific, measurable, achievable, relevant, and time-bound (SMART) goals. This necessitated regular meetings with all stakeholders to ensure transparency and collaboration throughout the process. Furthermore, I explored potential funding options and partnerships to support the implementation and ongoing maintenance of the new delivery system. I also prioritized the development of a robust feedback mechanism to ensure the system remained responsive to the evolving needs of our community.

Learning from Adversity

I'd like to share a reflection on resilience and personal growth. The challenges we face in life often serve as catalysts for significant personal development. Just as physical strength is developed through rigorous training, our character is strengthened through overcoming adversity. The process of adaptation and problem-solving in challenging situations fosters resilience and enhances our capacity to navigate future obstacles. While the journey may be difficult, the transformative potential of these experiences is undeniable. I believe that by embracing challenges and learning from them, we can emerge as stronger and more capable individuals. I look forward to continued collaboration and support as we collectively navigate the complexities that lie ahead.

Understanding Where to Begin

Let's start with recognizing that organizations are social units deliberatively constructed and reconstructed to seek specific goals. Organizations are characterized by: (1) divisions of labor, power and communication responsibilities, divisions which are not randomly or traditionally patterned, but deliberately planned to enhance the realization of specific goals; (2) the presence of one or more power centers which control the concerted efforts of the organization and direct them toward its goals; these power centers also continuously review the organization's performance and re-pattern its structure, where necessary, to increase its efficiency; (3) substitution of personnel, i.e., unsatisfactory persons can be removed and others assigned their tasks. The organization can also recombine its personnel through transfer and promotion.

Consider four organization ends or goals. The first is adaptiveness, or flexibility, and is to be measured by the number of new programs per year and the number of new techniques adopted per year. Flexibility in other contexts usually refers to adaptation to external influences or other disturbing factors, and environmental influences are important. At the same time, however, new programs and new techniques can be developed of the basis of internal considerations. The second organizational end is production, or effectiveness, measured by the number or persons served per year and the rate of increase in the number of persons served per year. This is clearly and internal consideration. The third goal is efficiency, or the cost factor, and is measured by the cost per unit of output per year and the amount of idle resources per year. The final end is job satisfaction, or morale. This is measured by the employee's' satisfaction with working conditions and by the turnover rate of job occupants per year. These ends involve more than just output; basically, they reflect internal factors they are also part of a conceptual model that views the organization as a system in and of itself.

Let's examine four organizational means: The first is complexity, or specialization, which is measured by the number of occupational specialists and the level of training required for them. Complexity is necessary because organizations must divide work into jobs in order to achieve their specific objectives. The second means is centralization, or hierarchy of authority, and is measured by the proportion of jobs whose holders participate in decision making and the number of areas in which they participate. The third means is formalization, or standardization, measured as the number of jobs that are codified and the range of variation allowed within jobs. The finale means stratification, or the status system. This is measured by the differences in income and prestige among jobs and the rate of mobility between low-and high-ranking jobs or status levels. As expected, these means are totally internal to the organization.

The rational model of an organization results in everything being functional making a positive, indeed an optimum contribution to the overall result. All resources, and their allocation fits a master plan. All action, and its outcomes and predictable.

Organizations must grapple with their environment. And an individual must be motivated to participate and produce in the organizational setting.

Every subsystem of an organization with its distinctive functions develops its own norms and values and is characterized by its own dynamics. People in the maintenance subsystem have the problem of maintaining the role system and preserving the character of the organization through selection of appropriate personnel, indoctrinating and training them, devise checks for endurance standard role performance, and so on. These people face inward in the organization and are concerned with maintain the status quo.

Functions of Leadership

Leadership involves critical decisions. It is more than group maintenance. The first involves the definition oof the organizational mission and role. This is obviously vital in a rapidly changing world and must be viewed as a dynamic process. The second task is the "institutional embodiment of purpose," which involves building the policy into the structure or deciding upon the means to achieve the ends desired. The third task is to defend the organization's integrity. Here, values and public relations intermix; the leader represents his organization to the public and to its own members as he tries to persuade them to follow his decision. The final task is the ordering of internal conflict.

The position I have taken is that leadership can occur in any group or organizational situation. And most importantly important for the organization is the leadership that occurs at the top of the organization, where the tasks of the leader have real impact on the organization. In most cases leader have real impact on the organization. In most cases leadership rests in the hands of more than one person. The use of human relations in leadership positions is no guarantee that any form of behavioral change by members of the organization will take place.

It is critical to note that leadership at the top of an organization is vastly different from leadership at the first-line supervisory level.

Leadership involves what a person does above and beyond the basic requirements of the position. It is the persuasion of individuals and innovativeness in ideas and decision making that differentiates leadership from the sheer possession of power. Individual characteristics are crucial for the leadership role.

Organizational leadership is a combination of factors. The most obvious is the high position in the organization. This gives the leader the power base and leads followers to the expectations that he has a legitimate right to that position and that he will in fact engage in the leadership process by shaping their own thoughts and actions and performing the leadership functions for the organization as a whole.

High level leaders tend to value job challenges and autonomy, while lower-level leaders tend to value security and stability. Followers value the leader who has influence with his supervisor, is identified with the organization, and demonstrates effectiveness in working for their welfare and comfort.

The supportive leader utilizes socioemotional appeals to his subordinates. This involves:

Consideration for Subordinated. The leader considers the needs and preferences of his subordinates, whom he treats with dignity and kindness, and is not punitive in his dealing with them. Such a leader is frequently referred to as "employee-centered" as opposed to "work-centered."

Consultive Decision Making. The leader asks his subordinates for their opinions before he makes decisions. Such a leader is consultative, participative, or democratic in his decision making.

General Supervision. The leader supervises in a general rather that a close manner, delegates authority to his subordinates, and permits them freedom to exercise discretion in their work rather than imposing tight controls and close supervision.

Supportive leadership is quite consistently related to several indicators of subordinate satisfaction and productivity.

1. This is less intragroup stress and more cooperation.
2. Turnover and grievance rates are lower.
3. The leader himself is viewed as more desirable.
4. There is frequently greater productivity.

Supportive leadership does lead to more positive attitudinal responses, particularly on the part of subordinates. Support leadership behavior is most effective when:

1. Decisions are not routine in nature.
2. The information required for effective decision making cannot be standardized or centralized.

3. Decisions need not be made rapidly, allowing time to involve subordinates in a participative decision-making process. And when subordinates
4. Feel a strong need for independence.
5. Regard their patriation in decision making as legitimate.
6. See themselves as able to contribute to the decision-making process.
7. Are confident of their ability to work without the reassurance of close supervision.

The closer one gets to the organizational center of control and decision making, the more pronounced is the emphasis on information exchange.

Intraorganizational differences are important. Equality vital are interorganizational differences. Four factors determine the importance of communications or intelligence for the organization:

1. The degree of conflict or competition with the external environment\
2. The degree of dependence on internal support and unity
3. The degree of which internal operations and external environment are believed to be rationalized
4. The size and structure of the organization, its heterogeneity of membership and diversity of goals, its centrality of authority.

Organizational Development

Organizational development refers to a long-range effort to improve an organization's problem-solving capabilities and its ability to cope with changes in its external environment with the help of external or internal behavior-scientist consultants or chang gents, as they are sometimes called. Organizational development is primarily aimed at the management levels or organizations with the specific intent of improving interpersonal skills and relationships.

Organizational development utilizes a total organization perspective. It attempts to work through repeated feedback of problems and prospects to key groups in the organization. The emphasis on organizational development is on units within organizations rather than on individuals, with the objective being units whose members elate to and understand each other and the objectives of their unit and the total organization.

Organizations as Registers to Change

Organizations are a major structuring component in society. Structuring takes place through the work roles of the members of the organizations and the values that organizational membership can impart. Organizations are a means of structuring the activities of the members.

Organizations also resist change. This resistance is directed toward change introduced from outside the organization. The organization attempts to protect itself. Obliviously, changes that are not important to the organization will not bring and organizational response and organizations by their very nature are conservative. When focus is shifted to how the organization itself operates, the point becomes even more clear.

It is important to note that the aims of the changes we are going through can be blunted without malice or intent. It is not a personal matter, but an organizational one.

How to Run a State Agency Like a Business

Developing a Strategic Plan

Developing and implementing strategic enterprise goals within a state agency requires a multifaceted approach. It necessitates a thorough understanding of the agency's mission, vision, and existing strategic plans. The process should begin with a comprehensive assessment of the current state, identifying key performance indicators (KPIs) and areas for improvement. This assessment should involve stakeholders across all levels of the agency to ensure a shared understanding of challenges and opportunities.

Once a clear picture of the current situation is established, the next step is to define specific, measurable, achievable, relevant, and time-bound (SMART) goals. These goals should align with the overall mission and vision of the agency, as well as broader state-level objectives.

Consider the agency's resources, both human and financial, and ensure that the goals are realistic and achievable within the allocated timeframe. It's crucial to involve key decision- makers in this goal-setting process to garner buy-in and commitment.

The implementation phase requires a detailed action plan, outlining specific tasks, responsibilities, and timelines. Regular monitoring and evaluation are essential to track progress and make necessary adjustments. This may involve the use of project management tools and regular progress reports to stakeholders. Finally, the establishment of a robust communication strategy is vital to keep all employees informed and engaged throughout the entire process. This includes transparent reporting on progress, addressing concerns, and celebrating successes. The ultimate success of this endeavor depends on effective communication, collaboration, and a commitment to continuous improvement.

Consolidation

My two-year deep dive into the operational structure of my state agency yielded significant insights. Initially, the complexity of our ten divisions presented a fragmented image to both internal staff and the public we serve. The numerous divisions, while historically functional, created a sense of disconnection, hindering efficient service delivery and fostering a perception of internal silos.

This realization prompted a strategic reorganization. My goal was not merely cosmetic; I aimed to fundamentally improve our agency's performance and public perception. Through meticulous analysis, I identified overlapping responsibilities and redundant processes across the ten divisions. This analysis revealed the potential for consolidation into a more streamlined and efficient structure.

The result was the creation of six integrated offices, each with clearly defined roles and responsibilities. This restructuring wasn't just about a name change; it represented a fundamental shift towards a unified and collaborative approach. By replacing "division" with "office of," I aimed to convey a sense of cohesion and shared purpose, reflecting the reality of our interconnected work and our commitment to seamless public service. This revised structure will enhance internal communication, improve operational efficiency, and ultimately result in superior service for the citizens of our state. I believe this change significantly enhanced our agency's effectiveness and its image as a united and responsive organization.

Learning How Employees Deal with Change

I want to discuss a topic of increasing importance in today's rapidly evolving workplace: employee learning and adaptation in the face of change. Understanding how employees acquire new skills and knowledge when confronted with shifting organizational structures, technological advancements, or evolving market demands is crucial for maintaining productivity, engagement, and overall organizational success.

This isn't simply about providing training; it's about fostering a culture of continuous learning and development. Several key factors influence how effectively employees learn in these dynamic situations. These include:

Learning Styles and Preferences: Recognizing the diverse learning styles within your workforce – visual, auditory, kinesthetic, etc. – is paramount. Tailoring training and development programs to accommodate these diverse preferences leads to significantly better outcomes.

Organizational Culture and Support: A culture that values learning, embraces experimentation, and provides ample opportunities for feedback and mentorship is essential for successful adaptation. Employees are far more likely to engage in learning when they feel supported and empowered.

Leveraging technology effectively – online learning platforms, collaborative tools, and knowledge management systems – can streamline the learning process and make it more accessible and engaging.

Clear Communication and Expectations: Transparent communication about upcoming changes, the reasons behind them, and the expected employee roles is vital. Clearly defined expectations reduce ambiguity and anxiety, fostering a more receptive learning environment.

Mentorship and Peer Support: Establishing mentorship programs and fostering peer-to-peer learning can significantly enhance the learning experience. Sharing knowledge and experience within the team creates a collaborative learning environment.

Understanding these factors allows organizations to proactively design effective learning strategies that equip their employees with the necessary skills and knowledge to thrive in a constantly changing world.

Cultivating a Culture of Trust

Cultivating a culture of trust within a government agency is a multifaceted endeavor demanding a comprehensive and sustained approach. It's not merely a matter of implementing policies but of fostering a fundamental shift in organizational ethos, impacting every level from frontline staff to senior leadership. This necessitates a multi-pronged strategy focusing on transparency, accountability, and consistent communication.

Transparency involves proactively disseminating information to the public and internal stakeholders. This encompasses open access to data, clear explanations of decision-making processes, and readily available channels for feedback. Accountability requires establishing robust mechanisms for oversight, ensuring that individuals are held responsible for their actions and that grievances are addressed promptly and fairly. This might involve strengthening internal audit functions, implementing whistleblower protection programs, and fostering a culture where constructive criticism is welcomed rather than suppressed.

Consistent and effective communication is the bedrock of trust. This means utilizing diverse communication channels to reach various audiences, ensuring information is accessible and understandable, and actively engaging with the public to address concerns and build rapport. Furthermore, active listening and responsiveness to feedback are crucial.

Beyond these core elements, success hinges on leadership commitment. Leaders must model the desired behavior, actively promote ethical conduct, and demonstrate a genuine commitment to transparency and accountability. This includes empowering employees to speak up and fostering a work environment where integrity is valued above all else. Regular training programs focusing on ethics, communication skills, and conflict resolution can also significantly contribute to building a strong foundation of trust.

Finally, consistent monitoring and evaluation are vital. Regular assessments of the agency's performance in terms of transparency, accountability, and public trust should be conducted to identify areas for improvement and ensure the long-term success of this crucial initiative.

Without ongoing evaluation and adaptation, the effort risks losing momentum and failing to achieve its ultimate goal.

Reading the Room

I want to share a crucial insight that can profoundly elevate the effectiveness of your meetings and interactions. While we meticulously craft our spoken messages, a significant portion of communication occurs silently, through the non-verbal signals conveyed by those around us.

Developing the skill to "read the room" by observing attendees' body language is an invaluable asset. It allows you to gauge engagement, understanding, and even unspoken concerns in real-time, enabling you to adapt your approach dynamically. Pay close attention to cues such as:

Open vs. Closed Postures: Are individuals leaning in with open arms, suggesting receptiveness and engagement, or are they withdrawn, perhaps with crossed arms, indicating skepticism, discomfort, or disinterest?

Eye Contact and Facial Expressions: Consistent eye contact and attentive expressions often signal active listening and agreement, while wandering gazes, furrowed brows, or a lack of expression might suggest confusion, distraction, or disagreement.

Energy Levels and Movements: Subtle nods can affirm comprehension, whereas fidgeting, restless movements, or a general slump in posture could point to boredom, anxiety, or a desire to interject.

By becoming adept at interpreting these silent signals, you can steer discussions more effectively. If you detect disengagement, you might strategically pose a direct question to draw someone into the conversation. If confusion is apparent, it's an opportunity to re-explain a point or solicit feedback. Recognizing subtle signs of disagreement allows for proactive addressing of concerns before they escalate.

This isn't about mind-reading, but about cultivating a heightened sense of awareness and empathy that fosters more inclusive, productive, and ultimately, more successful outcomes from our collaborative sessions. I encourage you to actively practice this observation during your upcoming meetings.

Have Fun

Maintaining a positive and productive work environment within your state agency is crucial to your success. While the responsibilities we shoulder are undeniably serious and demand our utmost dedication, fostering a workplace culture that incorporates humor and levity can significantly enhance your collective well-being and performance. A sense of camaraderie, built on shared laughter and mutual respect, can alleviate stress, improve teamwork, and ultimately lead to more innovative and effective solutions.

The challenges we face daily require a significant level of focus and commitment, but approaching our tasks with a balanced perspective – one that recognizes both the weight of our responsibilities and the value of a positive atmosphere – allows us to navigate those challenges more effectively. Humor serves as a powerful tool for de-escalating tension, promoting creative thinking, and fostering a sense of shared humanity among colleagues. By cultivating an environment where appropriate humor is welcomed and encouraged, you will contribute to a more engaged, motivated, and ultimately, more successful team. Actively work towards incorporating this positive approach into your daily interactions.

Personality Traits of Leadership

Developing Effective Leadership: An Exploration of Key Personality Traits

This document outlines a framework for understanding the essential personality traits that contribute to effective leadership. While no single set of traits guarantees success, cultivating these characteristics can significantly enhance a leader's ability to inspire, motivate, and guide their teams. We will explore several key areas, including:

Integrity and Ethical Conduct: The foundation of strong leadership rests on unwavering honesty, transparency, and adherence to a strong ethical code. Trust is paramount, and leaders must consistently model the behaviors they expect from their teams.

Vision and Strategic Thinking: Effective leaders possess a clear vision for the future and the ability to translate that vision into actionable strategies. This requires strong analytical skills, the capacity for forward-thinking, and the ability to adapt to changing circumstances.

Communication and Interpersonal Skills: The ability to communicate effectively – both verbally and nonverbally – is crucial. Leaders must be able to articulate their vision clearly, actively listen to others, provide constructive feedback, and foster open communication within the team. Strong interpersonal skills are necessary to build rapport, resolve conflict, and foster a positive and collaborative environment.

Decisiveness and Accountability: Leaders must be able to make timely and informed decisions, even in the face of uncertainty. Equally important is the willingness to take responsibility for both successes and failures, fostering a culture of accountability within the team.

Resilience and Adaptability: The ability to overcome challenges, learn from setbacks, and adapt to changing circumstances is essential for effective leadership. This involves maintaining a positive attitude, demonstrating perseverance, and embracing change as an opportunity for growth.

Empathy and Emotional Intelligence: Understanding and responding to the emotional needs of team members is critical. Leaders with high emotional intelligence can build strong relationships, foster trust, and motivate their teams through empathy and understanding.

This is a starting point for a deeper exploration into the multifaceted nature of leadership. Further research into specific leadership styles and models will enhance understanding and application of these traits.

Leading by Example

Leading by example isn't merely about actions; it's about cultivating a holistic approach to leadership that inspires and motivates those around you. It requires a conscious and consistent effort to embody the values and behaviors you expect from your team. This includes demonstrating integrity in all your interactions, both big and small. Transparency and open communication are key; sharing your decision-making processes and rationale builds trust and fosters a collaborative environment.

Furthermore, leading by example necessitates embracing continuous learning and self- improvement. Showing a commitment to personal growth encourages your team to do the same, fostering a culture of development and innovation. Finally, actively recognizing and celebrating the successes of others is paramount. By acknowledging their achievements and contributions, you reinforce positive behaviors and build a stronger, more motivated team.

Remember, true leadership is not about authority, but about influence and inspiration. Strive to embody these principles, and you'll find your leadership significantly more effective.

Cultivating Agency Executive Leadership Team

Cultivating a highly motivated executive leadership team is paramount to the success of any organization. It's not simply "your job" to motivate them; it's about fostering an environment where motivation thrives organically. This requires a multifaceted approach that goes beyond simple motivational speeches or performance-based incentives.

Consider these key strategies:

Understanding Individual Motivations: Each executive likely possesses unique drivers and aspirations. Understanding these individual needs – whether it's professional growth, recognition, increased autonomy, or a greater sense of purpose – is critical to tailoring your approach. Regular one-on-one meetings focused on their career development and aspirations are essential.

Clear Vision and Strategic Alignment: A shared vision, clearly communicated and consistently reinforced, provides a unifying purpose. Executives need to understand how their individual contributions directly impact the overall strategic goals of the organization. This alignment fuels intrinsic motivation.

Empowerment and Trust: Micromanagement is a surefire way to stifle motivation. Empower your team by delegating responsibility and trusting them to make decisions within their areas of expertise. This fosters a sense of ownership and accountability.

Open Communication and Feedback: Create a culture of open and honest communication, where feedback is both solicited and given constructively. Regular team meetings, both formal and informal, allow for the sharing of ideas, challenges, and progress. Active listening is crucial.

Recognition and Appreciation: Acknowledge and celebrate both individual and team achievements. Public recognition can be extremely motivating, but equally important is providing genuine appreciation for hard work and dedication.

Opportunities for Growth and Development: Invest in the professional development of your executive team. Provide opportunities for advanced training, mentorship programs, and challenging assignments that allow them to stretch their skills and expand their capabilities.

Motivating an executive leadership team isn't a one-size-fits-all proposition. It's an ongoing process requiring consistent effort, genuine care, and a deep understanding of individual needs and organizational goals. By focusing on these strategies, you can create a highly engaged and motivated leadership team capable of driving significant results.

Effective Delegation

Effective delegation is crucial for leadership growth and team success. It's more than just assigning tasks; it's about empowering your team members to own their responsibilities and develop their skills. To achieve this, we must consciously address the underlying issues that often hinder delegation – our ingrained tendencies towards micromanagement, fear of relinquishing control, and a reluctance to trust others.

Overcoming these barriers requires a multifaceted approach. Firstly, we need to cultivate a culture of trust and accountability within our team. This involves clear communication of expectations, providing adequate training and resources, and establishing a system for regular feedback and support. Secondly, we must consciously identify our personal obstacles to delegation. Are we afraid of mistakes? Do we believe we're the only ones capable of doing the task properly? Recognizing and challenging these limiting beliefs is critical.

Finally, effective delegation requires a structured process. Before delegating a task, clearly define the goals, deliverables, timelines, and resources needed. Select the right person for the task based on their skills and experience. Provide clear instructions and be available for support, but resist the urge to intervene unless absolutely necessary. Regular check-ins should focus on progress and problem-solving, not on micromanaging every detail. By actively working through these steps, we can learn to effectively delegate, foster team growth, and ultimately, improve overall productivity and efficiency.

Take a Mid-Day Break

Prioritizing your well-being is crucial for sustained productivity and overall health. Integrating regular lunch breaks into your daily schedule is a simple yet profoundly effective way to achieve this. Instead of viewing lunch as just a refueling stop, consider it a vital component of your workday, a time dedicated to rejuvenation and mental clarity.

Stepping away from your desk allows your mind to decompress from the demands of work. This break provides an opportunity to recharge your batteries, preventing burnout and fostering a more positive and energetic approach to the afternoon's challenges. A balanced, nutritious lunch contributes to sustained energy levels, minimizing afternoon slumps and enhancing cognitive function.

Think of your lunch break as a strategic investment in your overall success. Taking this time for yourself isn't selfish; it's essential. By incorporating mindful breaks into your routine, you'll find increased focus, improved mood, and a healthier work-life balance, ultimately leading to greater efficiency and accomplishment. Experiment with different ways to maximize your lunch break – a leisurely walk, a quick meditation, or simply a moment of quiet reflection – to discover what best supports your individual needs and contributes to a more fulfilling and productive workday.

Finding Happiness

This part deals with encouraging some introspection on a topic that's deeply personal and profoundly important: happiness. Instead of simply asking you to "examine what makes you happy," I'd like to propose a more structured approach to exploring this vital aspect of life.

Consider this a gentle invitation to embark on a journey of self-discovery. To truly understand what brings you joy, I suggest taking some time to reflect on the following:

Identify your core values: What principles guide your life? Understanding your values – such as creativity, connection, growth, or security – can shed light on the activities and relationships that bring you lasting fulfillment.

Recall moments of profound joy: Think back on moments in your life when you felt genuine, unadulterated happiness. What were the circumstances? Who were you with? What specific elements contributed to that feeling? Analyzing these memories can reveal recurring themes or patterns related to your well-being.

Explore different aspects of your life: Consider your work, relationships, hobbies, and personal pursuits. Are there areas that consistently bring you joy and satisfaction, and others that leave you feeling depleted or unfulfilled? Identifying these areas allows for conscious choices and potentially necessary changes.

Experiment and iterate: Don't be afraid to try new things and step outside your comfort zone. Explore new hobbies, connect with different people, and engage in activities that you've always been curious about. This process of experimentation is essential for discovering what truly resonates with you.

This isn't a task to be rushed. Allow yourself time for thoughtful contemplation and self- reflection. The goal isn't to find a singular answer, but rather to develop a deeper understanding of yourself and what contributes to a life well-lived.

Using a Balance Wheel

This is a reminder about the importance of utilizing the balance wheel as a tool for effective prioritization and time management. Instead of simply thinking of it as a "check," let's consider it a dynamic instrument for navigating the complexities of our various commitments.

Think of the balance wheel as a visual representation of your life's key areas – work, family, health, personal growth, finances, etc. Each segment represents a different aspect, and its size reflects the current level of attention and energy you're dedicating to it. When one area is disproportionately large, it's a signal that other areas are likely being neglected, leading to potential stress and imbalance.

Regularly reviewing your balance wheel allows you to:

Identify imbalances: Pinpoint areas where you're overextending yourself or neglecting important aspects of your life.

Set realistic goals: Develop actionable steps to re-allocate your time and resources more effectively.

Track your progress: Monitor your success in achieving balance and make adjustments as needed.

Promote well-being: Prevent burnout and foster a more fulfilling and harmonious life.

I encourage you to dedicate some time this week to creating your personal balance wheel and regularly assessing it. This proactive approach will significantly contribute to your overall well- being and success in achieving your goals.

Competition is Healthy

I'd like to expand on the idea that competition is beneficial. While it's true that a competitive environment can be healthy and contribute to individual growth, it's crucial to understand the nuances involved. Healthy competition fosters innovation, drives us to improve our skills and performance, and can lead to significant advancements within a field. Think of the advancements in technology spurred by the competition between tech giants, or the achievements in sports fueled by athletes striving for excellence. These are positive outcomes directly linked to competitive pressures.

However, it's equally important to acknowledge that unhealthy competition can be detrimental. An overemphasis on winning at all costs can lead to unethical behavior, stress, and even burnout. The pursuit of success shouldn't come at the expense of integrity or well-being. A truly healthy competitive landscape requires a balanced approach, emphasizing both the drive to excel and the importance of ethical conduct and mutual respect. It's about striving for personal best, not just surpassing others.

Creating a Roadmap to Success

Designing a roadmap for future success requires a multifaceted approach encompassing self- reflection, strategic planning, and consistent action. Let's break this down into actionable steps:

Phase 1: Self-Assessment and Goal Setting (1-2 Months)

Identify Your Values: What truly matters to you? What principles will guide your decisions? Defining your core values is fundamental to aligning your goals with your authentic self.

Skills Audit: What are your strengths and weaknesses? Which skills are marketable and in demand? Identify any skill gaps and plan for development (courses, workshops, mentoring).

Goal Setting (SMART): Set Specific, Measurable, Achievable, Relevant, and Time-bound goals. Break down large goals into smaller, manageable milestones.

Vision Board: Create a visual representation of your aspirations. This can be a physical or digital collage that inspires motivation and keeps your goals top-of-mind.

***Phase 2*: Strategic Planning and Resource Allocation (1-3 Months)**

Identify Opportunities: Research potential career paths, industry trends, and emerging technologies relevant to your goals. Network with professionals in your field to gain insights and identify opportunities.

Develop a Plan: Outline the steps necessary to achieve each milestone. Include deadlines, resources required (time, money, skills), and potential obstacles.

Resource Allocation: Prioritize tasks and allocate resources effectively. Learn to say "no" to distractions and commitments that don't align with your goals.

Build a Support Network: Surround yourself with supportive mentors, colleagues, and friends who can offer encouragement and guidance.

Phase 3: Implementation, Monitoring, and Adjustment (Ongoing)

Consistent Action: Take consistent, proactive steps towards your goals, even when progress feels slow. Celebrate small wins along the way to maintain momentum.

Monitor Progress: Regularly track your progress against your milestones. Are you on track? Do you need to adjust your plan?

Flexibility and Adaptation: Be prepared to adapt your plan as circumstances change. The ability to be flexible and resourceful is crucial for long-term success.

Continuous Learning: The world is constantly evolving. Commit to continuous learning to stay relevant and competitive.

This roadmap is a living document – continuously review and refine it as you progress. Remember, success is a journey, not a destination. Embrace the process, learn from setbacks, and celebrate your accomplishments along the way.

Consider Hiring a Consultant

The question of engaging a consultant during a period of significant transformation within a state agency is a critical one, often prompting careful consideration of internal capabilities versus external expertise.

Navigating organizational change, be it implementing new policies, integrating technological advancements, or undertaking comprehensive restructuring, presents unique complexities for state agencies. These initiatives demand not only a deep understanding of governance and public service mandates but also specialized project management, strategic planning, and often, stakeholder engagement skills that may not be readily available within an agency's existing internal teams.

Consultants bring a wealth of experience garnered from diverse projects across various sectors, including public administration. They offer an objective, unbiased perspective, free from institutional biases or internal politics, which is invaluable when assessing challenges and formulating effective solutions. Their role extends beyond mere advice; they provide proven methodologies, best practices, and dedicated resources to ensure a structured, efficient, and successful transition.

Furthermore, leveraging external consultants can mitigate risks associated with large-scale change, accelerate project timelines, and free up internal staff to focus on their core operational responsibilities. Ultimately, while the initial investment in a consultant may seem significant, the long-term benefits of avoiding costly missteps, ensuring smoother transitions, and achieving desired outcomes more effectively often far outweigh the initial expenditure, enabling the agency to adapt successfully and continue its vital service to the public.

I contracted after recommendations and full vetting with Sandra Hastings and Associates.

Hiring a Consultant to Coach Leadership Skills

The demanding arena of public service requires an unwavering dedication to its core mission and exceptional resilience in navigating constant public and political scrutiny. The complexities of governance and the imperative to deliver impactful results for citizens place unique pressures on leadership teams.

Team coaching initiatives are designed to empower government leaders to not only meet but exceed these expectations. These focus on meticulously strengthening three critical pillars:

Strategic Communication: Cultivating clarity, transparency, and influence in all interactions, ensuring policies are articulated effectively, public trust is maintained, and internal alignment is achieved across diverse stakeholders and departments.

Enhanced Collaboration: Fostering a culture of seamless teamwork that breaks down silos, leverages collective intelligence, and accelerates cross-agency initiatives to address multifaceted challenges more efficiently.

Adaptive Leadership Mindset: Equipping leaders with the mental fortitude, agility, and forward-thinking perspective required to embrace innovation, navigate rapid societal and technological shifts, and inspire their teams through periods of significant transformation.

By nurturing these foundational capabilities, this approach will enable government teams to operate with unparalleled effectiveness, proactively adapt to evolving circumstances, and consistently remain steadfastly aligned with the overarching mission of serving the public good. The ultimate outcome is a more responsive, efficient, and impactful public sector, truly capable of addressing the complex demands of today and building a better future.

I contracted after recommendations and full vetting, with Lou Tice and The Pacific Institute.

Take Time to Think and Reflect

It's crucial to remember that effective action starts with clear thinking. Before diving into your to-do list, allow yourself dedicated time for reflection and prioritization. This isn't about procrastination; it's about strategic planning. Consider breaking down large tasks into smaller, more manageable steps. Identify your most important priorities and focus your energy there, leaving less urgent items for later. Taking the time for mindful processing will ultimately enhance your efficiency and reduce stress, leading to better outcomes. Schedule this reflection time just as you would any other important meeting; treat it as an essential appointment with yourself. Remember, you are your most valuable resource, and taking care of yourself is a key component of success. Let's discuss this further if you feel you need support in prioritizing tasks.

One-Stop Approach

This outlines a proposal for a comprehensive modernization of our state agency's service delivery. Our current system presents challenges for citizens and internal staff alike, often requiring them to navigate multiple departments and platforms to access necessary information and services. This fragmentation leads to inefficiencies, frustration, and a less- than-optimal citizen experience.

A proposed "One-Stop Shop" initiative aims to consolidate all essential agency services onto a single, user-friendly platform. This unified system would offer a streamlined, intuitive experience, allowing citizens to access information, submit applications, and track progress with ease.

Key components of this initiative include:

Centralized online portal: A single website and/or mobile application serving as the primary access point for all agency services.

Integrated database: A unified database system to prevent data redundancy and ensure consistent, accurate information.

Improved customer support: Enhanced customer service channels, including live chat, email support, and a comprehensive FAQ section.

Data analytics and reporting: Tracking key metrics to identify areas for improvement and demonstrate the effectiveness of the system.

Phased implementation: A strategic rollout plan to minimize disruption and ensure a smooth transition.

This project will require significant investment in both technology and personnel training. However, the long-term benefits, including improved citizen satisfaction, increased efficiency, and reduced operational costs, far outweigh the initial investment. I would welcome the opportunity to discuss this proposal further and present a detailed plan for implementation.

How to Create a Culture of Loyalty

Cultivating a Culture of Loyalty and Commitment within a State Agency: A Strategic Approach

Creating a truly loyal and committed workforce within a state agency requires a multifaceted, long-term strategy that goes beyond simple incentives. It involves fostering a positive and supportive work environment where employees feel valued, respected, and empowered. This approach should focus on several key areas:

1. Invest in Employee Development and Growth: Providing opportunities for professional development, including training, mentorship programs, and tuition reimbursement, demonstrates a commitment to employees' future and enhances their job satisfaction. This investment fosters loyalty as employees see a clear path for advancement and growth within the agency. Regular performance reviews should be constructive and focused on both improvement and recognition of accomplishments.

2. Promote Open Communication and Transparency: A culture of open communication, where employees feel comfortable expressing their ideas and concerns, is crucial. This can be achieved through regular town hall meetings, open-door

policies for leadership, and anonymous feedback mechanisms. Transparency in decision-making processes, even when explaining difficult choices, builds trust and confidence in agency leadership.

3. Recognize and Reward Employee Contributions: A robust recognition and rewards system that goes beyond simply monetary compensation is essential. This could include public acknowledgment of achievements, employee-of-the-month programs, opportunities for increased responsibility, and flexible work arrangements where appropriate. Celebrating both individual and team successes reinforces positive behaviors and fosters a sense of collective accomplishment.

4. Foster a Positive and Supportive Work Environment: Creating a positive work culture requires addressing issues such as workplace harassment, discrimination, and burnout. This includes implementing strong policies and providing training to prevent these issues, and ensuring employees feel safe and supported. Promoting teamwork and collaboration, and fostering a sense of community among employees, is also critical.

5. Align Individual Goals with Agency Mission: Clearly articulating the agency's mission and vision and connecting employees' work to the broader societal impact will foster a sense of purpose and meaning. Employees are more likely to be loyal when they understand how their contributions directly benefit the community and align with their personal values.

By implementing these strategies, state agencies can cultivate a culture of loyalty and commitment, leading to increased employee retention, improved morale, and ultimately, more effective service delivery to the public. This is not a quick fix, but a continuous process of investment and improvement requiring consistent effort and attention from leadership.

My Experience Leading a State Agency

My experience leading the Nebraska Department of Labor involved extensive collaboration with the state legislature to successfully pass several key pieces of legislation. This included bills focused on workforce development and training, economic development, and education. My role encompassed not only developing and proposing the legislation, but also actively engaging in the legislative process. This involved:

Strategic Collaboration: Building and maintaining strong working relationships with legislators from both parties, understanding their priorities and concerns, and tailoring our proposals to address their needs and the needs of the state.

Effective Communication: Clearly articulating the benefits of our proposed legislation through presentations, testimony at committee hearings, and informal discussions with individual legislators and their staff. I successfully navigated complex political dynamics to build consensus and garner support.

Data-Driven Advocacy: Supporting our proposals with robust research, data analysis, and impact assessments to demonstrate the potential positive outcomes of the proposed legislation.

Lobbying and Negotiation: Working with legislative staff to address concerns, negotiate amendments, and compromise effectively to achieve the desired outcome. This required skillful negotiation and a deep understanding of the legislative process.

Post-Legislative Implementation: Overseeing the implementation of the passed legislation, ensuring its effectiveness and addressing any unforeseen challenges.

This experience honed my skills in strategic planning, political acumen, communication, negotiation, and collaborative leadership within the context of state government. The success of these legislative initiatives demonstrates my ability to translate policy goals into tangible results, effectively navigating the complexities of the state legislative process.

Embarking on a Continuous Journey

This message outlines my commitment to a transformative journey of continuous improvement. It's not just aiming for incremental changes; it's about striving for a fundamental shift in how we operate, fostering a culture of ongoing learning and adaptation.

This initiative will involve everyone, and its success depends on our collective participation and dedication.

You will need to implement several key strategies to support this journey. These include:

Enhanced Training Programs: You will be investing in new training opportunities to equip our team with the skills and knowledge needed to drive innovation and efficiency.

Open Communication Channels: You need to be committed to fostering a transparent and open environment where feedback is actively sought and valued at all levels. Your ideas and suggestions are crucial to this process.

Data-Driven Decision Making: You will leverage data analysis to identify areas for improvement and measure the effectiveness of our initiatives.

Regular Progress Reviews: You will conduct regular reviews to track our progress, celebrate successes, and address any challenges that arise.

I understand that change can be challenging, and you will need to be committed to providing the support and resources necessary for a smooth transition. I encourage you to actively participate in this journey and share your ideas and concerns with your team leaders or management. Together, you can achieve remarkable success.

My commitment to continuous professional development is a cornerstone of my approach to work and life. I believe in the importance of ongoing learning and self-improvement, not just for achieving immediate goals, but also for fostering long-term growth and adaptability in a constantly evolving environment. This commitment manifests in several ways, including actively seeking opportunities for skill enhancement through training, mentoring, and pursuing advanced certifications. I also consistently seek feedback, both formal and informal, to identify areas for refinement and leverage this insight to optimize performance and effectiveness. My dedication to this continuous improvement process reflects my desire to not only excel in my current role but also enhance my capacity for future contributions and leadership.

Dealing with the Status Quo

The inertia of the status quo can be a powerful force, a comfortable blanket that hides us from potential growth and unforeseen opportunities. We need to actively challenge this inertia, to rigorously examine the assumptions upon which our current situation rests. This isn't simply about change for the sake of change; it's about a conscious evaluation of our goals, strategies, and outcomes. Are we achieving what we set out to accomplish? Are there more efficient, effective, or ethical paths forward? What unseen risks are we accepting by maintaining the status quo? What innovations or improvements are we missing out on?

This process requires a thorough self-assessment. We must honestly analyze both successes and failures, identifying patterns and understanding the root causes of both. Only through this deep understanding can we formulate a plan for meaningful, sustainable progress. This might involve restructuring existing systems, embracing new technologies, or redefining our goals themselves. The challenge isn't merely to consider alternative approaches, but to actively seek them out, evaluate them objectively, and adapt with courage and resilience.

Cultivating a Culture

Cultivating a thriving organizational culture necessitates a strategic and empathetic approach, far exceeding a simple coaching role. To truly ensure success in organizational culture change, consider a multifaceted leadership strategy that blends coaching with other key elements. This requires actively shaping the environment, fostering open communication, empowering employees at all levels, and implementing measurable systems to track progress.

Instead of merely "coaching," focus on becoming a "Culture Architect". This involves designing a comprehensive framework that addresses the following:

Vision & Values: Clearly articulate the desired culture, aligning it with the organization's overall goals. This must be more than just a statement; it needs to be actively demonstrated through leadership actions and daily practices.

Communication & Transparency: Establish open and honest channels of communication. Actively solicit feedback, address concerns directly, and ensure transparency in decision- making processes. This builds trust and fosters a sense of psychological safety, vital for successful change.

Empowerment & Accountability: Delegate authority appropriately, providing employees with the autonomy to contribute their unique skills and perspectives. Simultaneously, establish clear expectations and accountability measures to ensure everyone is working toward the shared vision.

Training & Development: Invest in comprehensive training programs that equip employees with the knowledge and skills necessary to thrive in the new culture. This includes training on new processes, communication strategies, and conflict resolution techniques.

Measurement & Evaluation: Implement key performance indicators (KPIs) to track progress toward achieving the desired cultural changes. Regularly assess the effectiveness of implemented strategies and adapt your approach based on data-driven insights.

By embracing this holistic and proactive approach, you will move beyond simple coaching and become a catalyst for transformative organizational culture change. The outcome will be a more engaged, productive, and ultimately, successful organization.

Developing Effective Leadership

This document outlines a framework for understanding the essential personality traits that contribute to effective leadership. While no single set of traits guarantees success, cultivating these characteristics can significantly enhance a leader's ability to inspire, motivate, and guide their teams. We will explore several key areas, including:

Integrity and Ethical Conduct: The foundation of strong leadership rests on unwavering honesty, transparency, and adherence to a strong ethical code. Trust is paramount, and leaders must consistently model the behaviors they expect from their teams.

Vision and Strategic Thinking: Effective leaders possess a clear vision for the future and the ability to translate that vision into actionable strategies. This requires strong analytical skills, the capacity for forward-thinking, and the ability to adapt to changing circumstances.

Communication and Interpersonal Skills: The ability to communicate effectively – both verbally and nonverbally – is crucial. Leaders must be able to articulate their vision clearly, actively listen to others, provide constructive feedback, and foster open communication within the team. Strong interpersonal skills are necessary to build rapport, resolve conflict, and foster a positive and collaborative environment.

Decisiveness and Accountability: Leaders must be able to make timely and informed decisions, even in the face of uncertainty. Equally important is the willingness to take responsibility for both successes and failures, fostering a culture of accountability within the team.

Resilience and Adaptability: The ability to overcome challenges, learn from setbacks, and adapt to changing circumstances is essential for effective leadership. This involves maintaining a positive attitude, demonstrating perseverance, and embracing change as an opportunity for growth.

Empathy and Emotional Intelligence: Understanding and responding to the emotional needs of team members is critical. Leaders with high emotional intelligence can build strong relationships, foster trust, and motivate their teams through empathy and understanding.

This is a starting point for a deeper exploration into the multifaceted nature of leadership. Further research into specific leadership styles and models will enhance understanding and application of these traits.

Strategies for Empowering State Agency Employees

Developing a truly empowered workforce within a state agency requires a multifaceted approach focusing on individual growth, improved team dynamics, and a supportive organizational culture. This isn't simply about offering more training; it's about fostering a sense of ownership and purpose among your employees.

I. Fostering Individual Growth:

Invest in Targeted Training and Development: Go beyond generic compliance training. Identify specific skill gaps and provide opportunities for employees to enhance their expertise through workshops, online courses, mentorship programs, and conferences relevant to their roles and career aspirations. Consider offering tuition reimbursement for relevant advanced degrees or certifications.

Promote Internal Mobility: Create clear pathways for career progression within the agency. This allows employees to develop new skills and take on increased responsibility, boosting morale and retention. Regularly assess employee skills and interests to identify suitable opportunities for advancement.

Empowerment Through Delegation: Trust your employees to handle responsibility. Delegate tasks appropriately, providing them with the autonomy to make decisions within their scope of work. This fosters a sense of ownership and allows them to develop their problem-solving abilities. Provide clear expectations and support, but avoid micromanagement.

Encourage Innovation and Feedback: Create a culture where employees feel comfortable sharing ideas and providing constructive criticism. Implement systems for collecting feedback, such as regular surveys, suggestion boxes, or open forums. Actively consider and implement viable suggestions.

II.   Strengthening Team Dynamics:

Promote Collaboration and Teamwork: Encourage cross-departmental collaboration and teamwork to foster a sense of shared purpose and mutual support. Organize team-building activities and provide opportunities for employees to work together on challenging projects.

Establish Clear Communication Channels: Ensure open and transparent communication flows freely throughout the agency. Regular team meetings, transparent reporting mechanisms, and easily accessible information resources can facilitate this.

Recognize and Reward Achievements: Publicly acknowledge and reward individual and team accomplishments to boost morale and motivation. This can involve formal awards, bonuses, or simply a heartfelt thank you.

III.   Cultivating a Supportive Organizational Culture:

Lead by Example: Demonstrate the values of empowerment and trust in your own leadership style. Be approachable, supportive, and actively listen to your employees' concerns.

Foster a Positive Work Environment: Create a workplace where employees feel valued, respected, and supported. Address issues of harassment or discrimination promptly and effectively. Promote work-life balance and offer flexible work arrangements where possible.

Invest in Employee Wellness: Promote employee well-being through initiatives such as wellness programs, stress management resources, and employee assistance programs. A healthy and happy workforce is a more productive and empowered one.

By implementing these strategies, you can create a more engaged, productive, and ultimately, empowered workforce within your state agency. This will lead to improved efficiency, higher retention rates, and ultimately, better service to the public.

Listening to Your Employees

This message is to emphasize the critical importance of actively and genuinely listening to the employees within our state agency. This isn't simply about hearing their words; it's about understanding their perspectives, concerns, and suggestions. Effective communication and feedback mechanisms are essential for fostering a positive and productive work environment.

We must create a culture where employees feel empowered to share their insights without fear of reprisal. This requires a multi-faceted approach, including regular employee surveys, open forums, and one-on-one meetings with managers. It's crucial to actively solicit feedback at all levels of the organization and demonstrate that their input is valued and taken seriously.

The collective knowledge and experience of your employees represent an invaluable resource that can significantly enhance your agency's efficiency, effectiveness, and overall success. Ignoring their voices not only undermines morale but also limits our potential for growth and improvement. Let's prioritize developing a robust and inclusive communication strategy to ensure that every employee feels heard and valued.

Listening Skills

Developing effective listening skills is crucial for leading and managing employees within a state agency. This involves more than just hearing what your employees say; it requires actively engaging with their perspectives, understanding their concerns, and fostering a culture of open communication. Here's a structured approach to enhance your listening capabilities within this specific context:

I. Creating a Safe and Open Environment:

Establish Trust: Employees need to feel comfortable sharing their thoughts and feelings without fear of retribution. This requires consistent demonstration of fairness, empathy, and respect. Transparency in decision-making processes is also vital.

Regular Communication Channels: Implement formal and informal channels for communication. This could include regular staff meetings, suggestion boxes (physical or digital), anonymous feedback mechanisms, and one-on-one meetings. Make sure these channels are actively monitored and responded to.

Active Solicitation of Feedback: Don't just wait for employees to come to you. Proactively seek their input on relevant matters. Surveys, focus groups, and informal conversations can all be effective methods.

II. Active Listening Techniques:

Pay Attention: Minimize distractions, maintain eye contact, and focus your attention entirely on the speaker.

Show Empathy: Try to understand their perspective, even if you don't agree with it. Reflect back what you've heard to ensure understanding ("So, if I understand correctly, you're saying...")

Ask Clarifying Questions: Don't interrupt, but ask open-ended questions to encourage further elaboration ("Can you tell me more about that?")

Summarize and Paraphrase: Periodically summarize the speaker's points to demonstrate your understanding and ensure accuracy.

Avoid Interrupting or Judging: Allow employees to fully express themselves without interruption. Refrain from immediate judgment or offering solutions before fully understanding the problem.

III. Addressing Feedback and Concerns:

Acknowledge and Validate: Even if you can't immediately address a concern, acknowledge the employee's feelings and validate their experience.

Develop Action Plans: When appropriate, create actionable plans to address the issues raised. Keep employees updated on the progress of these plans.

Follow Up: Don't just listen and forget. Follow up with employees to demonstrate that their concerns are being taken seriously.

IV. Specific Considerations for State Agencies:

Understanding Bureaucracy: Be mindful of the bureaucratic processes and constraints within the agency. Explain how these processes impact the implementation of solutions.

Legal and Ethical Considerations: Ensure that all conversations and actions remain within the legal and ethical guidelines of the state agency.

Collaboration and Teamwork: Foster a collaborative environment where employees feel empowered to work together to solve problems.

By implementing these strategies, you can cultivate a culture of open communication and active listening within your state agency, leading to improved employee morale, increased productivity, and a more effective work environment.

Customer Feedback

Actively soliciting and incorporating customer feedback is paramount to your success. It's not merely a "necessity," but a foundational element of building a thriving business and fostering strong customer relationships. We need to implement robust systems for gathering feedback, surveys, focus groups, social media monitoring, and direct customer interaction – to ensure we're consistently capturing a wide range of perspectives. Furthermore, we must establish a clear process for analyzing this input, identifying actionable insights, and translating them into tangible improvements in our products, services, and overall customer experience. This commitment to customer-centricity will not only enhance customer satisfaction but also provide invaluable data to inform strategic decision-making, ultimately driving innovation and growth.

Compliance

This part concerns the crucial undertaking of fostering a positive and productive cultural shift within your state agency. Successfully navigating this process requires meticulous adherence to all applicable federal and state rules and regulations. You must ensure that all initiatives aimed at transforming the agency's culture are not only effective in achieving their desired outcomes but also fully compliant with the legal framework governing your operations.

To that end, establish a clear compliance protocol for all cultural change initiatives. This protocol should include:

A comprehensive legal review: Before implementation, each initiative should undergo a rigorous review by your legal team to identify and address any potential compliance concerns. This should encompass both federal and state regulations, paying close attention to areas such as employment law, ethics, and public records.

Regular compliance monitoring: Ongoing monitoring will be essential to ensure that your initiatives remain compliant throughout their lifecycle. This will involve periodic audits and reviews of relevant documentation, as well as proactive measures to address any emerging compliance issues.

Employee training: Effective communication and training are key to ensuring compliance. You should implement a program to educate all staff on the relevant laws, regulations, and internal policies related to cultural change initiatives. This will help ensure that everyone understands their responsibilities and the importance of maintaining compliance.

Open communication channels: Maintaining transparency and fostering open communication within the agency is vital to managing any compliance concerns. We should encourage employees to report potential compliance issues without fear of reprisal.

By establishing a robust compliance framework, you can effectively manage the cultural change process while ensuring that we adhere to all applicable laws and regulations.

Fostering a culture of compliance within your state agency while remaining fully compliant with all applicable federal rules and regulations. This isn't simply about avoiding penalties; it's about proactively building a strong ethical foundation for your work.

You need a strategic approach that goes beyond mere checklist adherence. This requires a multi-faceted plan encompassing training, improved communication, and a demonstrable commitment from leadership. Specifically, envision:

Comprehensive Training Programs: Regular, engaging training sessions covering all relevant federal regulations. These shouldn't be one-size-fits-all; rather, they should be tailored to the specific roles and responsibilities of our employees.

Enhanced Communication Channels: We need to ensure that information about compliance is readily accessible and easily understood by everyone. This could involve creating internal newsletters, online resources, and regular team meetings dedicated to compliance discussions. Clear and concise communication is paramount.

Leadership Commitment and Accountability: You must demonstrate, from the top down, an unwavering commitment to compliance. This means actively participating in training, setting clear expectations, and ensuring accountability for any lapses in adherence.

This isn't a quick fix, but a long-term commitment. I believe that by strategically focusing on these key areas, you can cultivate a culture where compliance isn't just a legal requirement, but an integral part of your agency's identity and a source of pride.

Doers and Non-Doers

I want to explore with you a concept I've been reflecting on: the distinction between individuals who actively pursue their goals and those who don't. It's not simply a matter of laziness versus diligence; the dynamic is far more nuanced.

The "doers," in my observation, exhibit a combination of traits. They possess a clear vision of what they want to achieve, coupled with a strong internal drive. This isn't necessarily ambition in the traditional sense; it could be a quiet determination to master a skill, contribute to a cause, or simply improve their own lives. Critically, they take consistent, proactive steps, even in the face of setbacks. They are adept at breaking down large goals into smaller, manageable tasks, celebrating small victories along the way. Their mindset is one of continuous learning and improvement, actively seeking feedback and adapting their approaches as needed.

"Non-doers," on the other hand, are not inherently lacking in ambition or capability. Often, they struggle with factors like fear of failure, procrastination stemming from perfectionism, or a lack of clarity in their objectives. They may also be overwhelmed by the sheer magnitude of their aspirations, leading to inaction.

Understanding this distinction isn't about judgment; it's about recognizing the potential roadblocks and finding strategies to overcome them.

I'm particularly interested in exploring how we can cultivate a "doer" mentality. This could involve identifying limiting beliefs, developing effective planning techniques, building support networks, and fostering a growth mindset.

Applying a Human Face to Public Service

Providing accessible and effective public services necessitates a fundamental shift in perspective. We must move beyond simply delivering services and instead focus on building genuine relationships with the individuals and communities we serve. This requires a deep understanding of their unique needs, challenges, and aspirations. It involves actively listening to their concerns, proactively seeking feedback, and tailoring services to be responsive and truly helpful. Ultimately, the goal is to create an environment where individuals feel valued, respected, and empowered to participate fully in society. This human-centered approach fosters trust and ensures that public services are not just efficient, but also equitable and effective in improving the lives of all citizens. I believe that by prioritizing this human- centered approach, we can create a more inclusive and just society.

Applying Common Sense in a State Government Agency

My recent experiences working within a state government agency have prompted me to reflect on the application of common sense in such a setting. While regulations and procedures are crucial, I've found that navigating the complexities of bureaucracy often requires a pragmatic approach that goes beyond simply adhering to the letter of the law. This involves several key aspects:

Firstly, understanding the underlying goals and intentions behind regulations is vital. Sometimes, a rigid adherence to a rule can actually hinder the achievement of the intended outcome. Common sense dictates that we should prioritize the overall objective, even if it means deviating slightly from a strict interpretation of a procedure, provided it's done transparently and responsibly.

Secondly, effective communication and collaboration are paramount. Common sense suggests that open dialogue with colleagues, supervisors, and stakeholders can uncover potential problems and identify more efficient solutions. This collaborative approach can help us avoid bureaucratic bottlenecks and achieve better outcomes through shared understanding and mutual support.

Thirdly, proactive problem-solving and risk assessment are essential. Instead of waiting for issues to arise, common sense encourages a proactive approach to identify potential roadblocks and develop mitigating strategies. This involves anticipating challenges and developing contingency plans, thereby preventing larger issues from developing.

Finally, data-driven decision-making is critical. While common sense provides a valuable framework, it should be informed by data and evidence. Using available data to inform decisions ensures that our actions are not only intuitive but also grounded in fact, leading to more effective and impactful results.

In conclusion, applying common sense within a state government agency requires a nuanced approach that balances adherence to regulations with a pragmatic, collaborative, and data- driven mindset. It's about finding the optimal path to achieving organizational goals while navigating the intricacies of bureaucratic processes.

Why Make Changes to Customer Service

The question of why a state government agency might resist adopting a culture of excellent customer service is complex and warrants deeper examination. Several factors could contribute to this resistance, ranging from systemic issues to deeply ingrained organizational behaviors.

Firstly, a lack of resources, both financial and human, can significantly hinder the implementation of improved customer service initiatives. Training staff to effectively interact with the public, upgrading outdated technology, and streamlining processes all require considerable investment. Budgetary constraints, coupled with competing priorities, often lead agencies to deprioritize customer service improvements.

Secondly, entrenched bureaucratic processes and hierarchical structures can create barriers to effective customer interaction. Rigid protocols and a lack of empowerment among frontline staff can lead to frustrating experiences for citizens seeking assistance. Employees may feel restricted in their ability to resolve issues efficiently, leading to delays and dissatisfaction.

Thirdly, a lack of accountability and performance measurement can perpetuate a culture of indifference towards customer needs. Without clear metrics to track customer satisfaction and identify areas for improvement, agencies may not have the incentive to prioritize customer service. This necessitates robust performance indicators and feedback mechanisms to ensure continuous improvement.

Finally, a lack of leadership commitment and support from within the agency is critical. Customer service excellence requires a top-down approach with clear expectations and active engagement from all levels of management. Without visible support and a demonstrable commitment from leadership, efforts to improve customer service are likely to be ineffective.

In conclusion, understanding the multifaceted reasons behind a state government agency's reluctance to embrace a customer service-oriented approach requires a thorough analysis of its resources, structure, accountability mechanisms, and leadership commitment. Addressing these systemic challenges is essential to fostering a culture that prioritizes the needs and experiences of its constituents.

Communications

Communicating truthfully and transparently with employees within a state government agency demands a multifaceted approach, carefully considering the legal, ethical, and practical implications. This isn't simply about telling the truth; it's about fostering a culture of trust and open communication. Several key factors need careful attention:

Legal Considerations: Before disclosing any information, a thorough understanding of relevant laws, regulations, and agency policies is crucial. This includes understanding privacy laws concerning employee data, whistleblower protection laws, and any restrictions on the release of confidential information. Consulting with legal counsel is highly recommended, especially when dealing with sensitive matters like budget cuts, restructuring, or performance issues.

Ethical Considerations: Transparency should be balanced with empathy and sensitivity. The manner in which information is delivered is just as important as the content itself. Consider the potential impact on employee morale, productivity, and overall agency well-being.

Avoiding jargon, using clear and concise language, and ensuring consistent communication across all levels are essential.

Practical Considerations: Effective communication requires a well-defined strategy. This might involve town hall meetings, departmental updates, individual conversations, or a combination of methods. The chosen approach should align with the specific information being shared and the audience's needs. Providing opportunities for questions and feedback is vital to building trust and addressing concerns. Regular and consistent communication, even when there's no major news, is crucial for maintaining a strong and informed workforce.

Building Trust: Open and honest communication fosters trust. Addressing concerns head-on, even difficult ones, builds confidence and credibility. Demonstrating accountability for actions and decisions also strengthens the bond between leadership and employees. A culture of trust requires ongoing commitment and effort.

Ultimately, the goal is not simply to relay information, but to cultivate an environment where employees feel valued, respected, and informed. A well-executed strategy involving legal counsel, ethical considerations, practical planning, and a commitment to building trust will ensure effective communication and a stronger, more engaged workforce.

The Middle and Staying the Course

Throughout my life, I've consistently prioritized mediation and compromise in resolving conflicts. This approach wasn't a conscious strategy initially, but rather an ingrained inclination. From childhood, I instinctively sought to de-escalate tensions among my peers, fostering a sense of unity and collaboration. This naturally extended into my academic and professional life, where I consistently strived to bridge divides and build consensus.

My experience as Labor Commissioner exemplifies this approach. I successfully facilitated numerous agreements between labor and management, focusing on identifying shared goals and building upon common ground. Rather than dwelling on irreconcilable differences, we prioritized areas of mutual agreement, addressing remaining disputes strategically and prioritizing the collective good.

This commitment to pragmatic cooperation also characterized my political career. Despite navigating partisan divides, my focus remained on forging bipartisan alliances. I actively sought common ground, transcending entrenched ideological positions to achieve tangible progress. This philosophy was instrumental in my successful appointments and reappointments by governors from both major political parties, a testament to the effectiveness of collaborative leadership. My three terms of office demonstrate the enduring value of seeking shared solutions above partisan divisions. I am proud of this record and believe it reflects a successful model for effective governance.

Ultimate Accountability

The question of ultimate accountability within a state and city government agency is complex and multifaceted, demanding a nuanced understanding of its organizational structure and operational dynamics. Unlike a private corporation with a clearly defined CEO at the apex, responsibility is often distributed across various branches and levels of authority.

Consider the interconnectedness of state and city agencies. A policy initiated at the state level might be implemented and enforced by a city agency, but ultimate responsibility for its effectiveness (or failure) might lie with the state-level decision-makers, the city agency's leadership, or even a combination thereof. This blurring of lines frequently makes identifying "where the buck stops" challenging, especially in the aftermath of a crisis or scandal.

Several key factors influence accountability:

Legal Framework: The specific legal statutes and ordinances governing the agency play a pivotal role. These documents often outline clear lines of authority and define responsibilities for various actions and decisions.

Organizational Chart: The formal structure of the agency, depicting the hierarchical relationships and reporting lines, offers a framework for assigning accountability. However, informal power structures and influence can often complicate this.

Political Landscape: The political climate and the relationships between elected officials, agency heads, and other stakeholders can significantly impact accountability mechanisms. Political pressures can sometimes impede effective accountability.

Oversight Mechanisms: The existence and efficacy of oversight bodies, including legislative committees, internal audits, and external reviews, are crucial in ensuring accountability. These mechanisms should be robust and independent to effectively investigate and address any shortcomings.

Ultimately, determining "where the buck stops" involves examining the interplay of these various elements. It's not always a single point of responsibility but often a complex web of interactions and dependencies requiring thorough investigation to ascertain culpability in specific instances.

What Constitutes a Successful Business Model

I'm writing this to discuss the multifaceted nature of a successful business model, a topic that's far more nuanced than a simple definition. There's no single answer, of course, as success is defined differently depending on the goals and context of each individual business. However, some key elements consistently contribute to a winning formula.

A robust business model needs to consider several crucial aspects:

Value Proposition: At its core, a successful business model delivers significant value to its customers. This goes beyond simply offering a product or service; it's about understanding customer needs, solving problems, and creating a unique and compelling experience. This requires market research, understanding your target audience intimately, and iteratively refining your offerings based on feedback.

Revenue Streams: How will you generate income? A diverse range of revenue streams often provides greater stability and resilience. This could involve direct sales, subscriptions, licensing, advertising, or a combination of several models. Careful consideration of pricing strategies and cost structures is essential here.

Key Resources & Activities: What resources – both tangible and intangible – are crucial for your business operations? This might include skilled employees, proprietary technology, intellectual property, or key partnerships. Equally important are the key activities required to deliver your value proposition. Efficient and effective processes are vital.

Customer Relationships: How will you interact with and retain your customers? This encompasses everything from customer service and support to building brand loyalty and community engagement. A strong customer relationship management (CRM) strategy is often critical.

Channels: How will you reach your target customers? This encompasses marketing and distribution strategies. Understanding your customers' preferred communication channels is critical to effectively reaching and engaging them.

Cost Structure: A thorough understanding of your operating expenses is fundamental. Minimizing unnecessary costs and maximizing efficiency can significantly impact profitability. Regular monitoring and analysis of your cost structure are essential.

Ultimately, a successful business model is a dynamic, iterative process. It requires ongoing evaluation, adaptation, and a willingness to embrace change in response to market dynamics and customer feedback.

Competition Is Good If Used for the Right Reason

I'd like to expand on the idea that competition is beneficial. While it's true that a competitive environment can be healthy and contribute to individual growth, it's crucial to understand the nuances involved. Healthy competition fosters innovation, drives us to improve our skills and performance, and can lead to significant advancements within a field. Think of the advancements in technology spurred by the competition between tech giants, or the achievements in sports fueled by athletes striving for excellence. These are positive outcomes directly linked to competitive pressures.

However, it's equally important to acknowledge that unhealthy competition can be detrimental. An overemphasis on winning at all costs can lead to unethical behavior, stress, and even burnout. The pursuit of success shouldn't come at the expense of integrity or well-being. A truly healthy competitive landscape requires a balanced approach, emphasizing both the drive to excel and the importance of ethical conduct and mutual respect. It's about striving for personal best, not just surpassing others.

Strategic Agency Transformation: Exploring the Edgerton Process

This part deals with the modernization and efficiency improvements needed at the state agency. I believe the Edgerton process offers a structured approach to tackling this challenge. It's not simply about adopting business principles; it's a comprehensive framework for understanding and implementing significant operational change.

Applying the Edgerton process would involve a thorough assessment of the agency's current capabilities, identifying areas where business-like practices can be implemented to improve resource allocation, streamline processes, enhance productivity, and ultimately achieve a better return on investment for the taxpayers. This would encompass a multi-faceted approach, including:

Process Optimization: Mapping out current workflows and identifying bottlenecks, redundancies, and inefficiencies that can be addressed through lean management techniques and technological upgrades.

Financial Management: Implementing robust budget planning, performance monitoring, and financial reporting mechanisms to ensure greater accountability and transparency in the use of public funds.

Human Capital Management: Assessing talent acquisition, training and development strategies, and employee performance management to foster a culture of continuous improvement and high performance.

Technology Integration: Evaluating current technology infrastructure and identifying opportunities for modernization through the adoption of innovative tools and systems that improve efficiency and productivity.

Stakeholder Engagement: Developing strategies to engage with key stakeholders, including employees, legislators, and the public, to secure buy-in and support throughout the transformation process.

The Edgerton process offers a structured methodology for guiding the agency through each of these stages. Its rigorous nature ensures a thorough review and implementation of changes, maximizing the potential for sustained improvements. The Nebraska Department of Labor was the first state government agency to go through the rigorous process.

Time is a Friend and a Foe

Most gubernatorial political appointees are lucky to get 4 years, which goes by in the blink of an eye. I, on the other hand, had 18 years in which to pursue excellence in service delivery to the public we served in Nebraska.

Time can be our greatest ally, providing the opportunity for steady progress and the space to learn and adapt. We can meticulously plan, strategize, and steadily chip away at our ambitions, utilizing each passing moment effectively. In this sense, time is indeed a friend, a patient companion on our journey.

However, time can also feel like a relentless adversary. Deadlines loom, opportunities slip away, and the pressure to achieve can feel overwhelming. Procrastination eats away at our precious reserves, and unforeseen circumstances can derail even the most carefully laid plans. The ticking clock can induce anxiety and create a sense of urgency that can hinder, rather than help, our progress. This is where time becomes your foe, a constant reminder of our limitations and the finite nature of your efforts.

Ultimately, navigating this duality is key to success. It requires both strategic planning and a flexible approach, allowing us to leverage the supportive aspects of time while mitigating the pressures of its constraints. We need to be mindful of both the long game and the immediate tasks at hand, maintaining a healthy balance between ambition and realistic expectations.

Managing Management and Labor Relations

Navigating the Complexities of Management and Labor Relations within a State Government Agency: A Strategic Approach

This memo outlines a strategic framework for effectively addressing management and labor issues within a state government agency. Given the unique legal and regulatory environment governing public sector employment, a proactive and comprehensive approach is crucial to fostering a productive and harmonious work environment.

This framework encompasses several key areas:

I. Proactive Labor Relations:

Early Conflict Detection and Resolution: Implementing robust mechanisms for identifying and addressing potential conflicts before they escalate. This includes regular communication channels, employee surveys, and open-door policies. Specific examples could include establishing a confidential feedback system or conducting regular focus groups with employees across different departments.

Strengthening Communication Strategies: Developing and implementing clear and consistent communication strategies to keep employees informed about agency policies, procedures, and upcoming changes. This should extend to utilizing diverse communication methods to cater to varying employee preferences and communication styles.

Promoting a Culture of Collaboration and Respect: Fostering a workplace culture that values collaboration, mutual respect, and open dialogue between management and labor. This could be achieved through team-building activities, employee recognition programs, and the creation of cross-functional teams to tackle shared goals.

II.   Addressing Existing Labor Issues:

Negotiation and Collective Bargaining: Employing effective negotiation strategies and adhering to all applicable collective bargaining agreements and laws when addressing labor- related disputes. This will necessitate a deep understanding of applicable labor laws, union contracts, and established grievance procedures.

Dispute Resolution Mechanisms: Establishing clear and accessible mechanisms for resolving disputes, such as mediation, arbitration, and grievance procedures. Training managers and employees on how to effectively utilize these mechanisms is essential.

Legal Compliance: Ensuring strict adherence to all applicable federal, state, and local laws and regulations governing employment practices, including fair labor standards, equal employment opportunity, and employee privacy.

III.   Continuous Improvement

Performance Monitoring and Evaluation: Regularly monitoring and evaluating the effectiveness of management and labor relations strategies. Key performance indicators (KPIs) should be established to track progress and identify areas for improvement.

Training and Development: Providing ongoing training and development opportunities for both management and employees on effective communication, conflict resolution, and labor relations best practices.

Seeking External Expertise: When necessary, engaging external consultants or experts to provide guidance and support on complex labor relations issues.

This strategic framework underscores the importance of proactive engagement, open communication, and a commitment to upholding legal and ethical standards in managing labor relations. By proactively implementing these strategies, the agency can foster a more productive, harmonious, and efficient work environment. To this end, I had regularly scheduled meetings with our union representatives to discuss agency issues.

Enterprise Goals

This outlines a collaborative approach to defining and implementing impactful enterprise goals for our state agency. Rather than simply stating goals, we need to develop a robust strategic plan that aligns with the overall mission of the agency and addresses the key challenges and opportunities we face.

This process will involve several key steps:

Stakeholder Engagement: We'll begin by engaging with staff at all levels, soliciting input on priorities and identifying potential roadblocks to success. This includes departmental heads, frontline staff, and external stakeholders such as community organizations and partner agencies.

Data-Driven Analysis: We'll leverage existing data and conduct further analysis to establish a clear understanding of your agency's current performance, identify areas for improvement, and measure the potential impact of various goals. This will ensure your goals are realistic, measurable, achievable, relevant, and time-bound (SMART).

Goal Development & Prioritization: Based on stakeholder input and data analysis, you will collaboratively develop a concise set of enterprise goals that reflect your agency's strategic priorities. This will involve prioritizing initiatives based on their potential impact and alignment with our overall mission. You will need to ensure transparency and clear communication throughout this process.

Implementation & Monitoring: Once the goals are established, you will need to develop detailed action plans with clear responsibilities and timelines. Regular monitoring and evaluation will be critical to ensuring progress and making necessary adjustments along the way.

Empowerment

Empowering your employees to make decisions isn't just a feel-good initiative; it's a strategic imperative for fostering a thriving and innovative workplace. To truly unlock the potential of your team, you need to cultivate a culture of trust, autonomy, and accountability. This involves more than simply delegating tasks; it requires a carefully planned and executed approach.

Consider these key elements:

Clearly Defined Decision-Making Authority: Establish a framework outlining which decisions can be made at each level of the organization. This transparency prevents confusion and empowers employees to act confidently within their defined scope. Use clear guidelines and job descriptions to delineate responsibilities and decision-making powers.

Invest in Training and Development: Equip your employees with the skills and knowledge they need to make informed decisions. This might involve training programs focused on critical thinking, problem-solving, and decision-making frameworks. Consider mentorship programs to pair experienced employees with those developing their decision-making skills.

Foster Open Communication and Feedback: Create a safe space for employees to share their ideas, concerns, and even mistakes. Regular feedback sessions and open dialogue are crucial for continuous improvement and learning. Implement systems for feedback collection that encourage honest and constructive input.

Provide the Necessary Resources and Support: Ensure employees have the resources, tools, and information they need to make effective decisions. This includes access to data, technology, and mentorship. Avoid micromanaging and allow employees the space to learn from their decisions, both successful and unsuccessful.

Recognize and Reward Good Decision-Making: Celebrate successes and learn from failures openly. Acknowledge and reward employees who demonstrate sound judgment and initiative. This reinforces positive behavior and encourages others to embrace their decision- making responsibilities.

By implementing these strategies, you can create a workplace where employees feel valued, empowered, and motivated to contribute their best work. This will not only improve efficiency and productivity but also foster a more engaged and satisfied workforce. Remember, empowering your employees is an ongoing process requiring consistent effort and adaptation.

Visiting Staff at their Workplaces

Building strong relationships with your state employees is crucial for effective leadership and a positive work environment. Regular in-person visits are invaluable for fostering trust, understanding, and a sense of connection that transcends emails and memos. My experience overseeing 500 employees in 22 offices across Nebraska highlighted the significant benefits of consistent, personal engagement. These visits weren't merely administrative; they were opportunities to learn firsthand about the challenges and successes of each team, to offer support and guidance tailored to their specific needs, and to recognize individual contributions. The mutual benefits extended beyond improved communication – they cultivated a stronger sense of team cohesion and boosted overall morale. Consider implementing a structured visitation schedule, incorporating opportunities for informal interactions alongside more formal meetings, to maximize the positive impact on both employee satisfaction and organizational effectiveness. Perhaps a rotating schedule visiting a specific number of offices per quarter, incorporating both planned meetings and informal drop-ins, could provide a good starting point for a more comprehensive strategy.

Working with Your Federal Partners

This outlines a proactive approach to fostering a strong collaborative relationship with your federal partners, crucial for the continued success of the state agency. Effective communication and information sharing are paramount to achieving your shared goals.

This strategy involves several key initiatives:

Regular Information Briefings: You will need to establish a routine schedule for briefings to ensure our federal partners receive timely and comprehensive updates on your progress, challenges, and any relevant developments. These briefings will be tailored to their specific needs and areas of interest.

Open Communication Channels: You will need to maintain open and accessible lines of communication, including dedicated contact points and regular scheduled meetings, to facilitate the prompt exchange of information and address any concerns promptly.

Joint Problem-Solving: You will need to proactively engage your federal partners in collaborative problem-solving sessions to identify and address potential roadblocks collaboratively, leveraging their expertise and resources to achieve optimal outcomes.

Strategic Information Sharing: You need to implement a systematic approach to sharing relevant information, ensuring that your federal partners possess the necessary data and context to provide informed support and guidance. This includes developing clear reporting mechanisms and using secure platforms for sensitive data.

By implementing these strategies, I am confident you can cultivate a robust partnership that will significantly enhance the effectiveness and success of the state agency.

Connection to National Organization

Connecting with your national organization. To make this process as effective as possible, let's consider what you hope to achieve. What specific resources are you seeking? Are you looking for networking opportunities, professional development support, information on upcoming events, access to specific publications, or something else?

Develop a plan to effectively leverage the national organization's resources to meet your needs.

Handling Brain Drain

Addressing employee attrition, often termed "brain drain," requires a proactive and comprehensive approach. A robust succession plan is crucial, but simply utilizing the community college system is insufficient. Instead, consider a multi-faceted strategy encompassing several key elements:

1. Proactive Talent Identification and Development: Implement a system for identifying high- potential employees early in their careers. This involves regular performance reviews with a focus on growth potential, mentorship programs pairing experienced staff with rising stars, and offering targeted training and development opportunities based on individual career aspirations and identified skill gaps.

2. Strategic Partnerships with Educational Institutions: While utilizing the community college system can be beneficial for certain skill development, consider forging broader partnerships with universities and other educational institutions offering advanced training relevant to your agency's specialized needs. This could involve sponsoring employees' further education or establishing customized training programs.

3. Competitive Compensation and Benefits Packages: A competitive salary and benefits package are paramount in retaining valuable employees. Regularly review market rates to ensure your agency remains competitive, and consider offering additional benefits such as flexible work arrangements, generous paid time off, and comprehensive health insurance.

4. Improved Employee Engagement and Retention Strategies: Create a positive and supportive work environment that fosters employee loyalty. This includes open communication, opportunities for professional growth, recognition of achievements, and a focus on work-life balance. Regularly solicit employee feedback to identify areas for improvement.

5. Detailed Succession Planning: Develop a comprehensive succession plan that goes beyond simply identifying potential replacements. It should include detailed training programs, mentorship opportunities, and clearly defined career paths for employees at all levels. The plan must also incorporate contingency planning to address unexpected departures.

6. Knowledge Management System: Implement a robust system for capturing and sharing institutional knowledge. This could involve creating detailed documentation of processes and procedures, establishing a knowledge base accessible to all employees, and conducting regular knowledge transfer sessions between employees.

By adopting this holistic approach, your agency can significantly mitigate the risks associated with employee attrition and build a strong, resilient workforce. Simply relying on the community college system is only one small part of a much larger and more critical strategy.

To this end, we formed a partnership with the Community College System in Nebraska to develop a "Leadership University" for employee growth.

Keeping Current with Computerization and Technology

The transformative power of computers in simplifying our daily lives is undeniable. From automating mundane tasks to facilitating seamless communication across geographical boundaries, their impact is pervasive. Consider, for instance, the efficiency gains realized through automated scheduling, data analysis, and information retrieval. These technologies drastically reduce the time and effort previously dedicated to manual processes, freeing up valuable time for more creative and strategic endeavors. Beyond the purely practical, computers also enhance our connectivity, enabling instant communication with loved ones, access to vast repositories of knowledge, and participation in global communities. However, this ease of access also presents challenges, highlighting the need for responsible digital literacy and awareness of potential pitfalls like information overload and digital divides.

Ultimately, harnessing the full potential of computers requires a mindful approach, balancing their inherent benefits with a keen understanding of their limitations and societal implications.

Preparing to Give Testimony to your State Legislature

Crafting compelling testimony for your State Legislators requires meticulous preparation. This isn't simply about presenting your views; it's about effectively influencing policy. Here's a structured approach to ensure your testimony resonates:

Phase 1: Understanding the Context

Identify the Legislation: Thoroughly review the bill or resolution you'll be addressing. Understand its specifics, intended consequences, and potential impact. Don't just read the text; research its history, the rationale behind it, and any related documents.

Know Your Audience: Research the legislators you'll be addressing. Understand their political affiliations, committee assignments, and previous stances on similar issues. This knowledge informs your approach and allows you to tailor your message for maximum impact.

Define Your Message: What is the core message you want to convey? Keep it concise and focused, avoiding jargon and overly technical language. What is the specific action you want the legislators to take?

Phase 2: Structuring Your Testimony

Create a Narrative: Frame your testimony as a story, connecting your personal experience or expertise to the legislation. This makes your testimony more engaging and memorable.

Use Data and Evidence: Support your claims with credible data, statistics, and examples. Cite your sources clearly and accurately. Strong evidence lends authority and persuasiveness to your argument.

Anticipate Questions: Consider potential questions the legislators might ask and prepare thoughtful, concise answers. This demonstrates preparedness and builds credibility. Practice delivering these answers aloud.

Time Management: Adhere strictly to any time limits provided. Practice your testimony to ensure it fits within the allotted timeframe.

Phase 3: Presentation and Delivery

Professional Attire: Dress professionally and respectfully. Your appearance contributes to your overall credibility.

Clear and Concise Delivery: Speak clearly and confidently. Maintain eye contact with the legislators. Practice your delivery to ensure a smooth and engaging presentation.

Passion and Conviction: Express your passion for the issue and your conviction in your message. Genuine enthusiasm is contagious.

Post-Testimony Follow-up: After your testimony, send a thank-you note to the legislators and reiterate your key points. Consider following up with additional information or resources.

Remember, effective testimony is about clear communication, compelling evidence, and a well-structured presentation. By following these steps, you can significantly increase your chances of influencing the legislative process.

Nebraska Worker Training Program

Because of my work with displaced workers earlier in my career due to layoffs, I floated the idea of a worker training program. The

Nebraska Worker Training Program (LB 1337), administered by the Nebraska Department of Labor, provided grants to assist firms in the retraining and upgrading of skills for existing employees.

This Program was designed to support the retraining and upgrading of existing workers, currently employed in, or being trained for, high-quality, long-term jobs that enhance business productivity. Worker Training Grants may also be used to train new employees of expanding Nebraska businesses and to recruit out-of-state new employees.

In Nebraska, we established the Worker Training Program, which included the Nebraska Worker Training Board, which provides grants to support job training programs aimed at expanding the state's workforce and increasing the pool of skilled workers. The program is funded by the Nebraska Training and Support Cash Fund, and grants can be used to train, retrain, or upgrade the skills of existing workers, train new employees for expanding businesses, and recruit workers to Nebraska.

Info Disc

Keeping Nebraskans informed about critical labor market data was a top priority. During my tenure, I spearheaded a significant initiative to enhance the dissemination of vital employment information, including unemployment rates, work trends, labor market analysis, available job opportunities, and crucial safety and labor standards. We created the disc in- house to keep production costs down.

This initiative resulted in the creation and implementation of the "Info Video Disc" program. This innovative approach involved the regular distribution of concise, informative video segments to radio and television stations statewide. The program was overwhelmingly well- received by news outlets across Nebraska, greatly improving the accessibility and reach of this crucial information to the public.

The positive response reflects the importance of readily available, accurate labor market data for both job seekers and employers in our state. We were committed to continuing to explore and implement methods of sharing this information effectively. We believed this ongoing effort contributed substantially to the economic well-being and informed citizenry of Nebraska. Our InfoDisk won several "Telly Awards" over the years. The award is a prestigious award honoring excellence in video and social information video across all screens.

Industry Tour

I spent several years traveling throughout Nebraska, leading the effort to celebrate businesses that demonstrably prioritize the well-being of their employees. Around Labor Day each year, this initiative culminated in a series of awards ceremonies. It was an incredibly rewarding experience, allowing me to directly connect with hundreds of employers who exemplify a commitment to fair labor practices, a positive work environment, and a genuine investment in their team's success. These businesses represent the best of Nebraska's spirit, and the awards were a small token of appreciation for their significant contributions to our state's workforce and economy. I remain deeply impressed by the dedication and innovation demonstrated by these companies, and I am proud to have played a part in acknowledging their achievements. Their commitment serves as an inspiration to us all.

Governors Summit on Workforce

My experience leading the Nebraska Department of Labor's annual Governor's Summit on Workforce Development. For several years, I had the privilege of overseeing this significant event, which consistently brought together over 450 key stakeholders from across the state.

These participants included influential business leaders, educators, economic development professionals, public officials, and other critical players in Nebraska's workforce landscape.

The Summit's purpose was to proactively address the evolving challenges facing our state's workforce. Each year, we carefully craft a dynamic agenda featuring insightful presentations, panel discussions, and interactive workshops. These sessions focused on crucial topics such as skill gaps, talent acquisition, workforce training, and the impact of emerging technologies on employment. The collaborative environment fostered at the Summit facilitated meaningful dialogue and the development of innovative solutions to promote a stronger and more robust workforce ecosystem in Nebraska.

The Summit's success was largely due to the dedication and expertise of the individuals who participated, and I am proud of the collective impact we achieved in fostering collaboration and innovation to address Nebraska's workforce needs.

Testifying Before a Congressional Appropriations Committee

I had the rare opportunity to testify before a congressional subcommittee on appropriations for the workforce development system. This part serves to outline a preparatory strategy for the opportunity to testify before the Congressional Appropriations Committee. The significance of this opportunity demands meticulous planning and execution. My preparation encompassed several key areas:

First, a thorough review of the committee's jurisdiction and past appropriations decisions is crucial. This will enable me to tailor my testimony to address their specific concerns and priorities. I intend to utilize publicly available information, including committee reports, hearing transcripts, and past appropriation bills, as primary resources for this phase.

Secondly, meticulously craft your testimony. This will involve not only a concise presentation of the key facts and figures but also a persuasive narrative explaining the vital importance of the funding request. The narrative will clearly articulate the potential impact of the requested funds on the intended beneficiaries and will be supported by robust evidence.

Thirdly, anticipating potential questions from the committee members is essential. I prepared comprehensive answers to a broad range of questions, both anticipated and less predictable. This preparation will involve simulating question and answer sessions with colleagues to refine my responses and ensure clarity and conciseness.

Finally, I would ensure that all supporting documentation, including data tables, charts, and any other relevant material, is meticulously prepared and easily accessible for both myself and the committee. This will facilitate a smooth and efficient presentation.

This multi-faceted approach aims to ensure that your testimony is not only informative and persuasive but also reflects the utmost professionalism and respect for the committee's time and consideration. I am confident that a well-prepared testimony will significantly increase the likelihood of a favorable outcome.

Handling Customer Complaints

Handling customer complaints effectively is crucial for maintaining a positive public image and ensuring the smooth operation of any state agency. This requires a multi-faceted approach that integrates proactive strategies with robust reactive mechanisms.

Proactive measures focus on preventing complaints before they arise. This includes clear and accessible communication channels, such as user-friendly websites with FAQs and online forms for submitting inquiries. Regularly reviewing and updating agency processes to identify and eliminate pain points will significantly reduce the volume of complaints. Investing in employee training that emphasizes customer service skills, empathy, and active listening is also vital. Staff should be equipped to handle a variety of situations with professionalism and efficiency.

Reactive strategies are equally critical for addressing complaints that do occur. A well-defined process for receiving, documenting, and resolving complaints is essential. This process should be transparent, accessible, and timely. Each complaint should be treated with respect and promptly investigated. Customers should be kept informed of the progress and the resolution of their complaint. Regular performance monitoring of the complaint resolution process allows for continuous improvement and the identification of any systemic issues contributing to recurring complaints. Data analysis from complaint records can be valuable in identifying areas for procedural improvement, preventing future issues, and allowing for the development of more effective customer service strategies. Finally, incorporating customer feedback into agency policy and procedures demonstrates a commitment to continuous improvement and strengthens public trust.

Facing the Public

This part outlines my strategic approach for upcoming community engagement regarding the program changes. Anticipate a range of reactions, from enthusiastic support to significant concerns and potentially strong emotional responses. Framing your communication effectively will be crucial for a productive dialogue.

Instead of simply "explaining" the changes, focus on a participatory approach. I began by acknowledging the community's investment in the existing program and the understandable anxieties that change often brings. Actively listen to their perspectives, allowing ample time for them to express their feelings and concerns. Emphasize your willingness to understand their viewpoints before delving into the rationale behind the changes.

When presenting the reasons for the modifications, I move beyond a simple list of benefits. Instead, I illustrated the positive impacts through concrete examples, emphasizing how these changes directly address community needs and contribute to improved outcomes.

I used data and case studies wherever possible to substantiate my claims. Where feasible, I involved community members in brainstorming solutions to potential challenges posed by the changes.

Prepare for difficult questions. Anticipate potential criticisms and formulate well-reasoned responses. Avoid defensive language; I maintained a respectful and empathetic tone throughout the interaction. Remember, your goal is not only to explain the changes but also to build trust and foster ongoing collaboration with the community.

Consider preparing a comprehensive FAQ document in advance to address common questions and concerns. This will streamline the meeting and allow for more in-depth discussions on individual issues. After the meeting, follow up with a summary of key points and next steps to maintain momentum and transparency.

Working at the National and International Level

Reflecting on my career, I'm deeply grateful for the opportunities I've had to serve at both the national and international levels. My election as President of the National Association of State Workforce Agencies (NASWA), twice, and the National Association of Government Labor Officials (NAGLO), also twice, provided invaluable experience and leadership opportunities. These roles allowed me to advocate for crucial policy changes and collaborate with influential figures within the workforce development landscape.

Furthermore, I had the privilege of representing the United States at several significant international events. My participation as a delegate to the Labor Exchange Conference in Taipei, Taiwan; the World Skills Competition in Helsinki, Finland; and the 5th World Congress and General Assembly of the World Association of Public Employment Services in Bergen, Norway, broadened my perspective considerably, exposing me to diverse approaches and best practices from around the globe. These experiences highlighted the global interconnectedness of labor markets and reinforced the importance of international collaboration.

I strongly encourage you to actively engage with your national professional organizations. These organizations offer unparalleled networking opportunities, access to cutting-edge information, and a powerful platform for advocating for your professional interests and driving positive change within the field. By participating, you can not only expand your knowledge base but also contribute significantly to the future direction of our profession. The opportunities for personal and professional growth are immense.

National Awards

During my tenure in state government, it was an experience far exceeding my expectations, and I'm profoundly proud of the collective achievements in employment and workforce development. To say it was a successful period would be a vast understatement – I was fortunate enough to receive "three" prestigious national awards!

The first, the "Building a World Class Workforce" award, recognizes the extraordinary success of the statewide apprenticeship program we spearheaded. This initiative wasn't just about numbers; it was about transforming lives. We weren't just aiming for growth; we were focused on building a pipeline of skilled labor to meet the state's evolving needs. Our efforts resulted in a remarkable 25% increase in skilled labor within a mere two years, a testament to the program's effectiveness and the dedication of the team. This award validates the transformative power of strategic investment in workforce development and its tangible benefits to the state's economy.

The William J. Harris – Equal Employment Opportunity Award is equally gratifying. This accolade reflects our commitment to fostering a truly inclusive and equitable workplace. The overhaul of our diversity and inclusion training program wasn't simply a box-ticking exercise; it was a fundamental shift in our approach. We invested in comprehensive, engaging training that addressed unconscious bias and fostered a culture of respect and understanding. This resulted in a significant 15% increase in the representation of underrepresented groups within state government employment – a measurable demonstration of our commitment to fairness and opportunity for all.

Finally, receiving the National Eagle Award from the National Association of State Workforce Agencies is truly the pinnacle of achievement. This award, recognizing excellence across all aspects of workforce development, is a testament to the unwavering dedication, collaborative spirit, and innovative strategies that defined my approach. It encapsulates the collective effort in building a far stronger and more resilient workforce development system for our entire state, creating lasting positive change for individuals and the economy.

These awards are not just personal accolades; they represent the collaborative spirit and dedication of our entire team.

In Conclusion

I want to reiterate my strong support for your initiative to transform your agency's culture.

Cultivating a work environment that prioritizes both efficient, productive meetings and exceptional customer service is crucial for your long-term success. This requires a multi- faceted approach.

To achieve this, I believe a phased implementation focusing on several key areas will be most effective. Firstly, you need to address meeting optimization. This includes establishing clear agendas beforehand, enforcing time limits, and actively encouraging participation from all attendees. Secondly, we must define and measure our commitment to excellent customer service. This might involve implementing new customer feedback mechanisms, training programs focusing on empathy and problem-solving, and establishing clear service level agreements. Finally, we need to foster a culture of open communication and collaboration, ensuring that all employees feel empowered to contribute to these improvements.

I'm confident that with careful planning, dedicated effort, and the collaborative spirit you're already demonstrating, you can create a truly exceptional agency culture.

Building a thriving agency culture requires a multifaceted approach, going beyond simple slogans. Let's break down how you can cultivate an exceptional environment that fosters both employee well-being and exceptional service to your taxpayers.

First, strategic planning is paramount. This isn't just about setting goals; it's about identifying the specific values and behaviors that will define your agency culture. You need to articulate these clearly and consistently, making sure they're integrated into your daily operations. This might involve developing a comprehensive cultural framework that outlines expectations, communication protocols, and mechanisms for feedback.

Second, dedicated effort translates to tangible actions. You need to invest in employee development programs, fostering a culture of continuous learning and growth. This could involve training initiatives, mentoring programs, and opportunities for professional advancement. Equally crucial is creating a supportive and inclusive environment where every employee feels valued, respected, and empowered to contribute their unique skills and perspectives. This includes actively addressing any issues of inequity or discrimination.

Third, collaboration is not just a buzzword; it's the cornerstone of success. You need to actively encourage teamwork and cross-departmental communication. This can be facilitated through team-building activities, open communication channels, and opportunities for collaborative projects. Creating a sense of shared purpose and collective ownership is crucial for achieving your agency's objectives.

Finally, remember that excellent customer service stems from our commitment to the public we serve. The "golden rule" – treating others as we wish to be treated – is fundamental.

However, you need to go beyond this principle and actively seek to understand the needs and expectations of your taxpayers. This requires incorporating feedback mechanisms, ensuring responsiveness to inquiries, and continuously striving to improve the efficiency and effectiveness of your services. By focusing on these elements, you can truly build an agency culture that is both exceptional and reflective of our commitment to public service.

Leaving Your Agency in Good Hands

Suppose you did your job right, and as you transition out of your role as head of your state agency. I want to emphasize the importance of legacy. The true measure of success isn't just the achievements during your tenure, but the enduring impact you leave behind. A well- structured, efficient, and thriving agency isn't built overnight; it requires foresight, strategic planning, and a commitment to developing robust systems and processes. By focusing on these areas—mentoring your team, documenting best practices, and identifying future opportunities—you can significantly contribute to the agency's continued growth and effectiveness long after your departure. Your attention to these details will be a powerful testament to your leadership and dedication. I commend your commitment to building a sustainable foundation for future success.

Life After Your Term(s) in State Government

Following my time as Commissioner of Labor, I accepted a position as the Omaha Mayor's Deputy Assistant, followed by accepting a position as the CEO and Executive Director for a school district's foundation. This role allowed me to leverage my experience to support teachers and enhance educational opportunities for students by securing vital funding for classroom resources and initiatives. This transition demonstrated my versatility and commitment to contributing to the betterment of communities through diverse and impactful roles.

After being in the employment and training business for several decades, what attracted me to the CB Community Education Foundation was the opportunity to work in the K-12 education environment to promote and enhance the community dialogue about the importance of career and technical education that leads to good jobs and careers through education and training.

Business and Education need to work hand-in-hand; parents need to get more involved, and students need to understand what education and skills are required for today's labor market at a much younger age. It is important to encourage students to make informed decisions about their future.

Since the time I arrive at the foundation in 2009, I organized the foundation into four business units, the foundation itself, which serves as the umbrella organization for its programs; the Kids & Company before and after school care program; the Council Bluffs Alumni Association; and the STARS Scholar program, which helps adults living in Pottawattamie County earn job certificates, associate and bachelor's degrees.

The Community Education Foundation also sponsored programs for students in need, a classroom teacher grants program, the Council Bluffs School District's teacher and staff recognition programs, annual awards, attendance incentives, and 30 scholarships for high school seniors graduating from the school district.

At the Community Education Foundation as its CEO and Executive Director, and during my tenure, I was named to the National Honor Roll by the American Schools Foundation Alliance.

THE END

About the Author
Fernando "Butch" Lecuona III

Is the Recipient of:

*The National Building a World Class Workforce Award

*The National William J. Harris, Equal Opportunity Award

*The Prestigious National NASWA Eagle Award

*The Edgerton Award of Progress, the first Nebraska state government agency to receive this Business Award

*The Patriotic Employer Award by the National Committee for Employer Support of the Guard and Reserves

*The Peace Medal from the Dallas Chief Eagle of the Rosebud (Lakota) Sioux Indian Tribe

*Inducted into the Packers Youth Football Hall of Fame

*Award from the American Red Cross as a Board of Directors in Appreciation for 6 years of service and Board Secretary.

*The Robert Danze Community Service Award by the Omaha Federation of Labor AFL-CIO
*The Outstanding Service Award from Creighton University
*The Outstanding Young Omahan Award from the Omaha Jaycees
*International Association of Workforce Professionals – Administrators Award
*Charitable Giving Campaign as Chairman of the Advisory Board

*Named to the National Honor Roll by the American Schools Foundation Alliance

*Inducted into the Omaha Benson High School Hall of Fame for my contributions to the city, State, and National government